The Beretta was up and tracking

The Executioner cut loose, the first round taking out the leader of the group, drilling through his skull and blowing his brains out the back of his head.

As Bolan swept the muzzle again, two other enemy gunners raised their assault rifles. His second shot punched a hole in the chest of his target even as the muzzles on the other two weapons spit flame.

The bullets struck him in the chest, but they didn't hit with the familiar burn of a regular round. The Executioner had been hit several times, but it had never felt like this.

Another moment passed before everything faded to black.

MACK BOLAN ®
The Executioner

DON PENDLETON'S
EXECUTIONER®
THE
ARCTIC BLAST

A GOLD EAGLE BOOK FROM
W☉RLDWIDE®

TORONTO • NEW YORK • LONDON
AMSTERDAM • PARIS • SYDNEY • HAMBURG
STOCKHOLM • ATHENS • TOKYO • MILAN
MADRID • WARSAW • BUDAPEST • AUCKLAND

First edition November 2002
ISBN 0-373-64288-1

Special thanks and acknowledgment to
Jon Guenther for his contribution to this work.

ARCTIC BLAST

Printed in U.S.A.

Every gun that is fired, every warship launched,
every rocket fired, signifies, in the final sense,
a theft from those who hunger and are not fed,
those who are cold and are not clothed.

—Dwight D. Eisenhower,
1890–1969

The spending of money in the arms race isn't the
real crime. It's the spending of America's dreams
for peace and the hopes of its children. Anyone
who does this will be subjected to some very
swift and direct consequences.

—Mack Bolan

To the Federation of American Scientists—
a wonderful and peace-loving organization

Prologue

White Sands Missile Range, New Mexico

There was a moment of awe in the room as the voice through the speakers announced the missile launch.

An ICBM had just lifted off its pad at Fort Huachuca, Arizona, headed on a direct collision course with a predetermined point on the range. It was the first test of the new Satellite Linked Anti-Missile System, and the men within the high-energy-laser systems test facility waited anxiously. Particularly Lieutenant Kyle Makowski, an Air Force systems controller who helped develop SLAMS.

Behind Makowski stood Colonel Ivan Wicker, creator of the new defense weapon. The deputy of Air Force for White Sands watched the electronic blip flash on the luminescent screen. Blue-white lines crossed one another in a grid; each was numbered vertically and horizontally within a glowing LCD. The yellow blip continued across the grid as it widened the gap between the orange *X*, which marked the position of Fort Huachuca, and drew closer to the green *X* marking the missile range.

Also present for the demonstration was the head of White Sands, General Jonathan Pordello. The general was a native of New Mexico, and he knew the area intimately. He'd monitored this project for the Pentagon from the get-go, and while he didn't pretend to understand the complexities like Wicker or Makowski, he *did* know one thing: this would prove to be the ultimate test of their missile-defense preparedness.

"Since this ICBM is capable of tremendous speeds," Wicker announced, "SLAMS has only a few minutes to perform the 3-D-F program, sir."

Pordello furrowed his eyebrows. "Which means what?"

Wicker turned and smiled at the general. Pordello couldn't say he thought much of the guy as a military man. Wicker was one of those types who thrived on attention. Oh, hell, who was he fooling? The guy was plainly an egomaniac and everybody knew it. Nonetheless, he was the USAF's whiz kid when it came to designing antimissile defense, so Pordello often found it necessary to entertain Wicker's whims.

However, Kyle Makowski was another thing altogether. A young, vibrant officer with undoubtedly a fine career ahead of him, Makowski knew how to take orders and keep his mouth shut. He cared only for the defense of the country and was duly respectful of his superiors, even if only by rank and not solely intelligence. Pordello knew Makowski was an electronics genius, but the young man never tried to flaunt it. Pordello could only respect him for that.

"The 3-D-F program is quite simple, sir," Wicker said with minor irritation in his voice. He sounded as he always did, as if he were having to explain a simple concept to a child for the fifth time in a row. "SLAMS must first detect the threat, deploy the defensive program and then deflect the object."

"I see," Pordello snapped, putting his hands behind his back and clearing his throat. "A perfectly logical explanation."

"Indeed," Wicker replied and then turned his back to Pordello so he could watch the screen.

"Phase one complete, sir," Makowski announced. "SLAMS has detected the missile and is counting down to deploy the program."

There was a renewed silence as the blue-white grid changed colors to a brilliant red. The lines seemed to merge out of the screen and then rotated sideways and vertically so that it was like looking into a cube of blocks. A new picture flashed onto the screen, a three-dimensional graphic of the SLAMS satellite.

The display alone was fascinating. Years of electronic engineering and secretive construction by some of the largest companies and government outsourcers in the country finally paid off. This was a monumental moment, and the feeling of pride almost overwhelmed Pordello. He wiped at his eyes when nobody was looking and took a deep breath to curb his anticipation.

Silence reigned, broken only by Makowski's clipped announcements. "Grid system is locked on."

Less than a minute remained before the missile would touch down in the center of the range. Everyone had been cleared from that area for the day, and most of the staff in the populated areas of the base were off for the Memorial Day weekend. Only key personnel were present for the test on this cool Saturday morning, and some civilian workers in the shopping and restaurant areas.

"Thirty seconds to execution," Makowski said.

"Excellent," Wicker whispered with glee.

"SLAMS is now sending the DQL and MXT deflection signals," Makowski reported. "Twenty seconds..."

The dot was now practically on top of the green *X*. The only way they could be sure the program would work was to test it under extreme circumstances. If an enemy ever found a way to penetrate the country's airspace undetected with the intent of delivering a nuclear strike—or any strike for that matter—it would have devastating effects. Rumor had it the Chinese were already working on a way to cloak bombers and missiles, as were the Russians, British and Middle Eastern countries.

Even the U.S. was into that. Technology, particularly in the areas of information systems and electronic circuitry, was advancing so rapidly that nobody could keep up with it. There were new technologies under development every day—both in the private and commercial sectors—that even their creators couldn't fully understand.

Now, in this moment, a new invention was about to be unveiled to the defense community. There would be very little threat of nuclear devastation if the American scientists could pull this off. As a matter of fact, there would be *no* threat from any air-based weapons of mass destruction. And Pordello knew he'd go down in the books as one of the main players in the development of SLAMS.

"Five seconds until execution," Makowski announced. "Four... three..."

As he counted down, Pordello could feel his heart beat in rhythm with the numbers. Within moments, his people would probably make history. It was going to be a memorable event.

"Ground zero, sirs," Makowski said. All of the sudden, the young officer jumped out of his seat. "The missile's changing course! It worked! It worked! The missile's changing course!"

Makowski began to jump up and down as a cheer went up from all others throughout the complex. He spun and threw his arms around Wicker, who returned the gesture with unabashed enthusiasm. They parted and each shook hands with Pordello, concluding their celebrations with salutes that Pordello rendered first.

"A job well done, gentleman," Pordello said, his voice cracking slightly as he dropped the salute. "Damn fine job."

"Lieutenant?" one of the technicians interjected before either Makowski or Wicker could reply.

The young officer turned. "What is it, Jake?"

"Sir, the missile has begun to fall again."

Makowski and Wicker rushed to the console and began to stab the assorted buttons and switches. They both stopped simultaneously, looking at each other wide-eyed before turning to peer at the grid. The dot had barely passed the green *X* and was definitely on the fall again.

"What's going on, men?" Pordello inquired, feeling the tension rise in his back and experiencing a new burning in his chest.

"I'm not certain, sir," Makowski said, punching some more buttons and studying a small screen. "The missile is falling, headed directly to grid 1-5-4 slash 2-1."

"Where's that at, son?"

"Oh, my God," he said. He looked at Wicker and Pordello with a ghostly expression, his face going completely white. "It's headed right for the main post."

Wicker swore furiously as he turned to a nearby phone and lifted the receiver. He started screaming into it as Makowski activated the post-wide alert system. Klaxons and whistles began to resound in their bunker complex, echoed by the speakers spread throughout the post.

Pordello whirled, ordering several men to follow him as he left the complex via the stairs and soon reached the exit. He pushed through the heavy security door after entering his pass code into the mounted lock. Everything went berserk in that few moments. The sun was at about 0800, and it burned hot rays into Pordello's eyes as he listened to the supersonic boom of the ICBM's passing.

Moments later, a reverberation cracked across the bleached, sandy grounds of the complex as the missile crashed through a barracks building. Hundreds of pieces of metal, brick and glass tore through the interior. Sparks flew from nearby transformers as power was cut from the building. Large fragments of metal continued through the barracks and traveled onward to a strip mall of AAFES shops along one of the main drags.

The adrenaline surged through Pordello's body as he rushed to a nearby staff car, his men sprinting on his heels. He jumped into the back seat as his aide climbed behind the wheel and another staff officer took the front.

"Get us to the main post. Now!"

"Yes, sir," the aide replied.

With gravel and sand spewing from the tires, they rocketed in the direction of what Pordello knew would result in senseless death and destruction.

It would be days before they could dig out survivors of the initial blast.

Mack Bolan sensed he was driving into trouble even before he reached White Sands.

He exited I-25 in Las Cruces where it met State Road 70, and drove to the front gates of White Sands Missile Range. Once he presented his credentials as Mike Blanski—operative with the SIGINT group—he followed directions to the range headquarters. Thus far, none of the devastation that had struck this quiet outpost in south-central New Mexico had reached the ears of the general public. That meant the Executioner had to look into the matter and come to some sort of quick resolution.

Stony Man was definitely counting on him to get some answers and deal with the situation. Back at the Farm, Bolan knew Aaron "The Bear" Kurtzman was working every angle possible. There hadn't been any conclusions yet, either through his technical team or those key personnel at White Sands. That's what had the boys in Wonderland up at arms, and Bolan was now involved because Stony Man believed there was something much deeper to this problem.

The soldier had to agree.

Several weeks had passed without a word from either investigator sent by the DOD. Members of the Defense Intelligence Agency, as well as the Senate Arms Committee and the Pentagon, were concerned that something treacherous lurked in the shadows surrounding the miserable failure that killed and wounded dozens of people. Moreover, the investigators hadn't sent back a single report; it was as if they had disappeared from the face of the earth.

When officials at White Sands were questioned, they claimed that orders had come stating investigators would soon be there, but nobody had ever shown. Their concerns were confirmed because multiple inquiries had been made by the post commander regarding their impending arrival.

So now they were sending in the cavalry. Bolan's mission was to find out what had happened to the two agents, as well as what or who was behind the failure of the SLAMS test.

His military background would give him an edge. The armed forces could be quite a closemouthed society—Bolan spoke their lingo. He understood their ways and their peculiar code of silence. Posing as an NSA hotshot might not make him the most popular person, but these were as much scientists as military men. He'd find a way to gain their confidence.

And if he ran into trouble, he would rely on instincts and the Beretta 93-R tucked in shoulder leather beneath his jacket. A satchel in the back seat contained additional firepower, including his trusted .44-Magnum Desert Eagle and a Belgian-made FNC. The Executioner had become quite attached to the assault rifle for its versatility alone. The satchel also contained additional ammunition for all the weapons and his Colt combat knife.

Bolan parked in a spot reserved for guests and made his way to the office of the range commander, General Jonathan Pordello.

The general had an impeccable record, according to Stony Man's information. His first commands had been spent in the usual manner, first as a field platoon leader, then company commander and finally a brigade-level commander. After a long and distinguished career, including multiple citations for the actions of his unit during Desert Storm, Pordello was awarded a command in his home state.

Now, with almost ten years as commander in chief of White Sands, and this being the first blemish to his untarnished record, the man was going to be reasonably defensive, although Bolan would have never detected it as he was shown into Pordello's office and greeted by the general with a warm handshake.

"Agent Blanski, welcome to White Sands Missile Range," Pordello said in a congenial tone. He gestured to a chair in front of his desk and Bolan accepted it. "May I offer you a drink?"

"No, thank you," the Executioner replied.

Bolan brushed at the dust on his pants. If he was going to fit in here, he would have to look the part. He was dressed in a gray suit, with a black tie and light blue shirt. He removed the mirrored sunglasses from his face, tucking them in his pocket.

"I'm sure you're anxious to get on with your investigation," Pordello continued as he seated himself behind his desk. "So I'll get right to the briefing."

"Excuse me, General," Bolan interjected, "but let's be straight from the start. I'm not here to conduct an investigation, I'm here to help."

Pordello's smile turned frosty. "Let me come right to the point, then, since you seem comfortable enough for candidness. I don't consider you any threat, but I'm afraid that Lieutenant Makowski and Colonel Wicker might see your presence here as interference."

"Then I'd have to wonder what they're trying to hide."

"Nothing. Granted, they're both strong-willed men...even pigheaded at times, but they're very knowledgeable when it comes to matters of this nature. And I can personally vouch for their allegiance."

"I don't question their patriotism or competence," Bolan countered. "How this missile failed isn't nearly as important to me as why. Your superiors agree with me."

"What are you talking about, Agent Blanski?" Pordello queried incredulously. "Don't tell me that Washington is concerned with a conspiracy."

"I didn't say that. I'm just saying that they wonder if the

failure was the work of an accident or not. I'm here to help make that determination."

"If this wasn't an accident," Pordello replied, "then it's the damnedest thing I've ever seen."

"Why don't you tell me what happened," Bolan suggested.

"I have a better idea," Pordello said, rising from his seat. "I'll show you."

The general led him outside and they climbed into a waiting M-998 High-Mobility Multipurpose Wheeled Vehicle. A driver accelerated smoothly and was soon speeding the two men across the base. Pordello spoke to Bolan from his position in the front seat.

"The test itself went fine," Pordello said matter-of-factly. "The missile was launched just as it should have been. Left the pad right on the money. SLAMS detected its presence, powered up and even went through deployment. It deflected the weapon for the moment, then all of a sudden it just failed."

"Sounds serious," Bolan offered.

Pordello eyed him sadly. "It *was* serious. I lost sixteen people, and we had to transport another seven to the area hospitals in Las Cruces because of burns that our base medical facility couldn't treat. If that warhead had been armed, the results could have been catastrophic."

"Doesn't sound too far from that now."

The driver deposited them in front of a bunker. The roof stuck out of the ground by barely a foot. They descended some stairs to a wide door guarded by two Air Force MPs wearing red berets.

Pordello turned to Bolan and asked, "Are you armed?"

Bolan nodded.

"You'll have to surrender your weapon to us, sir," one of the guards said.

The soldier shrugged and turned the weapon over to the MP without an argument. There was no point in trying to bully them, and he was comforted that if he wasn't allowed to bring a firearm inside, then nobody else would have one either.

Pordello signed them in and then handed the Executioner

a temporary admittance badge. "This will give you clearance into almost anything on the base. It's good for seventy-two hours. If you think you'll be here longer, let me know and I will have it renewed."

"Thanks."

Bolan attached the badge to the lapel of his shirt and then followed Pordello through the door, which one of the guards opened by entering a punch code. The interior was relatively cool to the heat outside. It was unusually dry for this time of year, even in a desert state, and Bolan could taste the dust in his mouth. It seemed to coat everything and left little doubt as to why they had given the range its name.

Pordello continued down a ramp to the dimly lit interior of the bunker. The place was absolutely amazing. Computer terminals sat everywhere, with a large, circular display taking up the center of the room. The crystal like screen was lit up with all kinds of three-dimensional graphics; it was a vibrant collage of colors that almost put Bolan in the Christmas spirit.

The atmosphere was as sullen as a library, the silence broken only by occasional bits of conversations or bursts of radio transmissions. Nearly every station was manned by a technician, some in civilian clothing and others in military uniforms from various branches of service.

One young man dressed in an Army uniform turned immediately toward them. He had sandy-blond hair, which glowed with an eerie green hue in the bizarre lights from the screen. There was something fresh and amiable about the guy, and he studied the new arrivals with a welcome smile.

"Lieutenant Kyle Makowski," Pordello introduced him. "Lieutenant, this is Mike Blanski. He's with the NSA Signal Intelligence group and he was sent to assist us in finding out what happened."

"Pleasure to meet you, sir," Makowski said, shaking Bolan's hand. He looked at Pordello before adding, "Although I think you may have wasted a trip."

"What do you mean?" Bolan asked.

Makowski pointed to the screen and gestured toward images of the missile and satellite. "We've been working on this for three days straight and we finally figured it out. We know what happened."

"So you've determined why the missile failed?" Pordello interjected.

"The missile didn't fail, sir," Makowski said. "SLAMS did."

"What? How did it happen?"

"Do you see this dotted yellow line?"

Both men nodded.

"That's the frequency signatures of our transmissions to the SLAMS satellite. They carry the encrypted codes that the system uses to send the laser grid down and cause interrupt requests within the homing signals of the missile. The signal was sent correctly, and the proper DQL and MXT signals replied and initiated the grid."

Bolan cocked an eyebrow at the whiz kid. "You want to try English for me?"

"Sorry," he replied genuinely. He turned and pointed at the red grid lines surrounding the missile. "See those? Those are initiated by the signals I mentioned earlier. The satellite sends laser beams down to the coordinates we feed it and creates a signal net using two different band signals."

"DQL and MXT," Pordello supplied helpfully. "Stands for Differing Quotient Light and Multi-Executable Timing, respectively."

"Precisely," Makowski continued. "DQLs are transmissions that run along the beams, thus creating the sort of grid shield denoted on the display. The MXTs are frequency pulses transmitted through particle emission technology. They actually alter the homing ability of the missile and turn it upward."

Bolan nodded with understanding. "And the missile does the rest, launching out of the atmosphere on its remaining fuel."

Makowski nodded. "However, when we looked at the MXTs more closely, we saw this."

He stabbed a button on the display main panel, and the

blue-white glow inside the grid enlarged twenty times, enough that Bolan thought it might leap right out of the circular screen and consume them all.

Makowski pointed to some darker spots that weren't visible before. There were seemingly billions of them inside the display, almost like flecks of pepper scattered throughout a sea of salt. "We analyzed these. They are ghosted signals with reversed frequencies."

"Almost like a virus," Bolan observed.

Makowski flashed him an impressed look. "In a sense. You must have an electronics background. That's a rather astute analogy."

The Executioner shrugged.

"MXT signals are what we call complex, in that they are constantly changing. It's this very nature that it uses to scramble set frequencies. All missiles are programmed with at least three numeric references—latitude, longitude and ground zero. MXT signals don't physically change those numbers, but rather alter the way those signals see the earth. By using MXT signals to change the convex of the earth to a cubed state within the grid, the ground zero default reference changes. Thus, the missile goes straight up."

"And that's where it goes above my head," Pordello admitted.

"Yeah," Bolan snapped. "I guess what you're saying is that those signals within this beam grid aren't ours, correct?"

"Exactly."

"Where did they come from?"

"We—"

"We aren't sure yet," a voice said to their right.

All eyes turned to see a tall, distinguished-looking man in a dark blue Air Force uniform. He had thinning black hair parted by a bald spot, and a thin mustache. He carried an aura of authority with him—enhanced by the rows of gleaming medals on his breast—along with a touch of arrogance. He walked with an almost sophisticated gait, one that belied more aristocracy than military proficiency.

"Agent Blanski, may I introduce to you the inventor of SLAMS, Colonel Ivan Wicker."

The men shook hands and then Wicker seemed to brush them aside as he studied the display for a moment. He seemed entranced by his own invention, impressed by his very presence in the room. The guy wasn't the kind who could be easily liked, and his very presence sent some bad vibes the Executioner's way.

Bolan had learned to listen to his sixth sense. Thus far, it seemed that Makowski was completely willing to cooperate. He still had that wide-eyed farm-boy innocence to him in many respects, but Wicker had been around the block a few times. Bolan immediately sensed this. He also immediately sensed he didn't like the guy.

Pordello obviously picked up on the wordless exchange of hostility between the two men because he immediately spoke. "So you haven't had any luck tracking the signals further, Colonel Wicker?"

Wicker turned and favored Pordello with a wan smile. "No, sir, and I don't know how long it will be if we can discover their origin." He turned to look at Bolan and added, "If ever."

"But you're certain they're malicious in nature?" the Executioner asked.

Something turned stony in Wicker's expression. Good, he had the guy on the spot and now there was no way around it. Bolan knew—as Wicker probably did—that if the Air Force officer reversed Makowski's initial speculation, it would look very suspicious. On the other hand, if he admitted to an outside force, it would confirm Bolan's theory that other powers were at work.

Wicker didn't say anything at first, but Makowski looked as if he were going to burst. He started to open his mouth after the moment of uncomfortable silence, but Wicker spoke before the younger man could utter a syllable.

"They're certainly not signals contained within the particle beam. To say more this early would be pure speculation."

"I'm interested to hear your speculation, Colonel," Bolan pressed.

"I am first and foremost a scientist, Blanski," Wicker huffed. "I do not guess."

"Then let me take a stab at it. I think that somebody planted that signal inside the particle beam of your SLAMS satellite. Now, in order to do that, they would have needed the access codes to the satellite. Besides you, who has those?"

"Only myself and Lieutenant Makowski," Wicker said.

"And a secure copy is kept in the safe vault," Pordello added, "which is under armed guard twenty-four, seven."

Wicker shot Pordello a furious look but kept quiet.

"Who has access to the vault?"

"Only me and the deputy post commander," Pordello replied. "But he spends the better part of his time at the Pentagon, so he's rarely here."

"We need to see if he's received access lately," Bolan said. "I would also like to see the logs of guard rotations."

"I can get on that immediately."

"Excuse me for asking, Blanski," Wicker interjected, "but what exactly is your position here? I thought you were supposed to *assist* us in discovering why this missile failed."

Bolan stared hard at Wicker, fixing the man with his ice-blue eyes. He said, "My function is simple, Colonel. If this missile was diverted by means other than failure of your system, and I now have reason to think so, it's my duty to find out."

"Aside from the National Security Agency, you have very little authority here, Blanski."

"Now, gentleman—" Pordello began, smiling and raising his hands.

Bolan stepped forward now and towered over Wicker with an expression he hoped would show he'd run out of patience with Wicker's impertinence. The guy may have been a brilliant scientist, but he was also a loudmouth. The Executioner was hardly intimidated by this guy. He'd run into the likes of Ivan Wicker before, and they always ended up squealing like a school bully who had met his match.

"Shut it down now," Bolan growled. "I'm here to do a job. In the meantime, I expect your full cooperation. I would hate to report to the commander in chief that you weren't helpful."

Wicker sneered. "You want us to believe you have the ear of the White House?"

Pordello cleared his throat and nodded when Wicker looked at him. Some of the smugness left the man's face in that moment, and he returned his gaze to Bolan. This time, his expression held a bit more respect, telling the soldier that Wicker got the message.

Bolan stepped back a pace, turned to the general and said, "I guess I'm done here for the time being."

Pordello chuckled and shook his head. "I would have to say so."

They left after a curt goodbye.

Bolan and Pordello didn't talk on the way back to the general's office. The Executioner used the time to reflect on what he knew so far. Apparently, Makowski suspected foul play, but it didn't as seem though Wicker wanted to commit to that idea. The soldier found that a bit strange, since the evidence of outside tampering would prove it wasn't an internal failure in the SLAMS program. Such news should have appealed to Wicker's ego, yet the Air Force deputy wanted to avoid such a theory.

That left Bolan with two possibilities—either Wicker had sabotaged the project himself, or somebody else had. But that wasn't the only thing that bothered the Executioner. It had seemed as if Makowski was holding back. He'd kept looking at Bolan as if he wanted to say something, but it seemed he clammed up when Wicker showed his face. Bolan knew he wanted a second opportunity to speak with Makowski. He'd have to find a way to get it.

When they arrived at Pordello's office, Bolan stopped short.

"Aren't you coming inside?"

"No, actually I'd like to grab a shower and quick bite," Bolan replied. "It's been a long day, and I could use a break."

"Good enough. I'll have my driver show you to your billet."

"Thanks."

"By the way, Blanski," Pordello said on afterthought, "I just want you to know that I'm glad you're here. Don't let Wicker scare you off. He's just eccentric."

"Yeah."

"I want to get the bottom of this, too. I know you realize that."

"I'm also concerned about the two agents who never made it here," Bolan remarked offhandedly. He wanted to test the waters, see how Pordello reacted.

The man nodded with a concerned expression. "I feel exactly the same way. It's been almost three weeks since I first received the phone calls telling me about their arrivals. That's why I became concerned and started calling back when they didn't show."

"I think somebody found out they were coming and headed them off."

"That's why they decided not to tell me about your little visit. Right?"

Bolan nodded.

"Well," he added with a smile, "I suppose that was best. When we were first told of the other arrivals, I told only my staff officer and the team assigned to the project. I can't believe we have a traitor in our midst."

"Maybe you don't," Bolan suggested. "Maybe whoever's behind these disappearances has your phone or office bugged. If these people found some way to foul up the SLAMS, placing a bug would be child's play."

"Perhaps you're right. Well, in either respect, have a good evening. I'll see you tomorrow."

"Count on it."

The men parted with a handshake and Bolan went to his car. When he had backed out of the space, the driver pulled ahead in the M-998 and Bolan followed him. They proceeded down a main road through the post and then the driver made a right-hand turn onto a gravel road.

The Executioner maintained a safe distance, certain to

keep back enough that he wasn't choked out by the sand, dust and pebbles spewing in the wake of the Hummer. Bolan was beginning to wonder where the hell he was actually quartered. They continued to drive almost two miles before the Hummer stopped.

Bolan started to ease on the brakes and slowed the vehicle as the dust settled. In the clearing air, he saw two more vehicles. They were also Hummers, their tops off, painted tan and marked with the insignia of military police. And they were filled with armed men. The gunmen wore desert-camouflage fatigues and expressions of murder, and toted a variety of deadly hardware.

Bolan stomped on the accelerator and jerked the wheel as he reached into the back seat and retrieved his weapons. Even as he pulled away from the group, he could hear the first reports of gunfire. Glass flew through the interior of Bolan's sedan as the back window imploded. It appeared the Executioner had shaken the enemy loose.

2

Mack Bolan barely detected the autofire, but he knew they were shooting at him.

He could hear the plinking sounds of bullets striking the trunk. One round came close—it tore a gash in the felt material of the roof interior and ricocheted through the windshield. The spiderweb effect, coupled with the dust and heat, blocked the warrior's field of vision and made negotiating the trail difficult.

Bolan estimated he had less than mile to go before reaching the main road. It was obvious to him who had been snooping around Pordello's business. His driver hadn't said a word to the Executioner, and the soldier cursed himself for not watching the guy closer. Well, there was nothing he could about it now. At least he had some idea of who was involved; the driver was a place to start anyway.

He wondered if they would break off the attack on the main road. Of course, nobody would stop a couple of MP vehicles on a missile range from chasing a nondescript car. Bolan could almost hear what they would say, telling Pordello later that they had seen Bolan violating law or entering a secured area. And that didn't even count the inflammatory information they would feed to any investigators.

No, the only chance the Executioner had was to get them into a position where he could deal with them head-on.

Rounds continued to slam into the back of the sedan or zip

past Bolan's head. He ran a zigzag pattern, lessening the chance of a lucky shot while still maintaining control of his own wheels on the slick gravel-and-sand road. Two more minutes passed before Bolan reached the road. He slammed on the brakes and jacked the wheel to the left, skidding the sedan onto the pavement.

He continued in motion, never losing a beat as he threw the sedan into Reverse and executed a J-turn. Now his vehicle was facing toward the enemy. They weren't visible yet through the dust and smoke that marked his trail. Bolan dropped the gearshift to Second and stomped the gas pedal. Tires smoked as he rocketed forward, heading straight toward his enemy.

The maneuver worked like a charm, causing both of the M-998 drivers to take evasive actions in order to avoid a collision. The erratic course of one driver took the Hummer over a deep rut that served as a makeshift drainage ditch. The right tire was caught in the rut and the speed of the vehicle did the rest. The Hummer flipped twice, tossing several of its occupants in every direction while the driver and man riding shotgun were crushed under the vehicle.

Bolan brought the sedan to a grinding halt. He reached into the satchel, withdrew the FNC, and then went EVA. The veteran combatant took in the scene with an expert eye in seconds, checking for any threat from the ground-pounders ejected from the first M-998 even as he prepared for the second group.

The Executioner heard the roar of another engine behind him and turned to see the general's driver behind the windshield. The soldier leaped from the Hummer and brought his side arm into view. The Beretta 92-SB was the predecessor of Bolan's 93-R, and a standard side arm for the modern American soldier. But it was no match against an automatic assault rifle.

Bolan raised his FNC, selecting burst mode as he brought the weapon to bear. His opponent managed to get off a single shot before falling under the blazing autofire. The flurry of 5.56 mm slugs punched holes through his belly and nearly eviscerated him. The impact sent him spinning, the pistol leaving numbed fingers as he body fell to the sand.

Bolan whirled to greet the next threat, which came in the form of four troopers from the upright M-998. Two charged him while the other duo tried a flanking maneuver.

The Executioner was too experienced to let that bother him. He took the head-on threat first, realizing the other pair had made a mistake. In trying to circle onto his back side, they had allowed him the cover of the sedan. Bolan dropped to one knee, switched to full-auto and leveled the FNC at his enemies. He depressed the trigger, feeling the weapon buck in his viselike grip as he took out the charging gunmen.

The first guy took several rounds in the thigh, which dropped him screaming to the ground. The second wasn't as lucky, his head snapping backward with the impact of each bullet. The guy looked as if he were having a seizure, and at least five rounds drilled through belly and chest before a final shot blew off the top of his skull.

The muzzle of Bolan's weapon smoked as he dropped to the ground and rolled away from the sounds of boots crunching along the gravelly surface. The maneuver saved his life as milliseconds later a flurry of rounds buzzed over his head. Bolan got to one knee, his FNC swinging upward as he squeezed the trigger. Both of the flanking soldiers never got shots to land close enough to pose any real threat to the Executioner. They died under a set of short, controlled bursts.

Even as they fell, more noise behind Bolan told the soldier he had enemies who still had to be dispatched. He whirled, watching as two of the "bodies" from the ejection rose up and tried to gain target acquisition. If nothing else, the Executioner had to admire their fervor.

It didn't do them any good, though. Bolan cut the pair down, popping off a steady stream of rounds and waving the muzzle in a corkscrew fashion. As the echoes of the gunfire died out, Bolan detected a new noise. A hot wind had begun to blow across the landscape, sending dust and sand into his eyes. He ignored the burning there, blinking his eyes to clear them while keeping a watch on the surroundings.

Nothing but the noise of the fresh breeze and the groaning of the one survivor greeted him. Dust rose in twirling patterns like minicyclones. Bolan could make out the blood clearly in the white sands as it seeped from the bodies. As he rose and began to inspect them, he was certain they weren't actually members of the U.S. military. They all had passports showing they'd entered the country from various global regions. It would take Stony Man some time to discover their origins.

Bolan finally marched over to where the wounded survivor lay. The guy was young, maybe twenty-five, with blond hair and blue eyes. There was something European in his appearance, maybe German, and he stared at the Executioner with a mixture of hate and fear. Quite a bit of blood poured from the wounds in his thigh.

Bolan used his colt combat knife to cut clothing from the man's deceased comrade. He tried to stem the bleeding, but the man pushed his hands away and began to yell at him in broken English. It was difficult to pin the man's accent at firs—Bolan's acute ear soon picked out the accent and dialect as probably Russian.

"All right, all right," Bolan finally said, stopping his care. "Just settle down. Where are you from?"

"It does not matter," the young man replied. "You will not live to see the dawn."

"If you don't let me stop this bleeding—" Bolan gestured to the bones sticking through the man's hip "—you won't, either."

"Then I die."

"That's not brave, it's stupid."

The light began to abruptly leave the man's eyes and his skin started to pale. He laid his head back and opened his mouth, taking several ragged breaths. He was moving his lips, as if to say something, and Bolan put his ear close, careful to keep the FNC out of reach in case the guy was playing possum. The dying man actually grabbed the lapel of Bolan's coat and pulled him close.

He whispered, "Nadezhda lives." Then he died.

Bolan rose and looked at the man's broken corpse. He wasn't sure what the hell to make of it. Sirens wailed in the distance as the real MPs approached. This wouldn't be a mess he could easily explain. While he had credentials and orders from the White House, it wouldn't be easy to explain the heavy firepower and the fact he'd just done battle with a dozen armed men and won. Bolan knew that Pordello was going to ask some very uncomfortable questions.

For now, he couldn't worry about it. There were more important things to consider, such as the source of this hit team.

IT WAS WELL after midnight when Bolan arrived at his billet. He'd spent the past six hours being questioned by the provost marshal and his men. Pordello had been present for the interrogation, as well, saying very little and nodding with consternation as Bolan was taken to task for his resistance to the terrorists.

The chief concern didn't seem to be the fact that a whole group of foreign insurgents had managed to penetrate a heavily secured military outpost. The provost marshal and the rest of his crew seemed more worried about what would have happened if the MPs had been real soldiers, not to mention the fact Bolan was toting enough firepower to start his own war.

The Executioner explained that he answered only to the authorities in Washington. He was allowed to make a phone call and he did—to Hal Brognola. Within twenty minutes, there were a half-dozen calls to the provost marshal's office, including one from the national-security adviser and one from the Man himself.

That changed the entire face of the operation from there out, and Bolan was granted full authority to proceed without molestation. Moreover, every person on White Sands Missile Range was to cooperate with him, or there would be hell to pay, and a lot of high-ranking officers would be collecting their pensions should any further "incidents" occur. Was that clear?

It was crystal clear to the provost marshal and his men.

Now Bolan was in his quarters—simple and sparse as they were—and ready to take a shower when he was interrupted by a soft knock at the front door. The Executioner snatched the Beretta from his coat and padded quietly across the room. He stood to one side of the door, weapon in battery and held at the ready.

"Yeah?" he said, just loud enough to be heard but not to reveal his exact position.

"Agent Blanski?" a familiar voice greeted him. "It's Lieutenant Makowski...Kyle Makowski. I met you today? I'd like to talk with you."

Bolan opened the door slightly, keeping the weapon in plain view. Makowski stepped back, still dressed in full uniform, and started to raise his hands. Bolan didn't let the young officer wait for an invitation. He grabbed him by the shoulders and yanked him inside. He took another look around before closing the door and holstering his weapon. Makowski stood there with a pained expression, his hands held high.

Bolan waved him down and said, "Relax, Lieutenant. I don't kill the good guys."

Makowski smiled and nodded as he lowered his hands. Bolan turned and peered through the wooden government-issue shutters painted the same OD green as everything else in the room. "Did you notice anybody following you?"

"No, I don't think so. Then again, I didn't really think to look. What's going on, sir?"

Bolan turned to face the young man and pinned him with a serious expression. "You don't have a clue what's going on around here, do you?"

"I guess not," Makowski said with a shrug, putting his hands in his pockets and seating himself on Bolan's bunk. "I'm just an expert in information technology. My father and mother were both career military. I was an Army brat, and I guess I just followed in their footsteps naturally."

"Nothing's by accident, Makowski."

"You're right, sir."

"Why don't you drop the 'sir' and just call me Mike."

"Cool. I heard about what happened today after you left the bunker. I thought I had better come by and talk to you. It's important."

"Okay. You want some coffee?"

"No, thank you, s— I mean, Mike."

Bolan nodded and pulled up a chair. He sat and studied this bright officer. There was something naturally likable about the kid. He was a whiz, probably looked upon as a nerd when he was younger. Bolan knew the type—average-looking boy with a high IQ. Add the pressures of all the things school-age boys and girls had to face in America today, and that made Makowski an outcast. It was a tough way to grow up—and damn lonely as the only child of a military family. Bolan had read his dossier before taking the mission.

"I'm guessing," the Executioner said, "that there was something you wanted to tell me today. Something held you back. Was it Wicker?"

Makowski's face turned an embarrassed hue. He didn't say anything, but just lowered his head and nodded almost imperceptibly. It was probably hard for a guy like Makowski. He had to kowtow to all the brass around him. He was probably smarter than Wicker and the rest of that group put together, but he was a junior officer and they treated him as such. An outcast once again.

"Don't worry about guys like Wicker," Bolan counseled him. "I spent quite a while in the service, and I've met officers like him before. He's not as smart as he thinks he is."

Makowski looked Bolan in the eyes, something deeper and more mature in his expression. "Some of those people who died in that missile crash were my friends, Mike. I think someone diverted that thing. I'm certain I know how and from where. I'm just not sure who."

"Go on," Bolan prodded.

"Colonel Wicker didn't tell you the truth about those signals. I asked him afterward and he said that you wouldn't understand. He claimed you would just poke around, snooping into our business and trying to find fault in the SLAMS program. Says he lied to protect me, him and the operation."

"Do you believe him?"

"I'm not sure. You don't seem like the kind of man looking out only for yourself. I think you are genuine, Mike. I think you really do care, and the fact somebody tried to kill you today convinces me that someone is out to sabotage SLAMS."

"You're right about one thing, Makowski," the Executioner replied. "I *do* care about SLAMS and what happens here. It's my job to care. I can help you if you let me."

Makowski nodded, an indication that he would trust Bolan. He took a deep breath, then said, "I discovered that those signals inside the particle beam didn't originate from the satellite. At least, not in the strictest sense. They were encoded into the system. Like you said, sort of a virus. I discovered a burst of UHF radio signals, transmitted directly to the satellite on a carrier beam. Those signals originated from Antarctica."

"The Antarctic's a big place," Bolan interjected. "Can you be more specific?"

"Unfortunately, I can't. The signals were sent in several series rather than one long transmission. Whoever tampered with the programming on the SLAMS computer not only knew what they were doing, but they made sure the tampering couldn't be traced."

Bolan nodded. "Someone in my organization could help you to narrow the search. The guy I have in mind is one sharp cookie when it comes to computers."

"No offense, Mike, but I have a degree from MIT."

"And this man has a degree from years of firsthand experience," Bolan said. "Give me the information anyway, and I'll pass it on to him."

Makowski nodded. "Fair enough. I've got it here."

The man reached inside his shirt and removed several thick

sheets of folded paper. He opened them and flattened the papers on the bunk, then pointed to some numbers and other data on the top page.

"These are the actual frequencies I traced that belong to the burst signals sent to the SLAMS satellite." He changed pages and pointed to a computer-enhanced drawing of the screen images Bolan had seen in the bunker. "This yellow line shows the signal transmissions, and the approximate times I determined they were sent."

Bolan furrowed his eyebrows. "According to this, those signals were sent days before the launch. Any significance to that?"

"A lot," he replied. "We wouldn't have detected it at that time because we were in the testing phases. The transmissions would have been masked by any simulations or test runs. Like I said, somebody knew what they were doing."

"And that somebody has a link to this base," Bolan murmured. "I don't think I've eliminated all of their resources."

"Can I ask you a question?"

"Shoot."

"Who do you think tried to kill you today? Who were those men?"

Bolan shook his head with a grin. "That's two questions. And I don't have an answer for either one of them. I do think this goes a lot deeper than anyone wants to admit."

"Could this be some sort of foreign power?"

"Only time will tell," the Executioner replied grimly.

AFTER MAKOWSKI LEFT, Mack Bolan drove to a truck stop not far from White Sands Missile Range. He used the fax machine in the owner's office to send the information over Aaron Kurtzman's secure, high-tech communications system. It was amazing how much cooperation could be solicited just by flashing a government badge. The cute redheaded waitress had even appointed the beefy maintenance guy to stand watch over the office and to insure the Executioner's privacy. Now Bolan sat at the desk on a second secure line, listening to the digital transmissions through which Kurtzman's voice resounded.

"Makowski's right, Striker," Kurtzman was saying. "Those signals originated in Antarctica. I managed to trace them to a much closer source, however. We're looking at somewhere in the central area of the continent."

"Mostly neutral territory. How close are we talking here, Bear?"

"Hard to say. I'll keep plugging away at it, but I don't know if I'll crack it. Those transmissions were just too short, even for a computerized triangulation. I imagine that's about the best I can do."

"Tell me a little more about SLAMS. How it works, for example," the Executioner said. "Maybe something you say will help me."

"Well, much of it is complicated. Basically, the program started with a public push for defense against air invasion by foreign powers. Some of it stemmed from this isolationist position American society seems to be taking, part out of fear from the sale of missile secrets by the last administration."

"So any number of Chinese or Arab allies might benefit by destroying the SLAMS project."

"You bet," Kurtzman replied. "There are still plenty of Marxist revolutionary groups willing to see us fall. This could be a terrorist group, or possibly an operation of a foreign government. What's most disturbing is the fact that not only does somebody know about SLAMS, they also evidently have the technical know-how to counteract it."

"Yeah, that bothers me, too. What about the Russians?"

"Hal has us looking into all options. For now, he's ready to take Jack and come out there. He wants to know if you're willing to fly to Antarctica and probe this further."

"Tell him I'll be waiting. And thanks, Bear. Hey, is Barb there?"

"Yeah, right here."

"Let me talk to her."

Price's efficient voice came on the line a moment later. "Hey, big guy. What's up?"

"Have you ever heard of Nadezhda?"

"Doesn't ring any immediate bells," she answered after a brief pause. "Sounds Russian."

"Probably is," the Executioner replied. "Could you look into it? I have no idea how it's spelled, but I think it might be important."

"I'll research it and send any information with Hal and Jack."

"Good enough."

"Take care of yourself."

"You, too," he replied.

3

The Gulfstream C21 Learjet lifted off the tarmac of White Sands Missile Range at 0632 hours the following morning.

As Jack Grimaldi leveled at a cruising altitude of thirty-five thousand feet, Bolan unbuckled his seat belt, rose and poured himself some coffee. He returned a moment later and noticed the watchful eye of Hal Brognola. The Executioner had seen that look before, and he knew something was up.

"What's going on, Hal?" Bolan asked. "You haven't said ten words since you got here."

"There's something you need to know about this mission," Brognola said around an unlit cigar. "I'm trying to figure out how to tell you."

"Why not just get it on the table?"

"I guess you're right," the Stony Man chief replied, pulling the cigar from his mouth and dropping the wet stump into an ashtray. "We've known each other too long for it to be any other way."

The soldier nodded and Brognola took his cue.

"I had Bear go over this thing, do some projection analysis and so forth. This is a bad time for Antarctica, seasonally speaking. You and Jack will be getting there just as a storm clears out. Another one is on its way in."

"And that means?"

Brognola sighed. "It means that you'll only have three

days to get in, figure out who or what is behind this, neutralize any threats and get out."

The Executioner was silent as he considered Brognola's statement. Seventy-two hours wasn't much time. If there *were* enemy forces operating deep in Antarctica, they probably had plenty of time to dig in and fortify their positions. The weather alone could pose hazards from which Bolan might not return—he knew that better than anyone. But it would be more difficult given he had to move through unfamiliar territory without assistance.

"My belief," Brognola continued, "is that the Russians are behind this. Barb agrees with me on that. One of the reasons we think so is because she looked into that word you dropped on her. Nadezhda is a woman's name. Translated from Russian it means 'hope.' "

"Hope lives," the Executioner murmured.

Brognola cocked his head as if he thought he was hearing things. "What's that?"

"One of those men I put down said 'Nadezhda lives.' "

Brognola's expression turned quizzical. "Hope lives? What do you think that means?"

"Don't know, Hal," Bolan replied, "but I'm sure it's significant. Any identification on that hit team?"

The big Fed shook his head and frowned. "Not yet, but we're working on it. That provost marshal with all his territorial crap slowed us down. We do know they were all European. The bodies were moved to Las Cruces, and we have some people doing autopsies. They'll try to find a common factor, but—"

"They might come up empty," Bolan finished for him.

Brognola nodded.

The Executioner took a sip of his coffee before asking, "Where exactly are we headed?"

"Well, Jack is going to drop me off in Florida. The President is at Cape Canaveral this week. I've agreed to meet him there on a possible mission for Phoenix Force. He's giving us full sanctions on this one. He wanted me to let you know he appreciates your involvement, and that he wants done whatever you think necessary."

"Sounds like he's as concerned about this as you are," Bolan replied.

"There is absolutely no reason why anyone outside the SLAMS project should even know about this, Striker. Stony Man only found out just before I contacted you with the request to go to White Sands."

"I'll agree this is going much further than I thought it would. Makowski is convinced someone reprogrammed the SLAMS satellite. Now that Bear's confirmed it, we need to find out who."

"Check," Brognola said with a short nod. "Once you're refueled, Jack's going to fly you to Vostok."

"Russian territory," Bolan commented.

"More or less. Actually, it belongs to the Commonwealth of Independent States, but I won't banter semantics with you. It's predominantly Russian territory, and its settlers are very proud to be Russians. Nonetheless, it's just one of many geophysical research bases scattered all along the ice shelf."

Brognola removed a dossier file and handed it to Bolan. Nodding toward the folder, he continued, "We've arranged for a contact who knows the area intimately."

The soldier opened the folder and saw a full-color glossy of a woman in military uniform. She had an ageless beauty that made her look somewhere between eighteen and forty. Her reddish brown hair was done up in a bun, and there were various insignia and medals on her Army dress uniform that the Executioner immediately recognized.

"Her name is Anika Faithe," Brognola stated. "She's a former member of the U.S. Army's meteorological team and an arctic-weather expert for the NSA."

"Why her?"

Brognola smiled. "Well, for one thing she's the most qualified to show you around. She's spent the past five years assigned to the Admundsen-Scott Station, which—as I'm sure you know—is owned by the U.S. and positioned at the South Pole."

"Geographically speaking?" Bolan added.

"Of course," the Stony Man chief replied with a shrug. "Also, she thinks you're another scientist assigned to the area. You're Michael Blanski, Ph.D., expert in geophysics. Antarctica is strictly for peaceful research, and this is the only way we can get you inside the continent with weapons. It's also the least conspicuous, since planes like these fly in the area all the time. Nobody, not even Faithe, knows why you're there."

Bolan dropped the dossier folder on the table and leaned back in his chair. "Do you think there's anything to this idea of sabotage, Hal?"

"I don't know what to think," Brognola said with a grunt, "but I do know one thing. Bear did see signals sent from the eastern area of the Antarctic region. You said yourself that Makowski felt there was validity to his claims."

"Maybe. But I'm convinced this isn't a terrorist threat. I've seen too many operate to be misled here. This has to be a foreign power."

"Who knows? I guess you'll find out soon enough."

"Yeah," Bolan murmured.

"HEY, SARGE." Grimaldi's voice broke through Bolan's subconscious.

The soldier was immediately awake and alert, ready for any possible situation that might present itself. Years of combat had fine-tuned Bolan's senses, and those instincts had saved his life on more than just a few occasions.

"What's up?"

"Slight detour," Grimaldi said. "That storm shifted direction. U.K. air control just told me we wouldn't be able to get into Vostok tonight. Looks like a layover in Halley Bay."

The Executioner scowled. "More time lost."

Grimaldi shrugged. "Well, at least it's in a British-controlled territory. They apparently saw this happening ahead of time, so your contact apparently flew to Halley before they were stormed in."

Bolan nodded. "Let's do it."

Jack Grimaldi touched down in Halley Bay with very little effort, a feat that could have bettered other pilots. It was more than just his friendship with the Executioner that made him an ace pilot and invaluable member of the Stony Man team. It was also his dedication to the cause of good. The meeting between the two men had been a life-changing one, and there was little hell he wouldn't go through to help the Executioner. Because Mack Bolan had once helped him—redeemed him not just from corruption but also from death. Death of his soul, which was something very few people knew. The soldier was one of them, and he didn't ever try to remind Grimaldi of that. They were friends and equals.

As they unbuckled from their seats, Grimaldi asked, "What's next?"

"We'll have to hole up with the locals. I guess this Faithe woman will take me the rest of the way in."

"Well, it's not your garden-variety vacation spot, but I guess I can wait it out here. But if you need me, just call."

Bolan nodded and slid out of his seat. He moved to the rear of the plane and grabbed his winter parka and his jacket. He knew the equipment brought by Brognola was top-of-the-line. Besides his standard weaponry and plenty of ammunition, there was a black duffel bag filled with things he needed.

There were three changes of winter-camouflage fatigues, two cold-weather coats and a cold-weather cap that was lined with rabbit fur and designed to drop down on the ears and wrap around the chin. Extreme-cold-weather boots were also included, with thick waterproof liners and special heating elements built into the soles. There were also plenty of socks and a couple of pairs of long underwear that would retain body heat and allow for dressing in layers, but not inhibit movement.

It might have seemed like too much, but Bolan had learned long ago to be prepared. The elements could kill you faster than any enemy.

This would be a stroll through a chilly park.

Yeah, right, Bolan thought as he hefted the bag onto his

shoulder and donned the glasses he'd been given. The frames were black, although the lenses were plain glass, and they gave him a mild-mannered geek look. It was all part of the ruse, and Bolan didn't mind playing the role. Actually, it was comforting to think that some people were able to lead very normal lives.

"Somebody's waiting for us," Grimaldi said as he peered out the portal window of the door.

Bolan and Grimaldi barely had the door open and the steps lowered when they were greeted by four men. They didn't appear to be armed, but they stood there with some apparent nervousness and they were shivering a little bit.

"Who's this," Grimaldi whispered, "the welcoming committee?"

Bolan shook his head to indicate he didn't know. He was immediately conscious of the Beretta now hiding beneath the parka he'd donned. They were on friendly territory, but something just didn't feel right. This greeting party couldn't have been put together that quickly. Nobody was even supposed to know about their arrival, and certainly not since they had just been diverted.

The Executioner smelled a trap.

One of the men stepped forward and offered a hand. "Dr. Blanski, welcome to Halley Bay, territory of Her Majesty."

"Thanks," he said, handing the duffel to the guy.

Bolan stepped out and moved easily down the steps. The tarmac was hard and cold, but there was no ice. A sheen of gray concrete reflected the sun, which brightened the midday. As to heating the area, though, it didn't seem to have much effect. The cold weather bit into Bolan's skin as he tried to retrieve his bag.

"That's okay, Doctor," the man said with a smile. "We'll carry that for you. We have quarters waiting."

Bolan nodded and then turned to Grimaldi. "Thank you for the lift, sir," he said in a clipped voice, trying to sound like the Harvard-educated man he was supposed to portray. "I'm sure I'll be in good hands now."

"Sure thing, Doc," Grimaldi said, although he nodded his immediate understanding. His expression showed he realized Bolan wasn't buying this little party, and that he should follow at a distance.

The Executioner turned and walked along the tarmac with his escort. He could almost sense them press inward as if closing on him. There were many telltale clues here that pointed to trouble. One thing Bolan was betting: he was presently surrounded by four of the biggest frauds that ever walked.

They rounded the corner of an outbuilding and proceeded toward a single-story brick structure on the outskirts of the airfield.

As he continued along with the group, Bolan gawked at everything, seeming to marvel at the sights. He had to keep up appearances if he were to stay alive long enough to determine the source of this threat.

The Executioner wondered for just a small moment if perhaps he was simply experiencing paranoia, but he quickly dismissed the idea. No, there was definitely something amiss here in Halley Bay, and he intended to find out what it was.

They reached the building and the one who had originally greeted Bolan started to open the door. As he did, strong hands suddenly seized the Executioner's arms and wrists, and the group made its move.

Bolan was ready.

He snapped a kick to the kneecap of the man on his right while swinging his left arm in a circular motion. Even as the leg gave out on his opponent, Bolan had the crook of his arm wrapped around the elbow of the second man. He yanked downward, snapping the man's elbow before twisting back and hitting him in the Adam's apple. The blow crushed the man's larynx, and he gargled blood as his hands reached for his throat.

The third attacker, who had been walking behind them wrapped a forearm around Bolan's neck. He was taller than the Executioner, and Bolan could feel the beefy arm constrict his windpipe. The soldier reached beneath his coat and thumbed the quick release strap on the shoulder rigging. The 93-R practically leaped into his grasp, and he produced the weapon just as the apparent leader realized what he was about to do. The man moved to stop Bolan but lurched forward with a surprised gasp and collapsed to the pavement before he could react.

Bolan saw Anika Faithe standing in the open door. He caught a glimpse of the muzzle of a pistol before it disappeared into a pocket of the long fur coat she wore. He twisted the muzzle of the Beretta backward and fired one shot. The behemoth restraining him screamed and released his hold as the subsonic 9 mm round drilled through his thigh. The Executioner whirled and fired a second shot at point-blank range. The bullet tore through the man's skull, splitting bone as it carved its ugly path. Blood and brain matter spewed everywhere, the scarlet splatters steaming as the body hit the pavement.

Bolan looked up to see Jack Grimaldi running toward them.

The pilot let out a sudden cry as he tumbled to the ground a millisecond before the Executioner heard the crack of the rifle.

"Get down!" Bolan said to Faithe, pushing her through the open door.

Bolan spun on his heel and rushed toward his friend. He didn't know who was shooting, or from where, and he didn't really care at that moment. A comrade was down, and he wasn't about to give his own life a second thought. The Executioner reached Grimaldi, and something within glowed at the pit of his stomach, warming him and transcending the bitter cold. The pilot managed a half smile as another round whizzed past the soldier's head and reminded them both that it was no time for happy reunions.

"Where are you hit?"

"In the leg," Grimaldi managed to say through gritted teeth.

"Hang on," Bolan said as he grabbed Grimaldi's jacket collar and dragged him across the tarmac.

He brought the pilot through the door and then retrieved his bag as the sniper popped off three more shots. The rounds ricocheted off the brick building, chipping at the red stone and mortar. The echoes of the gunfire boomed through the valleylike landscape, making it impossible to detect the sniper. Bolan's experience told him the shooter probably wasn't far away, concealed behind excellent cover and using a flash suppressor.

Bolan slammed the heavy wooden door to the small outbuilding. It was relatively warm inside, heated by some kind of generator the Executioner could hear humming in the near distance. The room was obviously a bunking area for travelers and tourists who were weathered in. It had a small eating area, several bunks and a toilet. It was dimly lit and there were no windows, but it was warm and cozy.

"*You* would be Dr. Blanski?" Faithe observed as Bolan helped Grimaldi to a bed.

"Hard to believe, isn't it?" Bolan replied as he ran his hands over Grimaldi's legs, trying to find the wound and expose it.

"You handle yourself more like a veteran soldier," Faithe said.

Bolan stopped pulling at the protesting pilot's pants and turned to study the woman a moment. She had an accent he couldn't quite place, but it definitely wasn't American. Perhaps her time spent in Antarctica had effected the changes in her voice. Nonetheless, she was a beautiful woman, although that wrap of hers wasn't exactly NSA standard issue.

"That's no cap gun you've got in your pocket," Bolan stated before he turned his attention back to Grimaldi.

"You're correct," she said. "But I wasn't always a scientist."

"I thought weapons were illegal in Antarctica," Bolan said as he found the gunshot wound.

"Knock it off, will you, Sarge?" Grimaldi said. "I'm okay. Just a bite."

Bolan studied the wound a moment and then eyed his

friend. "Just a bite that went right through your thigh, Jack. Although it missed the bone."

"I'll be all right."

Bolan could see the look in the pilot's eye, and he knew that he had to get the bleeding under control. It wouldn't be long before the shooting attracted real authorities.

As he withdrew a medical kit from his duffel and treated Grimaldi's wound by packing it with gauze sponges soaked with antiseptic, he thought about this new turn of events. The Executioner wasn't even sure what he'd stumbled into, but twice someone had tried to kill him. That didn't make the least bit of sense. Whoever was behind the curtains was very well connected. That belied someone of power and importance. Bolan knew the answers would reveal themselves soon enough—they always did.

When he was finished, Bolan turned to notice Faithe watching him intently.

"What's with the staring?"

"I'm just wondering who you work for. I would guess not CIA, and I know just about every field agent in my own organization. That leaves either the Defense Intelligence Agency or some other outfit."

"I work for myself," Bolan told her flatly.

The soldier stood and walked over to her. She was rather tall, taller than he had expected, but he still towered over her. There was something in the way she looked at him with those green eyes. Something intelligent and spirited and...something else he couldn't put his finger on. Was she hiding something? It was almost as if she looked at him with mockery or mischief.

"How did you know," she finally asked, "those men were fakes?"

"One, they didn't have British accents. Two, they were all shivering. They weren't dressed correctly or acclimated to the Antarctic. Not typical for men who work every day in this weather."

"You are very astute."

"Sure. You want to tell me how you know I'm not a scientist?"

She threw back her head and laughed. "Because I'm not a scientist, either. Not in the strictest sense anyway."

"Then who are you?"

"I'm just like you. I'm here to find out where those signals came from."

"What signals?" Bolan asked, trying to look confused.

"Let us not play that game, doctor."

"Fair enough," Bolan replied as he shrugged out of his parka.

The sound of roaring engines and tires skidding on pavement reached their ears. The Executioner went to his duffel bag and pulled out the FNC. He loaded a clip, brought the weapon into battery and slung it across his shoulder. He donned the cold-weather coat again and went to the door.

"Where are you going?" she asked him.

"To get some answers," Bolan told her.

"I already have them."

"New questions." And with that, he opened the door and charged out.

4

Pole of Inaccessibility, Antarctica

It towered above all else.

The cold gray skin of the metallic giant reflected the work lights and shone like pure silver as those lights were reflected against stark white walls of ice.

General Gavril Mishenka inhaled sharply, his broad chest and shoulders rising as he sucked in the frigid air. This was his dream child come to life: Nadezhda. The missile contained more than five hundred megatons of power—a sheer, destructive force of unthinkable energy. When she was unleashed she could wipe out one-third of the largest continent. She wasn't a plutonium weapon, no, not even really a hydrogen weapon.

Nadezhda was a neutron bomb, a weapon that had never been used in war. The neutron explosion was capable of even greater nuclear fallout, which would mean a greater spread of atomic energy.

The shock waves from a weapon like Nadezhda would not have as much force, but this missile was special. It contained a four-phase explosive core, creating a double fission-fusion effect. The critical temperature of Nadezhda could reach 35^2 million Kelvin in a matter of seconds, and the ramifications of such thermodynamic energy made even Mishenka think twice.

Yet only for a moment.

Mishenka's superiors had first realized the insanity of his dream, and a dozen of the country's top scientists agreed it couldn't be done. Mishenka refused to believe his colleagues, arguing his case before the Committee for State Security and a panel of former GRU members.

Many of those on the panel were colleagues with Mishenka through Komsomol, the All-Union Lenin Communist Youth League. Mishenka had spent many years in the organization, which involved educating students in the ways of Marxism-Leninism. As a result, Mishenka was a politically conscious soldier, as well as a vigilant statesman and loyal supporter of the Communist cause.

Nonetheless, he was part of a dying breed. He gagged on the idea of his country's loss of autonomy, its greatness rended into pieces like a fragile cloth.

Through the manipulation, or outright bribery, of some of the most impressionable and brightest minds in the world, the former Soviet military officer had created Nadezhda, the re-alization of all his dreams and aspirations. She was a titan, and Mishenka was bent on proving his worth and restoring the great name of his country.

Above the complex the winds howled relentlessly, but Mishenka wasn't concerned. He had become accustomed to the bitter chill—it mimicked the one in his breast. He was nei-ther a madman nor a diabolical creature. He didn't consider himself a victim of the Soviet collapse, but rather a messiah of sorts. No, not a messiah but a tool of resurrection and re-demption for his people. Of course, he constituted himself a mere mortal; he'd not lost his grip on reality.

Mishenka knew that in many respects he'd created Nadezhda solely because they had told him he couldn't. They had laughed in his faces, those of the Komsomol and the mil-itary scientists who had once held him in high regard. It was for this that Nadezhda would be born, and when he tested her against the Americans it would restore the honor and faith of the Russian people.

Mishenka turned from Nadezhda and walked through the

tunnel that led out of the launch bay. It had taken engineers months, using the latest in laser technology, to carve the halls, floors and walkways of the launch bay and the adjoining base. The complex was mammoth, powered by propane generators and buried beneath an almost infinite sheet of ice.

There were two gigantic computer labs within the complex, one used solely for the maintenance and readiness of Nadezhda. The other was a strategic work of genius in and of itself. Called Krai after the word *Krai,* which described territorial and administrative subdivisions within the Russian Republic, the lab monitored many of the subspace and atmospheric transmissions of multiple countries, particularly those of the United Kingdom, America and China.

The programs within this lab, after many hours of software development and hundreds of man-hours in signal intelligence, had facilitated sabotage of the SLAMS device.

While the Americans had worked furiously to develop an antimissile system, Mishenka had implanted observation right under their noses. Those fools at the testing facility in New Mexico were spoon-feeding him the information, and they didn't even know it. His moles were in place with the project, one particularly high in the chain of command.

Mishenka knew it was only a matter of time before they sent someone to stop him. They had no idea they were playing right into his hands.

The ice shelf of Antarctica accounted for more than seventy percent of the planet's water. In his "madness"—as it was labeled by men he'd once called friends—Mishenka accepted an assignment at the Pole of Inaccessibility for the very invisibility of the frozen wasteland. Maintenance of the Russian geophysical research station above them was provided by the Russian Department of Exterior, and it was on what Mishenka considered Soviet soil, despite the fact the Antarctic Treaty of 1959 considered the entire continent as neutral. The idiots in Antarctica actually thought that they were doing something, digging around the barren lands of this frozen hell and wasting what amounted to billions of dollars trying to determine how much the continent had to do with the Ice Age.

What did it matter?

Mishenka pitied them in their ignorance. He had a much grander scheme in mind, one that would make their paltry experiments come to naught. Within a few weeks, Nadezhda would be ready to make her solo flight deep into American territory. An hour after it struck, the bomb would decimate an area covering roughly three thousand square miles of the southwestern and western seaboard, causing fallout and irreparable damage from Phoenix, Arizona, to the Gulf of Mexico.

Yes, it was only a matter of time before he could show the awesome force of his weapon of war.

As Mishenka entered the lab, one of his aides rushed up to him and breathlessly saluted. The general returned the gesture sharply and then waited with a studious expression.

"We have a report from our people in Halley Bay, sir," the soldier said.

"What do they say?"

"The Americans arrived, just as you predicted."

"Were they eliminated, Moriz?"

"Unfortunately not, sir," he replied.

Mishenka had recruited young Moriz Ninakov from Komsomol, seeing the young man's bright future. For the past few years, the soldier had come to be Mishenka's closest protégé and an invaluable member of his team. While Ninakov's background was sketchy at best, there was no mistaking his brilliance and ingenuity. Ninakov had served with honor in his capacity, and in many respects he was more like Mishenka's progeny than just his trusted aide.

"What?" Mishenka demanded. "Then they are still alive?"

"Yes, sir."

Mishenka whirled and strode toward the barracks area of the compound as Ninakov rushed to keep up with his superior.

Mishenka was seething, and he could feel the heat rising in his blood. His breath came in short gasps as he marched along the corridor, barely able to control his rage. The complex had to be kept at freezing temperatures with the exception of the enclosed labs to prevent the structures from collapsing. Certain areas were reinforced with steel scaffolding, but the majority of the underground base was maintained in a natural state. It prevented detection from infrared signatures in satellite or spy plane photos.

Colonel Vasily promised results, but apparently that wasn't the case. The former Russian army officer was one of the best—or *had* been one of the best—but this was the final straw. If there was anything that Mishenka couldn't tolerate it was ineptitude. Vasily's men were falling under the skills of one American—a man they had yet to identify—and Mishenka wasn't about to let the farce continue.

He entered the barracks area and found Vasily engaged in a rather fancy meal with his executive officers. Most of the men were absent from the barracks, either working or conducting maneuvers on the inhospitable terrain above them.

Mishenka marched over to the officers and cleared his throat. The men jumped up and saluted, although Vasily only rose and stood at attention.

"Colonel Vasily, I have just been informed the American posing as a scientist is still alive."

"Begging your pardon, sir," Vasily snapped, "but that cannot be. I not only sent part of my team, but my most trusted sniper."

Mishenka turned and eyed Ninakov frostily. "Moriz, you are certain of this report?"

"Yes, sir," he said. "It has been confirmed at the highest levels."

"I see," Mishenka said coldly, and he returned a harder look to his chief officer. "There is no question that your efforts have failed. Again. Colonel, I am a patient man but I will not continue to endure failure. You have dishonored me and this unit for the last time." He turned to the nearest officer. "Captain, your pistol?"

The man didn't hesitate, reaching into his holster and retrieving the 9 mm Makarov carried by every senior commander in the complex. He passed the weapon to Mishenka, who immediately snatched it and cocked the hammer.

Vasily raised his hands, backing up as he realized what Mishenka planned to do. He reached for his own pistol at the last second, obviously intent on not allowing himself to die under such disgrace, but it didn't matter. Vasily had the weapon up with his thumb on the hammer before Mishenka fired twice.

Both 9 mm rounds took Vasily in the head, the gunfire in the confines causing Mishenka's ears to ring. The colonel's head snapped backward, striking the white wall behind him and smearing it with a pink-red haze. He slumped to the ground as Mishenka returned the captain's pistol.

The four officers who had been seated the table with Vasily stood frozen in place. Mishenka met the look of each one of them in turn, his heart thudding angrily in his chest. The blush he felt in his face and the throbbing in his temples made him seem impervious to the cold.

"I will let the remainder of you men decide who should be promoted to Colonel Vasily's position. This man," he spit, gesturing to the corpse, "is still deserving of a military burial. For the most part, he served with honor. See to it."

The men nodded and mumbled some "yes sirs" before Mishenka turned on his heel and left. The general couldn't help but spare a feeling of loss. Nonetheless, it was a waste to see one of his own men fall, particularly by Mishenka's hand, but that was the nature of discipline in his unit. He couldn't afford to let idleness slip by, and he hoped Vasily would serve as a reminder of the importance of the greater cause. Incompetence would win neither the respect of him as a leader nor the war for restoration of the Great Bear to its former greatness.

That was the way of things—the way of Nadezhda.

Halley Bay, Antarctica

EREK TROFIMOFF WATCHED the dismal scene with an unfulfilled feeling of satisfaction through the scope of the sniper rifle.

The Steyr-Mannlicher SSG-69 had been his trusted ally for many years, practically a decade now, and he had used this particular weapon to assassinate many a VIP. Yet nothing reeked of greater importance than the man shielded by the group of armed British soldiers now surrounding the outbuilding.

From his position within the rocks strewed cross the base of the Coats Land hills, Trofimoff wondered if it was worth taking another shot when the opportunity presented itself. The American was a worthy opponent, a challenge that the expert sniper could hardly resist. But Trofimoff knew it went beyond that.

Vasily had sent him with four of his very best, and Trofimoff had watched the American calling himself a scientist dispatch them as if they were nothing. What really bothered him was that one had fallen under the hand of the woman. She'd shot Renilt in the back, never thinking of facing the man before taking his life. It was a typically cowardly thing to do—and even more typical of a weakling.

Their actions against his comrades weren't just impudent; they were completely despicable. These Westerners thought themselves so superior to the rest of the human race. Trofimoff was hardly a purist in his views toward the Russian people, since his mother had been Polish. Nonetheless, the commando believed in General Mishenka's restorative cause, and he found himself bound to it as much by necessity as by a matter of patriotism.

Certainly, the Russian army had washed its hands of Mishenka and Vasily, but Trofimoff could distinguish the most promising plans. It made no difference that they were defending a people who had literally rejected them. Many like causes had been fought for such reasons, and the fighters were always put to rest with honor. So it would be with them—particularly when General Mishenka revealed the true nature of Nadezhda.

Personally, Trofimoff felt that they were putting a bit too much reliance upon such a devastating weapon. The ability to destroy millions of people in a matter of seconds was insignificant next to the powers of mind and body in a single individual. Regardless of the technology, it was the minds of the human race that were capable of both destroying civilizations and rebuilding them.

For Trofimoff, there was true wisdom in that line of thinking.

He smiled as he leaned his eye against the scope of the weapon. One of the Britons had actually moved enough to allow Trofimoff a clean shot. The Austrian-made rifle was primed and ready. If he took his shot now, the 7.62x51 mm NATO round would split the American's head clean in two from that short range. He would die a swift and merciful death.

Trofimoff couldn't bring himself to allow that. He wanted to make sure the Westerner died slowly...painfully...agonizingly. As he took his finger off the trigger and prepared to break down the rifle, he realized he was alone. He would have to find a way to get back to his unit and inform Colonel Vasily of their failure. He didn't look forward to that, yet he was already formulating a plan to do it.

And he did look forward to killing the American.

"THERE ARE NO unauthorized weapons allowed in Antarctica, Dr. Blanski," Captain Brigham Longworth said.

Bolan handed one of the enemy's 9 mm pistols to the British officer and replied with feigned distaste, "You should tell that to these men, Captain. I'm a scientist, not a murderer."

Longworth looked around before casting a disparaging glance at the Executioner. "I can see that is quite obvious."

The door to the outbuilding opened before Bolan could conjure a reply, and Anika Faithe walked outside, bundled in her fur coat. The sun was now starting to drop rapidly, and that meant trouble in a continent that experienced almost complete darkness six months out of the year. Because of its position, Antarctica rarely got above freezing—even in the summer months—and wind chills of anywhere from minus twenty to minus seventy-five degrees could occur within a half hour following sunset.

"Dr. Faithe," Longworth said, performing a perfunctory bow. "I didn't realize you were here. Are you all right?"

"I was fine, Captain, until these men tried to kill us," she replied. "I came all the way from Vostok to meet Dr. Blanski when they attacked us. I can assure you that it was unprovoked. Through some miracle, this man was able to save us with the assistance of his pilot. Who, by the way, lies inside this building wounded. He will need immediate medical attention."

"Yes, of course," Longworth said in a clipped tone, gesturing for his medic to go and attend to Jack Grimaldi.

He then turned his attention to Bolan again. "You have no idea who these men are or why they would want to attack you?"

"None," Bolan said. "It's as much a mystery to me as you, Captain."

"I see," Longworth replied, whipping out a piece of paper. "You say they greeted you as members of the airstrip crew?"

"Yes."

"And what about these weapons? At what point did they produce weapons?"

"They didn't at first. They acted as if they were escorting me here. They grabbed me and then all of the sudden the shooting started."

"I see. So the weapons you shot them with were ones they had, not any you were carrying."

"Right."

Longworth nodded and finally closed the pad. "I do apologize, Dr. Blanski. I obviously have made an error in judgment. It was thoughtless and arrogant of me to assume you would have brought weapons to Antarctica."

"Forget it," Bolan replied. "Will you take good care of my friend there?"

"I bloody well will, sir," Longworth replied. "You have my personal guarantee he will receive the best attention we can offer."

Bolan nodded and then reached into his pocket and withdrew a small card. It looked like an ordinary business card, embossed with a gold symbol and some fancy lettering. The number contained on it would be forwarded through five different switching areas and then secured with digital signature codes before ringing a line at Stony Man Farm.

"This is a number to the institute where I work," Bolan told Longworth. "Would you contact them and let them know my pilot was injured? They chartered that flight and would like to know that I'm okay."

"Of course, sir," Longworth said, taking the card hesitantly and adding, "But would you not perhaps wish to speak with them personally?"

"Time is of the essence here, Captain," Bolan answered. "I have a limited amount of time to conduct my experiments. You will understand when I say that our investors expect results. My employer is completely funded by charity, and every dime counts. I wonder if these men were after my data or even my equipment."

"Of course, sir," Longworth said with a nod. "I'm in the know about such issues."

"Thank you for your consideration, Captain Longworth," Faithe interjected, holding out her hand, which the officer kissed gently. "It was most agreeable to see you again."

"You are leaving, Dr. Faithe?"

"We must depart before the next storm sets in," she said. "I have arranged for us to leave by hydroplane."

Faithe looked at Bolan. "We shall have to stay here tonight, Doctor, and leave at first light."

Bolan nodded.

"Very well, Dr. Faithe," Longworth said. He turned and began barking orders at the remaining soldiers, who had fanned out and were checking the dead for identification.

The Executioner turned with Faithe and entered the building. The winds were starting to kick up outside, and Bolan would appreciate the warmth. It was damn cold, to be sure, and the soldier knew that it would be a lot colder when they arrived in Molodeznaja.

"You going to be okay until I get back?" Bolan asked Grimaldi as several soldiers came in with a litter.

"I'll be fine," Grimaldi said with a slur in his voice.

"He's had some morphine, sir," the medic explained. "The bullet went through and through. Missed the bone by a narrow margin, but I should think this old boy will be up before you know it."

He turned to Grimaldi and winked. "You're a tough bloke."

"Thanks," the Stony Man pilot replied with a drug-induced cheeriness.

"Take it easy, Jack."

"Will do, Sarge."

Bolan hoped the other men didn't catch the slip, and he looked at each face in turn. Nobody appeared to give it another thought, obviously focused on their task as they moved Grimaldi onto the litter under the careful eye of the medic. As they were leaving, Bolan called for the man who had introduced himself as Richmondson.

"Where are you taking him?"

"We have a general surgeon at the base," Richmondson replied. "It is just a few miles from here, Dr. Blanski. You may come see him if you wish. He'll be fine. Under the best care any chap can be."

Bolan nodded and the medic left him alone with Faithe.

The Executioner looked down at her and said, "Okay, how about those answers you promised me."

She smiled as she sat at a nearby table and replied, "Of course."

5

Dr. Anika Faithe had led an interesting life by any measure.

Mack Bolan knew she served with distinction in the Gulf War, winning several medals including the Distinguished Service Cross and two Bronze Stars. Once she graduated from warrant officer's school, Faithe attended UCLA while on stateside tours and completed her degree in meteorology. Afterward, she continued to progress as a military scientist, even spending a brief time at the Advanced Research Institute in Virginia before leaving the military.

Her next assignment was with the National Security Agency as a weather satellite adviser. She was involved with several top secret projects and presently held a GS-18 rating with a security clearance so high that only a select few knew the official name of the clearance.

Presently, she was working for the NSA as a field agent and serving U.S. defense purposes here in Antarctica.

While she didn't tell the Executioner most of this, he already knew it and she knew he did. She gave him the pertinent details and he realized that she was doling out more information than actually required. The soldier didn't feel any need to mince words in that case, so he decided to show some of the same forthrightness without compromising himself or the Stony Man group.

"So you are *not* a scientist. This much is obvious to me,"

Faithe said. "Would you care to explain your true presence here?"

"I need you to get me inside CIS territory so I can pinpoint those signals."

"And what territory specifically are you referring to?"

"Molodeznaja," Bolan replied. "My people are convinced that's the closest habitable point to what we're looking for."

"And what exactly are you looking for, Blanski?"

"You tell me," Bolan said, "since you obviously aren't here to collect rock samples."

Faithe smiled and sipped a steaming liquid from her mug. She'd heated some apple cider sprinkled with powdered sugar and spiced with cinnamon sticks. It was a favorite concoction in that part of the world, and no wonder. Bolan held a mug of his own, and the cider seemed to ooze down his throat and warm his insides. The outbuilding was actually stocked with quite a bit of food—mostly dry staples that could withstand not only the temperature extremes but also the time between visitors.

"I know about the signals that were sent to the SLAMS satellite," she finally said. "I also know they didn't originate from Admundsen-Scott Station, although they appeared to have originated from there."

Bolan nodded. "My people said the central part of the continent, but they couldn't be more specific. How do you know about SLAMS?"

"Come now, Blanski," she said with a snort. "Do you really think there's anything the NSA doesn't know? Our job is national security, and antimissile systems are matters of national security."

"Go on."

"Those signals came from an area known as the Pole of Inaccessibility. Ever heard of it?"

"Sure," Bolan said. "I've heard of it."

Faithe rose and began to pace the room, grabbing her arms and rubbing to improve circulation. She was dressed in a bulky turtleneck sweater that flowed past her waist. She'd stripped from her snow pants to reveal a pair of woolen stretch trousers beneath them, and removed her boots. The soldier could glimpse just a hint of the thermal underwear beneath the pants. Bolan had lit a fire in the large brick fireplace against one wall, and she stood in front of it. The crackling flames lit her face and cast a warm glow across her timeless features.

The Executioner could see that keen mind working, although he had to admit he was a bit suspicious. Brognola had said that Stony Man hadn't known about the SLAMS project; not even Price had heard about it through her NSA connections. It seemed a bit more than coincidence that Faithe now stood here talking about it as if it had been her own from the beginning.

"It is some of the harshest terrain in Antarctica, to be sure," Faithe continued. "The Pole of Inaccessibility lies at a height of about twelve thousand feet above sea level on the sixty-degree longitudinal axis. It is covered by a sheet of ice approximately forty-one inches thick at this time of year. Not a nice place to visit."

"How did you manage to trace the signals so precisely?" Bolan asked, rising from a chair and dropping into a cushioned loveseat in front of the fireplace. He'd stripped down himself, donning long underwear before sliding into a pair of wool pants and a plaid shirt made from quilted flannel

"Whoever sent those signals wasn't expecting someone to intercept them on short-range waves from a local area. I believe whoever's behind this was only planning on monitoring from a distance."

"So because you were already here, it made it easier to pinpoint the location?"

Faithe nodded. "Exactly."

"Well, they must know something. This is the second hit team sent for me, and we're only in day two," Bolan pointed out.

"It is probable that they know about *you*," Faithe said. "However, they obviously have no idea that I'm involved."

"Don't be too sure."

Faithe stared at him. "No one has made any attempts on

my life, which means they don't know I've traced the signals directly to them."

"I'd buy that except for one thing," the soldier stated. "Whoever sniped Jack managed to escape. I'm sure the sniper got a glimpse of you."

"Meaning?"

"Meaning you might have been anonymous but you aren't anymore."

Bolan could see Faithe swallow hard as she stopped pacing and returned her glance to the fire. "I see your point."

"Well," Bolan said as he rose and took both their mugs to the kitchenette for a refill, "now that we know where the signals came from, how do we get there?"

"I have equipment waiting for us in Vostok. Plenty of cold-weather gear and a pair of snowmobiles."

"Snowmobiles?" Bolan said, returning with her cup. She nodded her thanks as he handed it to her and he added, "If I'm not mistaken, that trip would take us quite a few days. We don't have that kind of time."

"I know that, Blanski," she snapped. "There's a pilot I know there. He's from Croatia. Very knowledgeable of the area and very trustworthy."

"Okay, supposing you can convince this guy to take us in. Are you planning to score a chopper or fixed wing, too?"

"He owns one," Faithe replied easily. "It's a conversion from some kind of old military helicopter. A Russian cargo ship if I'm not mistaken."

"Then we'd better get some sleep," Bolan said, plopping onto the couch and propping up his feet. He laid his head on the backrest of the couch, the mug cradled between his big hands on his stomach.

"It gets awfully cold at night," she said.

"I'll get a blanket if I need one."

"Are you suggesting we keep each other warm under the covers?" Faithe asked him.

Bolan opened his eyes and stared at her—a cold blue stare. "Not at all."

She gave an appearance of frosty indignation as she turned and marched toward one of the far bunks. "Very well, then... good *night,* Blanski."

Bolan returned to his relaxed position. He couldn't afford to get involved with Anika Faithe in any respect, especially considering there was an enemy close. The Executioner could just sense the sniper looking at him through the scope when he was talking with the British troops. The soldier had to wonder for a moment why his opponent hadn't taken the shot.

Perhaps he hadn't wanted to risk detection, bringing the whole British task force down on his head and the like. Yet, as a marksman in his own right, the Executioner just couldn't buy that. In some respects, whoever was out there was almost an alter ego to Bolan—a shadowy reflection with a black heart and a mind for murder.

The soldier knew it was only a matter of time before they met again.

AS THE SUN ROSE over the peaks of the Coats Land hills, Bolan and Faithe boarded the Lockheed P-3C Orion.

Through her connections with the various scientific groups scattered throughout the continent, Faithe had managed to get a crew stationed at Vostok for a few days. In this environment, pilots were a rare and precious commodity. Nonetheless, Faithe had made all of the arrangements, and they flew from Halley Bay to Vostok without incident.

Bolan still couldn't shake the nagging sensation that something was amiss. Even for someone with a Ph.D., Faithe seemed to command quite a bit of respect. This was unusual in such a huge place. Her assignment with the Admundsen-Scott Station had only been ongoing for about two years, which was hardly enough time to achieve rank in the scientific hierarchy. The P-3C, painted stark white with the markings of the WMO, British, American and various other scientific symbols, was a pretty nice charter.

Then again, Faithe had mentioned she was still working with the NSA, which would have given her considerable pull in this frozen outpost. He knew that being so suspicious of her was counterproductive to his goals. He was going to need Faithe if he was to accomplish his mission. Nevertheless, he planned to keep a close watch on her movements.

Bolan noticed it was much colder as he disembarked from the plane in Vostok. The sun was already disappearing and the temperature dropping rapidly the Executioner noted as he and Faithe lugged their equipment to a waiting SUV.

"Sure gets dark fast."

Faithe nodded. "And cold, too, Blanski. You're lucky to be here when there's any sunlight at all. Six months out of the year, it's almost continuously dark."

"What do you do for fun in a place like this?" Bolan asked her as a driver helped them load their equipment into the back of the SUV.

"It can be difficult at times," she said as they climbed into the back seat. Faithe said something in Russian to the driver, who nodded and left the airstrip.

Bolan could hear the chugging sound beneath him as the driver put the vehicle in 4-wheel drive. They had left the makeshift airstrip and were headed toward a cluster of buildings barely visible in the distance and waning light.

"Boredom runs rampant at the stations," Faithe told him. "Sometimes it results in high rates of suicide, drug abuse and alcoholism. Although we try to keep such things out of the press."

"I'd guess that's pretty easy to do in this environment," Bolan cracked.

"Yes," she said with a cool smile, but he could see the amusement in her eyes.

The Executioner was quickly coming to understand Anika Faithe. She was in her element, since she carried an almost natural air of indignation and superior intellect. Not that she didn't have every right—she was considered quite intelligent by her peers and superiors. Her file was full of references to her genius and ingenuity, traits that had sent her down troublesome paths on occasions.

Still, there was something dignified and honorable about

her, and Bolan wasn't about to count her faults. He'd experienced a few of his own in his career, some to the detriment of others.

"What about you?" he asked.

"What about me?" she replied matter-of-factly.

"Do you get out of here much?"

"Enough to remember how the rest of the world lives," she shot back. "And every time I do, I cannot wait to get back here."

"Sounds like you're running from something."

"It would be best not to analyze me so closely, Blanski."

"Maybe so."

He didn't push the matter, electing to focus at the sights ahead. As they entered the Molodeznaja research station, Bolan found himself hard-pressed to show any interest. It consisted of four nondescript buildings, constructed of what he could only guess, and all of them were linked by some kind of sheltered walkways.

Tall antennae extended from every building, and there was an isolated tower at one end that Bolan guessed at about a hundred yards high. The base of the tower had a door built into the side, and Bolan guessed it was there to allow work and maintenance from some relative shelter.

The driver left them off in front of the second building and then departed once their bags were unloaded. By the time they had reached the interior warmth of the building, it was completely dark outside.

"We must hurry," Faithe replied. "The temperature will be at minus 30.2° Celsius within a matter of two hours. We must be down and settled in by then."

"You plan to leave right away?" Bolan asked with disbelief.

"Most of our stuff will be safe here, Blanski," she said. "But you already said that we haven't much time. We have to get as close to Inaccessibility as possible before we are trapped for another night here."

"What do you mean trapped?"

"The winds pick up at night on the ice shelf," she explained rapidly as she started to pack their gear. "Speeds can be achieved as high as seventy-five miles per hour within a few minutes. Now help me pack. My friend will be here within a half hour, and we must be ready."

Bolan helped her change out their gear into a couple of weatherproof knapsacks attached to rigid plastic frames. It made absolute sense to use plastic, since metal in that extreme temperature would have more associated problems. There was the chance of freezing to skin and material, not to mention the chances of warping.

The Executioner had to admit that Faithe definitely knew how to survive in the hostile climates of Antarctica. Bolan had seen his own share of hellholes, but nothing like this. He'd been to Antarctica on a couple of previous occasions, and even performed missions in the North Pole and Greenland.

But this was entirely different. He was on a timetable now, and there was no way to predict what would happen once they were in the middle of Antarctica on their own. One thing Bolan knew for certain—his enemy was dangerous and resourceful. Although he hadn't experienced any more encounters, Bolan believed his opponents knew his every step.

He took some comfort in the fact that the enemy would have to endure whatever he did if they still wanted to kill him. Bolan could sense that his prey was closer and closer. Once he determined the threat, neutralizing it wasn't the problem. It was getting out of harm's way before the approaching storm hit.

When he and Faithe finished, she directed him to follow her through one of the sheltered walkways to the neighboring building. Several men and one woman—all in various modes of dress—greeted Faithe warmly. Once handshakes and hugs were dispensed, and introductions made, Faithe studied the satellite readouts and computer-enhanced images.

The whole of the continent seemed fairly clear, except for some isolated patches of solid green on the radar. There were also some red spots on the readout.

"Those are natural sinkholes containing heated water beneath the ice shelf," she explained.

One of the scientists, who had a heavy accent and had introduced himself as Pyotr from the Ukraine, interjected, "We call them the oasis of the frozen desert."

"They're actually volcanic pipelines that go so deep we cannot measure them," Faithe continued, smiling at the man. "It's believed that they might account for the sudden changes in temperature, but we've already attributed this to Antarctica's relationship to Earth's rotational axis."

"There's lava beneath the ice shelf?" Bolan queried.

"No, not actually," Pyotr interrupted again. He reached forward and pointed to the different areas in red. "We just know these are heat sources. Drilling probes dropped at certain points have revealed temperatures that would indicate holes, roughly thirty meters in diameter, that contain heated water. The only plausible explanation for this is the same theory as applies to natural springs."

"Like hot springs in the Alps," Bolan replied.

"Exactly," Faithe said. She looked at her watch and told him, "It's time for us to leave."

"Are you going away, my dear?" Pyotr asked.

"For a few days," Faithe explained. "I'm going to take Dr. Blanski here out to the shelf and let him obtain some geological samples. Capek will be here any minute, and we must return to the airstrip."

"I wish you luck, Anika. Be careful."

"As always, Pyotr."

TROFIMOFF WAITED PATIENTLY for nearly an hour before squeezing himself from behind the crates tied in with cargo nets. There was a stillness in the cold and dark of the P-3C Orion plane he'd stowed aboard. The pilots were probably in their bunks at the Molodeznaja station, which gave Trofimoff the perfect opportunity to contact his master.

Once he'd disentangled himself, the sniper made his way to the cockpit of the plane. He engaged the auxiliary power, keeping the instrument lights as dim as possible while he punched in the encoded frequency on the communications panel.

The signal was transmitted in a burst of static, and there was an immediate connection to the base of operations beneath the geophysical research station.

"Korsakoff One to Mentor, Korsakoff One to Mentor," Trofimoff whispered.

"Korsakoff, proceed with transmission."

Before he could reply, Trofimoff noticed a flash of light on metal.

The chopper suddenly appeared overhead and touched onto the runway after passing the landing pad and doing a 180-degree maneuver. Trofimoff immediately recognized the converted Mil Mi-6 "Hook" helicopter. One of the largest cargo choppers in the world, there was no mistaking the lines and superior engineering of the special aircraft. Trofimoff knew it was piloted by a Croat named Luva Capek, who hired his services out to the highest bidder.

The sniper had to duck behind the control panel to keep from view as the searchlight passed through the cockpit. He had been discovered! No...wait.

"Korsakoff, we are reading you. Proceed with your transmission."

Trofimoff hissed at the transmitter before returning his attention to the airstrip. A vehicle arrived a moment later, and the American and woman scientist emerged from it. They loaded packs aboard the chopper and then boarded themselves. The entire operation took less than a minute before they were lifting off. So that was it! That clever woman had obviously hired Capek to take her and the American agent to the Pole of Inaccessibility.

Trofimoff smiled to himself with sadistic satisfaction as he leaned close to the transmitter. "I have something to report."

6

"Dr. Mike Blanski, meet Luva Capek," Faithe said.

Bolan nodded at the pilot, and for a moment the man's devil-may-care grin reminded the Executioner of Jack Grimaldi. He was worried about his friend, but he tried to put the distractions from his mind. The ace pilot was in the best hands now, and he could survive without Bolan standing over him like a mother hen.

"It is a pleasure, sir," Capek said, extending his hand.

Bolan returned the gesture. The pilot had a firm but unthreatening grip, and his dark eyes sparkled in the lights of the cockpit. It was hard to tell in the dimness of the Mi-6, but it looked as if his hair was stark black. The soldier estimated Capek stood nearly as tall as he did, and the guy was under thirty years of age. There was no mistaking the pistol tucked into shoulder leather under his armpit.

With the formalities dispensed, Capek turned back to his job of preparing for lift off as Bolan and Faithe moved to the back to store their gear. When they were out of earshot, the soldier inclined his head in Capek's direction.

"What's with the pistol?"

"Don't panic, Blanski," Faithe said. "He's carried a side arm as long as I've known him."

"And that's been how long?"

"Long enough," she said with a shake of her head. "Are you always this paranoid?"

"I prefer careful."

"And I would prefer someplace warmer, but we don't always get what we wanted."

The interior of the chopper was actually quite warm, and Bolan realized the aircraft had probably been equipped with special heaters. He pulled off his coat and placed it across a jump seat. They sat and Faithe reached into her pack and withdrew a large relief map of the entire continent, which she spread on the floor. The map vibrated with the movement as the chopper rose into the air, leveled off and increased speed. Within moments, Bolan knew they were on their way to the thick ice shelf covering a majority of the western continent.

Faithe reached down and pointed to an *X* drawn in red marker on the map. "This is the Pole of Inaccessibility." She gestured to another in blue. "There's a ridge here, which is where Capek is going to drop us."

"How far is that from the Pole?" Bolan asked, studying the whites and grays of the map that distinguished elevations.

Faithe shrugged. "Perhaps twenty kilometers, but not more than twenty-five."

The Executioner canted his head with a grunt. "Ten or fifteen klicks on foot in that? You drive a hard bargain."

"There is no other way to do it," she said, laying her hand on his arm. Bolan was aware of the gesture but he didn't move from her seemingly electric touch. "Capek could not get us any closer than that. Even during the day, the winds are too much. Putting us where he will is risky enough. However, I promised that we would have snowmobiles, and I will make good. They will be located only two kilometers from the drop site."

"Good enough," Bolan said with a nod. "I knew whoever was dug in there already would have the advantage. We'll have to wing it."

"Why, Dr. Blanski...you're not concerned?"

"I've been through tougher than a little walk in the brisk morning air."

"Oh, I can assure you that this will go beyond brisk. Even with the sun up, the temperatures will easily stand at minus 15° to 20° Celsius."

Bolan could hardly fathom that kind of temperature. Their gear was designed to resist it, although only fools would have attempted such a journey. The Executioner hadn't exaggerated his experiences. He had crossed nearly every kind of terrain imaginable. With only a few hours of sunlight available to them, it promised to be a challenging trip all the same. Nonetheless, he'd been through much worse trials and come out the other side.

Something spurred the Executioner to move beyond seemingly impossible odds. In some respects, Mack Bolan was almost superhuman in his abilities. Of course, he could fall like anyone; he wasn't bulletproof. He was simply a man in command of himself—a driven man—propelled by his mission to protect the innocent people in the world. Bolan believed he had a duty to fight for those who couldn't fight for themselves, and he knew he could survive as long as he believed that.

Then again, there were occasions where circumstances miraculously unfolded to his advantage. The warrior had never been able to explain, and probably never would, his unbelievable luck. When it seemed the enemy was about to deliver the fatal blow, destiny prevailed and he was spared to fight another day.

Perhaps it was the hand of God. If some wanted to believe that, that was okay by him. He knew that each person's path was preordained by the nature of his or her spirit. Bolan wanted to believe that everyone was inherently good, but he knew the reality of it. There were some just born to be evil. And when they reared their heads, Bolan would swing the sword to end the terror. It was his duty and his destiny.

A RED LIGHT with a loud buzzer started winking on and off. Faithe and Bolan awoke with a start. Capek had to have activated some sort of signaling switch in the cockpit. The Executioner checked his watch as the pair got up and proceeded to the front of the Mil Mi-6. They had been asleep for nearly two hours; they had to be near the drop-off point.

When they pushed their way into the cabin, Capek pointed straight ahead of them. Through the cockpit, they saw several sets of flashing lights. They seemed to be on a direct course with the chopper, and it wouldn't be long before contact.

"I think we have company," Capek said.

"Can you tell what they are?" Bolan asked.

Capek nodded as he furrowed his brows and studied his instrumentation. "I would say Hind helicopters based on the scope signatures."

The Mil Mi-6 was quite a piece of work. Capek had obviously made a few modifications to the older Russian craft. One thing to his advantage was the fact that the Hook helicopter had a reputation as a workhorse. It had probably been modified to resist the cold of the Antarctic, not to mention the electronic enhancements Bolan could observe firsthand. They sure as hell hadn't come standard with the refit.

"How far are we from the drop zone?" the Executioner asked quickly.

"Not far," Capek said. He looked back and fixed the Executioner with a grim look. "The winds are getting stronger. This would not be the best time for an encounter, I think?"

"Is there ever a best time in Antarctica?" Bolan queried.

"Come then," Faithe said. "Perhaps you can outrun them, Capek. We will go back, return to Vostok."

"No, we won't," the soldier replied. "We need to get out of here, right now."

"And how do you propose we do that?" she asked.

"Capek, can you get us to within a few yards of the ground?"

"Of course," the pilot said with a grin and a shrug.

"Without lights?"

Capek's smile quickly faded. "What you ask is almost impossible."

"Maybe not," Faithe suggested. "If you were to turn on infrared and find a lava aperture, you could use instrumentation and echo signals to bring us down."

"It is good," Capek said in his broken, accented English. He flipped a few switches on the instrument panel, let the infrared sonar light up and then killed the exterior lights.

Bolan nodded with satisfaction as Capek brought the chopper into a steep dive. There was no telling how high they were, and the Executioner hoped the faith he had in this young hotshot was justified.

There wasn't a time more than now that the soldier wished it were Jack Grimaldi behind the stick. Nonetheless, Capek seemed quite skilled in handling the controls of the Mi-6. In fact, he'd piloted the chopper to this point like a veteran. Perhaps he'd flown in combat before, being from a country that had experienced its own strife and warring in the past few years.

But even if their little trick worked, Bolan couldn't imagine why anyone would be out here. It was crazy. It meant somebody was on to them already.

The enemy had been relentless, and now they planned to send Bolan to an icy grave by shooting the chopper right out of the air. This time, he couldn't be suspicious of Anika Faithe. She hadn't been out of his sight since the beginning of the trip, so she wouldn't have had time to warn anyone.

It was possible one of the scientists at Vostok could have led the enemy here, but that didn't really wash. Moreover, Bolan had seen Faithe give the coordinates to Capek the minute they boarded. The pilot hadn't known about the destination previously.

That left out the obvious, and the Executioner knew he now had to consider the obscure. Somebody had obviously followed them to Vostok, and that somebody had somehow known of their destination.

The mysteries surrounding these mission were deepening by the minute. There had to be a connection between whoever was behind these attacks and the incident at White Sands. Bolan was already betting his cards on Ivan Wicker, but in a sense that seemed too obvious.

Brognola had planned to look deeper into Wicker's background upon his return to Stony Man, but that information would be too little too late in helping the Executioner.

The chopper swung into a level position and shook with unbelievable force as Capek tried to hold it against the buffeting winds.

"I am unable to hold long," he said, jerking his head toward the compartment. "If you leave, do so now."

Bolan didn't wait for an engraved invitation. He whirled and rushed out of the cockpit, practically dragging Faithe with him. The Executioner ordered her to stand still as he passed her a pack and a large bag. He then shrugged into his own pack and grabbed the remaining two duffel bags.

"Get to the door. Now!" he hollered over the noise of the shimmying craft.

She did as instructed, but not before throwing him a furious look. The two opened the door of the Mil Mi-6, the high winds blasting their faces with a merciless bite. Bolan went out first, bracing himself for the landing that came much sooner than expected. Faithe collapsed onto the snow-packed ice shelf a moment later, a dark and almost formless shape.

A moment later, the chopper moved up and away from them. Bolan fumbled with the packs, struggling against the chilling winds. It was as if they were biting through his jacket and gloves like angry wolves with razor-sharp fangs.

The Executioner looked around them, trying to see if he could spot the choppers, but visibility was zero in the winds and blowing snow. He reached into a side pocket of one of the duffels and withdrew a flare.

"What are you doing?" Faithe shouted over the blustering winds. "They will see us!"

"I can barely see you, lady," Bolan snapped, "and we're over a lava hole. Remember?"

Faithe nodded and fell silent.

Bolan worked feverishly to get the shelter out of the pack. The flare provided him enough light by which to see, but he knew it wouldn't last long and he wanted to conserve the rest of them. It only took him ten minutes—with Faithe's help—to get the shelter in place.

Once they were safely inside, Bolan rolled out a heavy Mylar mat with spikes in one side. It served as a makeshift floor, preventing the transfer of heat from their bodies to the icy ground beneath, or vice versa. Within a minute, he had the heater frame in place. Bolan dropped three, crystallike rocks into the center of the special stove and lit them with the dying flare. The rocks gave off an immediate glow and radiated consistent heat.

Faithe removed her gloves and put them close to the stove as Bolan hauled in the rest of the gear and buttoned the shelter.

"This is amazing," she said. "What is it?"

"Not sure exactly," the Executioner said with a shrug. "Some sort of special compound mixed by a guy I know. It contains magnesium oxide, for one thing, and some other chemicals I wouldn't care to guess."

"And someone you work with created this? It's ingenious."

The Executioner smiled. "We call him Gadgets."

"I'm not surprised."

They sat in front of the heat and listened to the winds howl.

Faithe finally said, "It will continue like this for a while and then the winds will pipe down. We should get some sleep."

"Yeah," Bolan agreed. "We've got a long walk ahead of us tomorrow."

THE NIGHT PASSED without incident. Bolan was up with the sun and he woke Faithe, who seemed to be sleeping soundly. Within minutes, they were fully dressed and breaking down their equipment. Once the stove was encased in its protective sheath and the mat rolled up, Bolan struck the shelter and packed it, as well.

"You ready?" he asked her as he donned his pack.

"Yes." She produced a compass and marked their position. "I will have to realign, but I'm sure the shelter holding our transportation is in that direction."

She pointed to a slight ridge in the distance.

Bolan nodded as he lifted their two bags. "I'm glad I won't have to haul these more than that. Otherwise, we'd be leaving them."

Faithe nodded as she cinched her backpack tightly and

hefted her own duffel. "I cannot argue with you on that point, Blanski."

The two set out in the direction of the alleged snowmobiles. As they walked, the Executioner had to wonder why Faithe had gone to such great lengths.

"It seems like you went to some trouble doing things this way," he remarked. "Why?"

She huffed and puffed as she hauled her own weight. There was no doubt that Anika Faithe wasn't used to such physical exertion. Not to mention that the mere act of breathing hard could practically freeze the lungs. On the other hand, Bolan was more accustomed to such things and he made his way along with relative ease.

"If those signals were generated by an enemy of the United States," she replied, "then I do not want us to be the ones who are surprised."

"That makes sense," Bolan agreed.

"Plus, as I explained before, the winds are very unpredictable, and I knew that only Capek could have done what he did last night. I did not want to involve the innocents."

"That's commendable of you," the Executioner said. "I avoid the same kind of situations myself."

"How long have you been doing your kind of work?"

The question seemed offhanded. "A long time."

"You have never considered retirement?"

"Someday, I suppose, but not yet."

"No family or children."

"No."

"A girlfriend, perhaps?"

He shook his head. "Nothing steady."

"It would seem you do not have much of a social life."

"I get around."

They spent most of the remainder of their trek in silence. As the reached the peak of the ridge almost an hour later, Bolan spotted the shelter. It was nearly impossible to see except for the tall, willowy antenna that rose from it and the large orange dot emblazoned on one side.

"I had the snowmobiles airlifted in two days ago when I was told you were coming. They managed to get them out here before the storm passed through."

"Good thinking," Bolan retorted.

Within minutes, they reached the shelter. It was really a plastic- and wooden-frame with ventilated sides that allowed air to flow through but kept out snow and ice. Faithe dropped her bag and disengaged the thick wooden dowel that served as the door bolt.

She ducked her head inside and then peered at Bolan with a mischievous expression. "They are here and look to be in good order. It might take some time getting them started, however."

"Let's get on it."

Bolan dropped his bags also and then went about the task of getting the snowmobiles extracted from the shelter.

As they worked, Faithe explained how they used the shelters year-round to store testing equipment and other supplies. There were only certain times they could get into or out of that area, and the shelter came in handy during those times.

"On several occasions, it has even saved people's lives who were trapped in sudden storms that were not predicted."

"Hell of a way to live," Bolan said.

It took nearly an hour of precious daylight before the Executioner could get both of the snowmobiles started, but he finally managed to accomplish the task. As they warmed up, he lashed their equipment securely to the cargo pads attached to the back of the snowmobiles.

That accomplished, he extracted the FNC from the bag and loaded it. He sprayed a protective and lubricating silicone-oil mixture onto the action, then did the same for the Beretta before returning it to the holster beneath his parka. He slid the Fabrique Nationale carbine-style weapon into a special insulated sheath he'd strapped to the snowmobile and then climbed onto his mount.

He withdrew the scarf at his neck and wrapped it twice around his face before donning the cold-air filter. He then adjusted his goggles, cinched the parka tight and looked over at Faithe, who was preparing her own gear for the cold ride ahead.

"With any luck," he told her, "we'll make it to the Pole by nightfall."

She pulled back a fur-lined mitten and looked at her watch. "We only have two hours left. We should go."

Bolan nodded and let the engine on the snowmobile roar a few times before popping the clutch and putting the thing into gear. The snowmobile launched from its spot, and it wasn't long before Faithe was leading him along the length of the ridge.

They reached a break in the rocky terrain and Faithe turned so that they passed through it. Nothing but a pure sheet of white lay before them and a peak loomed in the distance: the Pole of Inaccessibility. It seemed unreal to find himself rapidly crossing some of the most inhospitable country on the face of the world, but the terrain could hold such breathtaking views. In many respects, the Executioner felt as if he were on another planet—or perhaps as if he'd traveled back in time to the Ice Age.

Heavy-caliber gunfire rocked the ground ahead of them and interrupted Bolan's musings. He steered the snowmobile to the right, splitting away from Faithe's own evasive path as a thick line of tracers ran past them. The red-orange tips struck the ground and quickly subsided in the bitter chill. They burned hot, and even through the filter mask the soldier immediately recognized the unmistakable scent of burning phosphorous.

Bolan looked around but saw nothing. He glanced skyward and searched for aircraft, but it was also empty and blue. A quick look to the rear and he finally spotted the threat. A Mil Mi-24 Hind helicopter had completed its turn and was now on a direct intercept course.

And the Executioner prepared for the challenge.

7

Mack Bolan nearly flipped his snowmobile as he turned it into the Hind's path.

It was much more difficult for a helicopter to take out a target directly below it, and the combined speeds of the aircraft and snowmobile would decrease overall maneuverability for the pilot. Eventually, the chopper crew would wise up and swing out far enough to take their target at a distance.

The Executioner didn't plan to give them that time.

As the Hind crossed overhead, the starboard-side 30 mm cannon winked orange flame, spitting a flurry of rounds in Bolan's direction. The soldier knew at that position there was little chance they could hit him this time, although the next pass would be a completely different story.

The twin Isotov engines whined as the Hind crossed directly over him, and a quick inspection revealed launch pylons on the port side for Swatter missiles. There was no question he was looking at a Hind-D model, the most advanced of the Russian-made combat helicopters.

The Mil Mi-24 was an impressive aircraft, capable of function in just about any terrain. Its versatility held much of the appeal, and it was configured with some of the most advanced weaponry and electronic surveillance systems available. These facts confirmed Capek's thoughts that the choppers who had pursued them the night before were probably Hinds, as well.

The Executioner spun the snowmobile to a halt as he snatched the FNC from its protective sheath. He snapped the folding stock into place and raised the weapon to his shoulder as the chopper made another tight turn.

Bolan took careful aim, leading the aircraft just slightly, and took a deep breath before depressing the trigger. He sent three short bursts in the direction of the chopper and gauged each shot for maximum effect. Finally, Bolan held the trigger for a long burst. The 5.56 mm slugs landed on target, shattering the Hind's lower windscreen.

The soldier immediately engaged the clutch and put the snowmobile into forward motion, ducking as the chopper skimmed overhead. The auto cannon was silent, and the Executioner knew he'd hit the gunner.

While the measure was only temporary, Bolan knew it had a psychological effect on his enemy. He'd taken out half the crew of the Mi-24, and that would buy him an extra minute. Bolan scanned the area for Faithe, but he didn't see her. Perhaps the battle had given her the chance to find cover—hard to believe, given the flat and open terrain. The Executioner risked a backward glance and saw the Hind was continuing to move away from him.

He thought furiously, trying to find a reason to justify the pilot's maneuver, but nothing seemed to make sense. Then he spotted the reason ahead of him. A half-dozen specks on the horizon grew larger as they approached. Bolan already had an educated guess as to what they were even as he decreased speed and reached to his pack to retrieve a pair of field glasses.

The Executioner studied the shapes in the 30-power enhancement. They were armed men, riding snowmobiles in pairs and wearing ominous-looking cold-weather masks. Their snowfield camouflage contrasted with their surroundings, but there was no mistaking their intent. They sought blood—probably his.

The soldier knew he stood little chance of flanking them at that distance. The other thing that continued to nag at him was the absence of Anika Faithe. Bolan increased speed as he made a beeline for a large outcropping on his left. He deduced that it was the only logical place Faithe could be hiding. His pursuers changed course, approaching steadily and keeping pace with him. If he reached the outcropping first, it would be a miracle.

Bolan beat the snowmobile team by less than a minute. He rounded the back side of the rocky cluster and found Faithe clutching a smooth, handled tube painted flat black. It took the Executioner only a moment to recognize the device, and he studied her for a moment with relative surprise.

"A grenade launcher?" he asked as he leaped from the snowmobile.

"You are not the only one who came prepared, Blanski."

The soldier had sensed a hardness beneath Faithe's rigid and proper exterior, and he knew she had more combat experience than he'd guessed. Obviously, her entire time in the military hadn't been spent monitoring weather patterns.

Bolan snatched the weapon and traded her his FNC. He ignored the furious look she gave him. He quickly inspected it even as the roar of the snowmobiles reached his ears. It was a CIS 40GL, a model very similar in design to the M-203. The Executioner had heard the weapon was manufactured for a certain number of undisclosed countries by the island republic of Singapore. It was strange that Faithe had managed to get her hands on one.

Bolan checked to make sure the grenade was loaded, then popped up and aimed for center mass even as Faithe took up a good firing position between a V-shaped break in the rocks. He sighted toward the center of the group and depressed the rubber booty. The high-explosive 40 mm charge rocketed toward the group and exploded on impact. The grenade destroyed one pair and knocked a second from their snowmobile.

The remaining four pairs split off on divergent courses, and Faithe set up a heavy field of fire as Bolan reloaded. Although the soldier had never fired the 40GL before, he knew the weapon was simple in its construction. He depressed the charging lever, which cocked the firing pin and applied the safety catch. The barrel swung aside with a simple tug, and he indicated he needed another grenade.

Faithe jerked her thumb to her backpack where the top flap was undone. Bolan reached inside and withdrew a 40 mm shell that was tipped with a gold-colored cap and had a bronze-type center with an OD-green base. He popped the grenade into the chamber and slammed the barrel home.

Bolan set up a second shot and pulled the trigger. The cushioned butt of the 40GL was similar to the top portion of a crutch. It added a certain amount of decrease to the recoil, unlike the hard plastic stock of an M-16/M-203 combo. The grenade didn't hit any of the crews this time, but it created havoc and that was enough to keep their attackers off balance.

The sound of helicopter blades beating the air commanded the Executioner's attention. The Mil Mi-24 gunship was now on a direct course for them once again, but Bolan didn't detect any fire coming from the 30 mm cannon. The pilot had obviously decided that an AT-2 Swatter would do the trick nicely, and Bolan realized that's why he was maintaining such a distance. The minimum charge time range was 250 meters, and the soldier figured the pilot at about 300 plus.

Faithe realized what was about to happen even before she saw the flash.

"Oh—"

The Executioner never let her finish. He threw down the GL40 while simultaneously grabbing her by the collar and hauling her over the large cluster of rocks. They landed on the other side and Bolan rolled, Faithe keeping pace with him even as the missile impacted the area where they had been standing just seconds earlier. The hollow-charge HE warhead struck just short of the snowmobiles, but the explosive in a single Swatter was enough to penetrate 500 mm of armor. The warhead detonated on impact and the heat and flame washed over them.

Superheated metal and rock rained down on them, and one rock struck Bolan hard enough in the head to cause stars to dance in front of his eyes. The blow staggered him and he fell to his knees, waves of nausea sweeping over him. He looked to his right and saw Faithe lying nearby. She looked unconscious, and there was a large gash on her face.

Bolan shook his head to clear his vision, but it only seemed to make matters worse. He looked around and quickly spotted the FNC. It lay about ten yards from Faithe's body. The Executioner willed himself to get on his feet, and he staggered to the weapon. The concussion had practically knocked him senseless, and only his iron resolve kept him going.

He reached the FNC even as the remaining snowmobiles converged on their position. Bolan snatched the weapon, swung the muzzle in the direction of the closest pair and opened fire. The 5.56 mm rounds took the driver in the belly and chest, causing the man to slump against one handle. The snowmobile spun to one side, abruptly knocking the rider off and onto the icy plain.

Bolan tracked on another pair and loosed a burst. The driver managed to avoid the hail of slugs as his rider opened up with an AKSU assault rifle. Although a shortened version of the AK-74, the AKSU had a cyclic fire rate exceeding 800 rounds per minute. It was like a bullet hose in many respects, and difficult to control under sustained fire. This was the only thing that saved the Executioner's hide as he shoulder rolled to avoid the enemy's return fire, the 5.45 mm rounds passing overhead.

The Executioner came to one knee out of the roll and readjusted his aim. He held the FNC at his hip as he triggered a fresh volley. The rounds punctured the thin shell of the snowmobile, ripping holes through the gas tank and the thigh of the driver. The man howled in agony as he steered from Bolan's assault.

The angry buzz of the 30 mm cannon resounded through the cold afternoon air as the Mil Mi-24 Hind rushed overhead. The heavy-caliber rounds came too close for comfort, and Bolan knew he was going to have to grab himself a ride. He turned to see the snowmobile of the first pair he'd taken down had stopped thirty yards from him. Its driver was hanging almost completely off, only his legs elevated on the seat where he'd collapsed.

The man who had been thrown from the snowmobile rose at just about the same time that Bolan started for their mount. He tried to bring his weapon to bear, but the Executioner was a little quicker. He stroked the FNC's trigger on the run, dropping his would-be assassin with a burst to the gut that eviscerated him. The gunner collapsed to the ice, down and dead.

Bolan reached the snowmobile. It was clutched into Neutral, but the engine was still running. He turned at the roar of another pair approaching. They charged him directly, the driver's body hunched in a position of preparation while his rider leveled another AKSU at the soldier. The muzzle winked as the rounds burned past the Executioner's head.

The warrior dropped behind the snowmobile and clutched the FNC close to his body. He swept the muzzle in their general direction and fired a trio of short bursts. He didn't hit either one of the pair in his haste to avoid having his head blown off, but they steered away from him. The maneuver had its desired effect, and as they turned off course, the Executioner reached into his pocket and retrieved one of the Diehl DM51 fragmentation grenades supplied by Stony Man.

Designed by the Germans, the Diehl contained a two-ounce filling of PETN high explosive. It was surrounded by a removable plastic sleeve that was hollow and filled with thousands of 2 mm steel balls. The Executioner had used the grenades rather effectively in past missions, since without the sleeve they were excellent concussion devices, and with the sleeves they were most effective as antipersonnel weapons.

This time was no exception. He yanked the pin and let fly, jumping onto the snowmobile as soon as the bomb had left his fingers. The grenade exploded in midair, its more than six thousand balls showering the duo of attackers with high-velocity fragments. The rider's back was shredded, and the concussion nearly flipped the snowmobile.

Bolan was in motion, performing a one-eighty and rushing to where Faithe lay still out cold. The Executioner used the snowmobile as cover while he dismounted and tossed her limp form across the back. He turned to the sound of another approaching snowmobile and triggered the FNC in one fluid motion. The weapon chugged repeatedly, spitting hot lead at the attackers until the bolt locked back on an empty breech.

The 5.56 mm high-velocity rounds ripped through the driver and continued into the body of the rider, as well. The two men were literally blown off the seat by the impact, knocking them onto their backs as the snowmobile skittered out of control and flipped end over end.

Bolan reached into another pocket of his parka, ejecting the spent magazine and substituting it for a fresh load. He gunned the engine on the snowmobile, cinched his hood tightly around his head and tore away from the hellzone.

The remaining snowmobile laid in a pursuit course, with the Hind riding shotgun above them. The 30 mm cannon on the Hind rattled incessantly, dumping the large rounds at close range. It began to seem to Bolan that the chopper was only trying to keep him off balance. The pilot had to fly the damn thing now, and try to take them out, but it should have been easier with all the weapons at his disposal. Not only that, but he'd had a couple of good opportunities and missed.

It almost seemed as if they were only trying to keep them on the run, as if like they were trying to keep the pressure on. It had been just too damn easy thus far, and now on this open plain of thick ice it should have been child's play for that pilot to knock them down, but he hadn't.

Bolan glanced behind him and watched as the snowmobile drew steadily closer. The make of his snowmobile was identical, but it seemed they were slowly gaining. It was probably weight. The Executioner was toting a lot of hardware, plus his survival pack. He also had the deadweight of Faithe and her pack, as well, although the scientist-turned-soldier was moaning, slowly regaining consciousness.

The soldier reached into his coat pocket and withdrew another Diehl, holding on to the fuse cap with one hand while removing the plastic sleeve with the other. He pocketed the sleeve, then yanked the pin and slowed some. He waited until the snowmobile was about four seconds behind and then nonchalantly dropped the grenade off the side.

If either one of the pair of pursuers saw the bomb, they saw it too late to do much about it. The grenade exploded on cue, its HE PETN rocking the left skids off the ground and tipping the machine onto its side. The driver was thrown clear but the rider was crushed under the machine, his back bent at an awkward angle with enough force and weight behind it to snap his spine.

Bolan pressed onward, quite aware that he still hadn't neutralized the greatest threat. That chopper was a thorn in the flesh. Despite the fact he'd rendered the gunner helpless, there was still a tremendous threat. The chopper stayed behind far enough to keep the heat on. More rounds of 30 mm ammunition chopped up the ground immediately behind or ahead of him, forcing the Executioner to use every evasive maneuver he could think of.

Then the firing suddenly ceased and an unbelievable explosion resounded in his ears. Bolan maintained speed and looked back in time to see the flaming wreckage of the Hind as it fell from the sky and crashed into the tundra. Through the smoke of its path came the familiar shape of an old Mil Mi-6.

Capek's chopper buzzed overhead and moved in advance of Bolan's course. The chopper turned, its metallic hull gleaming in the sun that dipped rapidly toward the horizon. Within an hour it would be completely dark, and the winds were already starting to pick up speed. The Mil Mi-6 began to drop and Bolan changed course, slowing considerably to avoid being pelted with debris from the turbine-powered blades. Once the Mi-6 Hook was on the ground and the blades had slowed, the Executioner drove his snowmobile into the LZ and came to a stop. He jumped from the vehicle and turned his attention to Faithe.

The blood had congealed into a dark streak on her face, and

her cheeks were red from the cold. She was thrashing about but seemed to wake up when Bolan grabbed her by the shoulders and assisted her into a sitting position.

He looked her in the eyes, checking for any signs of shock or hypothermia. She appeared no worse for the wear, and the wound on her face didn't look as if it would leave any sort of noticeable scar. Not that she wouldn't have worn it with as much class and style as she seemed to wear everything now.

Faithe smiled and laid a mitten on one of Bolan's shoulders.

"You all right?" he asked.

"I'm okay."

"Anything broken?"

"I do not know," she said. "I did not bring my X-ray glasses with me."

Bolan nodded at her quip. "Full of sass as usual. You're all right."

She smiled and got to her feet. "What happened?"

"I had to get us through that mess while you were loafing."

"Who sent them?"

The Executioner shook his head. "I'm not sure, but I would have to guess they were Russians."

"You are convinced they're behind this?"

"Given the weapons they used and that Hind, I would have to say it leaves little doubt."

The door to the Mil Mi-6 opened, and Luva Capek stared at the duo with a half smile. The Executioner turned and tossed a casual salute at the Croat. The man nodded ever so slightly, but Bolan could immediately see something in his eyes that didn't quite gel. He looked down to the man's chest as he reached for Faithe to assist getting her on her feet. The pistol was gone, and the echo of Faithe's words came back to him in a moment.

He's worn a pistol as long as I've known him, Blanski....

Bolan reached into his belt just as a quartet of troops dressed identically to the snowmobile crews pushed Capek aside and emerged from the Mil Mi-6. The Beretta was out and tracking before they could do much else.

The Executioner cut loose, the first 9 mm slug taking out the leader of the group, drilling through his skull and blowing his brains out the back of his head.

Bolan swept the muzzle again, firing at the next nearest target just as he noticed the other two raising their rifles. His second shot punched a hole in the chest of his target even as the muzzles on the other two weapons spit flame. The bullets struck him in the chest but they didn't hit with the familiar burn of normal weapons. The Executioner had been shot several times, and it had never felt like this.

A moment passed before the world faded to black.

8

Stony Man Farm, Virginia

"Striker's in trouble, Hal," Aaron Kurtzman announced.

The aftermath of his words caused a hush to fall over the War Room.

The Stony Man chief turned and looked at Kurtzman as the man wheeled himself into the room. His eyes flashed as he mulled over the statement. He was exhausted—he didn't mind looking it and he didn't mind showing it. The urge to remain in eternal vigil while his men were in the field fighting to keep the free world free had passed a long time ago.

The reality of the situation was that Hal Brognola was just damn tired. He knew that eventually he would have to pass the torch onto someone else, then sit back, sipping tea and watching the sunset without a care in the world. That was, of course, if he lived long enough for that day to come.

But for now, he would do all he could to support the soldiers of Stony Man.

"What's happened?" Barbara Price asked.

Kurtzman looked at her and shook his head sadly. "I just got off the horn with Grimaldi. They were hit as soon as they landed."

"Are they all right?"

"Jack got shot in the thigh," Kurtzman said, "but it was through and through."

"And Striker?"

"Untouched. Apparently, Dr. Faithe met them and she's a bit more than she was cracked up to be. Personally saved the big guy's bacon, from what Jack says. She also told them that she had some answers regarding those signals, but the medics hauled him away before he could hear more."

"So where are they now?"

"Well, Striker has apparently left with Faithe for Molodeznaja. The surgeon at the medical facility in Halley Bay patched up Jack. He's under good care, and they've told him he'll be fine."

"We'll send someone to get him as soon as the weather's stable," Price told Brognola.

The big Fed nodded and then returned his attention to Kurtzman. "What about this hit team, Bear? Any link to Striker's friends back at White Sands?"

"Our information is still sketchy on this crew," Kurtzman replied, "but from what Grimaldi said they were heavily armed. Machine pistols and whatnot, not to mention the unseen who got him. Doctors told Grimaldi that the cavitation effect and path of the bullet that hit him suggested a heavy-caliber, high-velocity round."

"A sniper rifle."

"Probably."

"You know," Price interjected, "it would seem that these two issues are related."

Brognola turned to look her, acutely aware that she was on to something. Little escaped her notice. Barbara Price was mostly introspective. Not quiet in a demure sense but more because of her high intelligence and background in the espionage world. Brognola had learned to listen to her with careful attention.

"Explain," he prompted her.

"The first two agents sent by the White House to investigate the problems at White Sands disappear. Then we send in Mack and someone tries to put him down less than twelve hours after his arrival. Now we're barely on the ground in Antarctica, and a second group looks to finish things before they get started."

"What's the point?" Kurtzman asked, shrugging his shoulders.

She looked at him and smiled. "The point is that whoever's behind this has not only been onto us from the beginning, but they're willing to expend a considerable amount of risk and resources to see to it we don't find out anything more than we have."

"That hardly narrows the list, Barb," Brognola replied.

"Sure, it does."

"How so?"

She pinned him with a studious gaze. "We know that most of these attacks have been made by Europeans from rather dubious origins. We also know that the signals that corrupted the SLAMS system came from Antarctica, *and* there's some reason to suspect a mole within the project group at White Sands."

"So that means our mystery man had somebody feeding information from the start."

"Or mystery woman?"

"Uh-oh," Kurtzman groaned. "Please don't tell me that Mack went out of the frying pan and into the fire with this Anika Faithe."

"That's just it," Price admitted. "I can't be completely sure."

"What do you mean?" Brognola asked.

"Prior to Dr. Faithe's work in the military and her schooling, I can't get a thing on her. No W-2 forms, high-school transcripts...not even a birth certificate. She doesn't have any fingerprints, or at least she's never been fingerprinted, and if she drove a car before entering college, then she did it without a license."

"A mole?"

"It's possible," Price said, "but then it might also have something to do with the nature of her work. She's served with advanced research in the area of meteorological weapons development."

"So she knows a lot about satellites."

"Exactly."

"Say what?" Kurtzman said, exchanging glances between his two colleagues.

"Meteorological weapons are a thing of the past now," Price said, "but at one time the government took the idea quite seriously. Scientists theorized that satellites might be equipped with certain devices capable of creating earthquakes or thunderstorms."

Brognola nodded in agreement. "The idea of particle-beam weapons that could cause seismic disturbances or change the molecular density of air and humidity. The thought was to find cost-effective ways of repelling major attacks, particularly by aircraft. Instead of shooting them out of the sky with expensive missiles and antiaircraft guns, we could just push a button and create a tsunami or hurricane between us and them."

The big Fed could see the wheels turning by the expression on Kurtzman's face.

"What a fascinating concept," the computer expert replied.

"But a pipe dream all the same," Price continued, shushing both of them with a look that said she was on a roll and not to interrupt. "In any case, that leaves very little doubt regarding Faithe's abilities. It doesn't, however, explain why this woman didn't exist before 1987."

"What about your connections inside of the NSA? After all, she still works for them."

"They were as baffled by it as I was. My main connection there said that she was going to dig deeper into this, but for the time being it's still a mystery."

"What about all of the people involved with the SLAMS project?"

"Only one small discrepancy, but an interesting one," Price said, reaching for a stack of file folders. "These are complete military jackets and personal-history dossiers on every individual who has either knowledge of or direct access to the SLAMS project. I've spent the past twelve hours going through them with a fine-tooth comb. I didn't find a thing out of the ordinary except Pordello."

"And that was?"

"Prior to military service, he doesn't seem to exist, either."

"What the hell is going on here?" Kurtzman chimed in.

"That's a good question," Brognola said, rubbing his chin thoughtfully.

"The connection between no background on Pordello and Faithe seems to be too much of a coincidence."

"I'd agree," Brognola said. "But I'm wondering if this is someone's attempt to throw us off the trail of the real culprits here."

"How so?"

"Striker told me on the flight from White Sands that he was suspicious of Ivan Wicker, the project leader and cocreator of the SLAMS technology. Makowski told him that Wicker lied about the origins of those signals under the pretense Striker was really there to find cause to shut down the project."

"That sounds like paranoia, Hal," Price replied.

"Maybe, but it's a legitimate concern."

"Is it?" she shot back. "I meant the paranoia response literally, Hal. Wicker has a history of paranoia and depressive behavior, and on one particular bout he even had to take medication. The man is a genius, but he's also a borderline paranoid schizophrenic. He acts the way he does because he suffers from a mental disorder."

"How on earth did he get clearance to work on SLAMS?" the Bear asked.

Price shook her head and tossed him a lopsided grin. "That's just it. It was through all of his illness that Wicker first came up with the idea for SLAMS. He managed to get out of the military's mental-health clinic by pretending he'd regained his sanity, then pressed one defense contract after another until he was able to get the project off the ground. Ever since then, it's been his obsession."

"He protects it like it was one of his own kids," Brognola observed.

"Exactly."

"So that rules out Wicker," Kurtzman said. "He's bright

enough and dangerous enough, but he's a kook and nobody would want to use him as a tool of espionage, short of outright exploitation."

"What about Makowski?" Brognola asked.

Price shook her head. "Recruiting-poster Army officer and a genius in his own right. Makowski's as faithful and patriotic as they come. Military upbringing as both parents served with honors. Graduated from MIT under the advanced GI bill, and entered the Army at age twenty-six with an MIS. Sharp as a tack, highly decorated and clean security record."

"Seems almost too good," Kurtzman said. "That's suspicious in and of itself."

"Maybe not," Brognola countered. He closed his eyes, leaned back in his chair and rubbed at his eyelids. They burned with the length of the day and the stress of the night. Every time it seemed as if they were getting somewhere, they hit a dead end. It wasn't the first time, though, and it certainly wouldn't be the last.

There was no question that Striker's missions didn't turn out to be the hit-and-get as they had in the early days of his campaigns. Those had been simpler times, when fighting the Mafia or KBG, where the Executioner could just go in, kick ass and take names. Now it was a different time and a different world. Nobody cared about what was really happening in the background. The nastier it got, the less people wanted to know about it, and that made Brognola's job harder.

America had reached a state of paralyzing apathy. Politics threatened to swallow up the senses of patriotism, justice and decency. Now, when covert groups were caught operating outside the parameters of the laws and Constitution, the public wanted to string them up from the highest trees. Things like this tied the hands of the Stony Man group tighter and tighter, although the damage wasn't always visible. There were moments where Brognola and his people had to make decisions that would compromise the security of the country, or leave their covert operations open to congressional scrutiny. It was no small wonder that Stony Man had survived as long as it had in a world gone awry. And he owed it to the spirit of dedication and honor present in all its members. A spirit modeled after Mack Bolan, aka the Executioner. It was only his dedication and perseverance that drove the rest of them to continue in the good fight.

"So where does that leave us, Barb?" Brognola asked.

"I think this link between Pordello and Faithe is where we should start," she said. "If this is some sort of deception, I'll figure it out soon enough. If these two *are* connected in some way, it would help us to figure out why we've been shadowed at every turn, and bring us one step closer to finding out who's behind the sabotage of the SLAMS project."

"Fair enough. I'll leave that one to you," Brognola replied. He turned to Kurtzman and added, "What about your assessment of those signals? Did your team come up with anything else?"

Kurtzman nodded. "We started running down possible foreign insurgents that might have access to the kind of technology and materials needed to pull off such an elaborate sabotage. That helped us narrow it down considerably."

"What do we know?"

"I've downloaded the information into our database." Kurtzman used a switch built into a panel on the table to dim the lights, then activated the computer-enhanced projector.

The pudgy face of a middle-aged man appeared on the screen. He was dressed in a three-piece suit, and wore a large gold pin on his lapel that was emblazoned with a yellow hammer and sickle on a red background.

"This is Borysko Luvanovich, a former Soviet military intelligence officer and a current known member of the Russian mob," Kurtzman explained. "Since Striker dropped the name Nadezhda on Barbara, we've focused our efforts on the off chance it was the Russians behind this problem. Luvanovich has mostly been playing small-time business, but we think he might be a key player to what led up to the present crisis."

"How so?" Price asked.

"As assistant director of the Soviet military's R&D department, Luvanovich had to evaluate and approve all requests for funding on any new project. MI-6 reports taken from a defector to Britain indicate he used to serve with the main political directorate of the Soviet army and navy. The British were told that a secret weapons project was submitted several times by this man." Kurtzman stabbed a button and a new face appeared. "General Gavril Mishenka."

This time the picture was of a slightly younger, much leaner and broad-shouldered man in a Soviet uniform. Several stars adorned the man's epaulettes. He had salt-and-pepper hair and beard, and a jutting nose. A scar ran down one side of his cheek and disappeared into the beard. His eyes were light gray, and they reflected in the flashbulb. The face looked as if it had been chiseled from granite, and the man held a pompous, consternate expression.

"Age forty-eight, status at present is unknown," the Bear continued. "Listed as deserted from the Soviet military and presumed dead. He was a graduate of Komsomol and a former Russian army officer. Highly decorated with numerous medals for heroism. Mishenka was headstrong, if anything—his military record reflects this. He tried every way possible to get his project past funding, from enlistment of Komsomol graduates to bribes and threats. He even manipulated select members of the GRU to facilitate political intimidation. But every time he was shot down by Luvanovich. Take a wild guess what the project was code-named."

"Nadezhda?" Brognola offered.

"Bingo." Kurtzman pushed the button again and brought up a diagram of a missile. "This was extracted from an MI-6 database archive about four years ago. It was supposedly a rough blueprint prepared by an amateur developer that the defector is convinced had close ties with Mishenka. We pored over this drawing, looking for any clues, and finally one of our people saw this."

Kurtzman hit another button, which enhanced the photograph a hundredfold. There was a set of initials inscribed into the very corner of the drawing: PK. "We have no idea who this refers to as of yet, but we're still plugging away at it."

"This doesn't fit any of the usual suspects?" Brognola asked.

Kurtzman shook his head. "None. We're almost sure the defector's allegation that the creator of the blueprints was an amateur is incorrect. We don't even think that MI-6 discovered this. It was flashed into the blueprint layers with a microlaser etcher. The same kind used for eye and brain surgery."

"That doesn't sound like the work of any amateur," Price said.

"No, it doesn't," Brognola agreed.

"Well, whoever created it knew what they were doing," the computer expert added.

"What exactly is it about this project that was supposed to be so special?" the big Fed asked.

"We're not sure," Kurtzman replied. "The plans don't specify anything regarding the nature of the missile, or describe any special features." He queued the computer back to the original diagram, then withdrew a laser pointer from his shirt pocket and gestured toward the nose cone.

"Based on our analysis of the diagram and warhead configuration, we figured this design was specific for a nuclear warhead. There's no question this missile is capable of such modifications, but that wouldn't make it all that special. In many respects, the specifications of the warhead and launch body are identical to earlier ICBM designs."

"In what way?"

"Well, many of the missiles equipped in Papa- and Oscar-class SSGN Russian submarines fire 200-kiloton warheads. Land-based ICBMs are capable of twice that capacity, and this thing doesn't look to be any different in its configuration. We ran this by quite a few of our DOD ballistic experts at the Pentagon, and they all agreed on one thing. There's nothing at all remarkable about this design. As a matter of fact, many mentioned it was a bit outdated."

"What about Mishenka?" Price interjected. "What happened to him?"

"That's another mystery," Kurtzman said, killing the computer projector and raising the lights. He wheeled himself over to the filing cabinet and pulled a folder off the top. He handed it to Brognola and then poured himself a cup of coffee before continuing, "Official military records say he went AWOL and was never heard from again, but we're not buying it."

"You know, it's funny how some of this is starting to fall into place," Brognola huffed. "We have no history on Faithe or Pordello, we have some inconsequential plans drafted by someone who allegedly doesn't exist and now we have a decorated Russian army officer who just disappeared off the face of the earth."

"Something is definitely rotten in Denmark, Hal," Price agreed.

"You're not kidding. I want you two on this around the clock. We need to find out what's going on and find out quickly. Striker's out there in God knows what kind of circumstances, and we need to do everything we can on this end to figure out just exactly what we're up against."

"I already have my people working around the clock to find out everything we can about this Nadezhda project," Kurtzman told him. "It's only a matter of time before we crack it."

"Good. I'm convinced this is more than just coincidence." The head Fed turned to Price. "Barb, we can start doing some digging on our end. While I'm in meeting with the Man, you take care of getting Grimaldi extracted out of Halley Bay. He'll be in better hands stateside."

Price nodded. "And safer. What then?"

"Get everything together you possibly can on Pordello, and have it ready when I get back. Also, give Katz a ring and see what he can tell you about Russia's extracurricular activities around Vostok. Maybe his contacts can shed some light on any terrorist goings-on in Antarctica. I want some extra insurance, just in case we're barking up the wrong tree on this thing."

"What do you plan to do with Pordello?"

"I'm planning to get some solid answers. This closemouthed game they're playing out there at White Sands is about to come to an end. They keep putting people off and I'm tired of it. We're going to get to the bottom of this thing, or Pordello is going to spend some quality time under interrogation by a Senate Arms Committee inquiry."

"You're going to White Sands, Hal?" Kurtzman said. "That could be dangerous."

"I'll be fine. Besides the fact, I'm taking somebody along. I'm not intimidated by military brass and I'm certainly not a fool. It's time for some answers, Barb, and I'm going to get them. One way or another."

9

Pole of Inaccessibility, Antarctica

As consciousness returned, the first thing Mack Bolan realized was that it was freezing and dark. The next thing he realized was that he wasn't outdoors—somebody had moved him.

He was groggy but immediately recalled the events preceding his shooting. There was no question that whatever those soldiers had fired at him had contained significant quantities of tranquilizer. Enough to probably bring down a horse, considering the headache he was enduring right at that moment. The most common drug used for sedation was Thorazine, but Bolan was feeling side effects that went beyond that.

The sound of heavy but steady breathing reached his ears, and he turned to see the ghostly outline of someone lying next to him. He leaned close and squinted, waiting for his eyes to adjust to the gloom.

Well, it wasn't completely dark. A look upward revealed a square-shaped crease of light coming from far above. They were underground, and the sunlight meant that night and morning had already come to Antarctica again. This put odds against Bolan. He had less than twenty-four hours remaining before a new storm would hit Antarctica, making escape from this frozen hell a virtually impossible.

Bolan ran his hands quickly under Faithe's outer garments,

checking her armpits, groin and the back of her neck. All were quite warm, and he relaxed some. There was the sound of scraping behind him. Bolan turned and came to his feet, jumping off the stonelike bed he'd been lying on.

A dark and almost ominous shape drew nearer, and the Executioner waited until it was almost on top of him before launching a fist. The opponent barely had time to move out of the way, and Bolan could feel his knuckles scrape along the right side of the newcomer's chin.

"Wait, Doctor, it's me!" the man cried in a heavily accented voice.

Bolan immediately recognized it. "Capek?"

"Yes, it is me, Luva Capek," the Croatian pilot replied. Between his panting from the sudden surge of adrenaline he added, "You are one touchy bastard, Dr. Blanski."

"You can drop the 'doctor' stuff, Luva," Bolan replied. "We both know I'm no scientist."

The soldier could see Capek nod in the half light filtering down to them. "I know this, but I did not wish to make you suspicious."

"Little late for that," Bolan growled.

"Listen, Blanski, I did not betray you. Someone betrayed *me*. When I got back to Vostok and put down, they were waiting for me."

"Who?"

"I do not know his name, but he is apparently part of the Russian armies. Or at least he used to be."

"The Soviet military is involved in this?"

"Yes."

"Any idea where we're at?"

Capek shook his head. "After they put you and Anika to sleep, they blindfolded me."

"There's something I don't understand here."

"What's that?"

"It was you who took out that Hind chopper, right?"

"Yes."

"But I thought they were on the side of whoever ambushed you."

"I do not think so," he said. "I think that this helicopter I shot down come from Vostok. I think it was true Soviet patrol."

That might have made sense to Capek, but the Executioner wasn't buying it.

Whoever had been behind this dogged trailing of Bolan and Faithe had known what was what. There was a consistency—some kind of tactical repetition—to the ambushes his unknown enemy had initiated. All of the groups, from the trap sprung at White Sands to the attack on the ice shelf, had worked with perfectly executed maneuvers and nearly identical tactics. Each team had worked in pairs, carried the latest hardware and moved with the precision of practiced veterans. That didn't indicate tactical deficiency, and it certainly didn't point to any ordinary terrorist group. No, the soldiers Bolan had faced to this point had been just that— soldiers.

Still, it was a little difficult to believe that they would create such an elaborate and expensive hoax to capture a few insurgents. This group wouldn't blow an expensive piece of equipment to kingdom come unless the benefits far outweighed the disadvantages.

Maybe Capek was correct, and the Mil Mi-24 hadn't been coordinating an attack. Perhaps the shots it had fired initially had been a warning. After all, they hadn't actually fired for effect until Bolan killed the nose gunner. The Executioner cursed himself when he thought about that. He'd potentially fired on a peaceful Soviet gunship, never taking into account it might have had nothing to do with the enemy.

Well, there was very little he could about it now. He'd just have to start dishing out what the enemy had when the chance presented itself. The priority now was to figure out where the hell they were and who the real enemy was. Then Mack Bolan would do what he did best—judgment by fire.

"Okay," he conceded to Capek, "let's say you're right. You saying this is some sort of Soviet coup?"

"Or perhaps a secret military project," Capek suggested.

"So secret that the Soviets don't want anyone else to know about it."

"Including their own people," Bolan finished with a nod. "It's possible you're onto something."

"I did not spend all of my time flying tourists, my friend," Capek replied with a smile.

"I didn't think so," the Executioner remarked. "You flew in the war?"

"Two tours with the RAF during the Gulf. Then I returned to my own country to fight against our oppressors. I was pretty good with a rifle. I guess carrying a pistol became a bit of a habit. I wish I had one now, so that I might kill whoever these people are."

"There'll be a time and place," Bolan assured him.

"What do you think they will do with us?"

The Executioner shook his head but said nothing. He had to admit he didn't really know. Much of it depended on the enemy's motives. If their captors were behind the sabotage of SLAMS, then there was a direct link to his being a prisoner. It might be they were saving Bolan and his allies for torture. If his cover was holding, they might suspect he and Faithe knew something of value. If the opportunity arose, Bolan would use this to his advantage.

The sound of a door opening caught their attention.

Bolan and Capek turned to see several armed guards enter. They were dressed in the same arctic-camouflage suits Bolan had noticed during the ice-shelf encounter. They toted AKSU assault rifles, and as the soldier noted that he began to wonder if these weren't former Spetsnaz commandos. The AKSU weapons had become the signature firearms of Spetsnaz troops, and these guys weren't strangers to Soviet military tactics.

Another man followed the entry of the three guards. He was about Bolan's height, maybe slightly taller, with dark hair and cold blue eyes. In many respects, the way he carried himself and his features made Bolan think he was looking in the mirror. The man cast an icy stare at Bolan, smiling with an expression as frozen as their prison cell. The soldier thought he read a silent sign of respect in those features but he said nothing and neither did the man.

The last man to enter carried the aura of authority. He wore the uniform of a Russian army general, with red stars strung across his gold epaulettes. An infantry tassel hung from his left breast, along with a score of medals. There were white streaks of hair running alongside either temple, and he had a scar that ran down one side of his face.

The once dark beard was now almost pure white, which looked out of place against the dark hair and eyebrows. Apparently, the guy still dyed that part of his hair, choosing to leave the white streaks. The salt-and-pepper effect was extreme, and had it not been for the stern expression, his features might have generated some laughter on the Executioner's part.

"Good," he said in a clipped, barking tone. "You are awake. At least two of you. It would appear our fine Anika is still a bit on the sleepy side. That's quite all right, though. The amphetamines will wake her up."

"Who the fu—?" Capek began to ask, but Bolan put his hand on the pilot's arm to silence him.

"You will not speak to me unless I address you directly!" the man shouted. "Is that clear?"

Capek nodded, obviously stunned by the general's sudden and violent temperament.

It took Bolan a little time to search his mental files, but he finally recognized the aged face. He was staring at none other than General Gavril Mishenka. The Executioner recognized him from Stony Man records kept during his war against the KGB and Greb Strakhov. At that time, Mishenka had served as chief adviser for the Main Intelligence Directorate, also known as the GRU. Mishenka had coordinated military strategy and R&D with members of both political entities within the Soviet army and navy, as well as those with the Committee for State Security.

Shortly after Strakhov's death, Mishenka had disappeared

and was never heard from again. The official story was that Mishenka had deserted and was later found dead by suicide, but nobody within either American or European intelligence departments had ever been able to confirm this. Yet here he stood before them now—alive and well.

It didn't surprise Bolan that Mishenka was alive, nor was he surprised the Russian general could be involved in the sabotage of the SLAMS project. Mishenka had been close to Strakhov, among many other agents and personnel eliminated by the Stony Man teams during the hottest times of the cold war. He was probably seeking revenge—it was the oldest motivation in the book.

What Bolan hoped was that Mishenka didn't recognize *him.* There had been a point when every KGB and GRU goon in the Russian intelligence field knew his face. In fact, he had killed one of their top moles right there in the White House—right in front of the Man himself. The kill-on-sight order was still in effect, as far as Bolan knew, and he could only hope that if Mishenka didn't recognize him, things would stay that way.

"You have been a meddlesome one, Dr. Blanski. Or should I say *Agent* Blanski? Perhaps neither of these?"

"You only have one guess left," Bolan said tauntingly.

"Oh, I can assure you that before my people are through with you, I will have your real name, along with anything else I wish."

"You're scaring me," he replied.

"You do not think I will make good on my promise?"

"I think you'll have to kill me before I tell you anything."

"Brave words coming from someone in your position."

"And just what is our position?" Capek interjected.

Mishenka looked at the Croatian pilot and delivered a frosty smile. "You are now prisoners of the Supreme Soviet Socialist Republic." He raised his finger to ward off any comments from them, then placed his arms behind his back and began to pace. "I know what you are thinking. That I am some insane madman with a twisted and indulgent plot to overthrow your government." Mishenka stopped pacing and looked the men in the eye now. The light that came in through the open door reflected off the medals on his uniform. "The fact is I am a soldier and statesman, not a crazed terrorist. I do not aspire to overthrow America. I am simply going to destroy it."

"And how do you plan to do that?" Bolan asked.

"Why, with Nadezhda of course."

"You're delusional," Capek spit.

"You think? You doubt me after I have been so ingenuous with you?" Mishenka said, his voice climbing in pitch. He turned to the guards and nodded. The soldiers moved forward and bound Bolan and Capek, shackling them with thick plastic cuffs. They had obviously had practice functioning in such a hostile environment.

Everything around them appeared to be made of wood or plastic, now that it was light enough to make a visual inspection. Such an environment was hard on metals, and Bolan noted that even their pistols were coated with a silicone material similar to what he'd used to protect the metal and moving parts of his FNC.

They proceeded down the hallway, their guards joined by two more at some point through the tour. The walls were lined with what appeared to be braces built directly into the wall. The hum of generators was barely audible, powering the lights through the icy caverns. Eventually, they reached a reinforced portal that opened onto a catwalk standing about thirty yards above the floor. It was built directly into the wall, reinforced below with wooden cross braces and suspended by thick plastic poles.

The monstrosity filling the cavern dwarfed the catwalk, however. The missile stretched upward a good seventy or eighty yards. It wasn't as thick as the Executioner might have expected, maybe three yards in diameter, but it wasn't his first time seeing something of this sort.

Capek stared at the missile with awe, then whispered, "What is it, Blanski?"

"ICBM," Bolan answered quietly. "A nuclear missile."

"*Not* a nuclear missile," Mishenka cut in, "but a neutron cruise missile. Yes, I can see the surprise on your faces. Nadezhda is the most powerful weapon of mass destruction ever created."

"You are insane," Capek said matter-of-factly.

"I am not insane!" Mishenka screamed, clenching his fists, his pale features turning beet-red. "That is what my colleagues once thought. At every turn, they denied me the chance to restore the glory of our country. We have been torn apart because of the decadence of capitalism and the greed of those with no vision. Nadezhda will change their minds."

"What exactly are you hoping to accomplish with this?" Bolan asked, inclining his head in the direction of the missile. "You actually think that you will get this past our missile defenses? One missile is hardly enough to worry the American government. We'll shoot this thing out of the sky before it comes anywhere near U.S. airspace."

"Oh, really?" Mishenka asked. "I do not think you shall. If you are speaking of your pathetic SLAMS project, you need not bother. I have thoroughly evaluated this system and rendered it useless. I am afraid that your beloved fellow scientists will be quite unable to repel snowballs when I have finished disabling their defenses, let alone a virgin weapon of war like Nadezhda. She will lead the way."

"Yeah, right," Bolan replied sarcastically.

He was trying to goad Mishenka into an argument. He recalled how hot-tempered the Russian general could be, and he was hoping to push Mishenka over the edge. The guy wasn't that far from it now, and it was Bolan's experience that once men bordering on insanity actually lost it, they made mistakes. It had happened to Nero, Hitler, and Stalin— Mishenka would be no different. Bolan knew it was simply a matter of having the patience and insight to push the right buttons.

Then when Mishenka fell on his face and the time was right, the Executioner would make his move.

"I do not think you understand," Mishenka said quietly, his face becoming impassive. It appeared he was over his tantrum as quickly as it had come. "Nadezhda is much more than just an ordinary missile. It is a neutron bomb, capable of destroying nearly half of your country's Eastern Seaboard."

Bolan was educated when it came to nuclear weapons, but he was unfamiliar with the technology Mishenka was spouting now. The thought of a weapon that could do that kind of damage was impossible to fathom. The Executioner considered that Mishenka was bluffing, and that his expectations of the weapons capabilities were as inflated as his ego. Nonetheless, if what Mishenka was boasting were true, then the American people were in trouble. Such destruction would more than likely throw the country into a panic and a retaliatory strike would be implemented without question.

"I can see you think carefully now about what I have proposed," Mishenka continued. "When your country realizes what kind of weapons we are capable of deploying, and that they are hopelessly defenseless against *any* strike, I think they will discuss terms of surrender. Then my country will be restored to its former greatness, and we will once again be the rich and deserved people we were."

"The Americans will not surrender that easy. They will cut you down," Capek interjected.

When his comments were greeted with a death's-head look from Mishenka, the Croat looked at Bolan for support and said, "Right?"

"Take them back to their cells," Mishenka growled. "I grow tired of these games."

The tall one dressed in thick pants and a leather parka nodded and instructed the guards to follow. It didn't appear in the least that their captors would allow for any chance of escape, but Bolan formulated a plan anyway. It wouldn't work to try taking out all five of them at once. He would have to wait until his hands were free and Faithe was awake.

The guards unshackled the pair and shoved them roughly into the cell. The heavy door closed after them, the slamming noise echoing in their high-walled prison. Footsteps of several of them faded, and the Executioner waited for some time, shushing Capek when he spoke and keeping his ear pressed closely to the door.

"Who is that?" a slurred voice asked.

Faithe was finally awake, and they detected just a hint of her outline as she sat up. Bolan moved quickly over to the concrete table that had served as their makeshift bed. He knew she was probably feeling the effects of the sedative, but his head had cleared now and he sat down and put his arm around her in comfort.

"It's me," he said quietly. "Capek's here, too."

"Oh...my head is killing me," she replied quietly. "They must have tranquilized us. I remember them shooting, and I saw you fall. I thought you were dead. And then they shot me and I thought I was dead."

"No, they want us alive."

"Who wants us alive?"

"He did not tell us his name," Capek replied.

"He didn't have to," Bolan said. "I recognized him from pictures. His name is Mishenka. He's a former general of the Russian army, and now he's just a nutcase."

"Mishenka?" Faithe said. "General Gavril Mishenka?"

"How did you know that?" Bolan asked.

"I have heard his name," she replied. "As a military scientist, I was trained on different components of research and development. It was part of the training required when we were working on meteorological weapons. Mishenka was credited with some of the earlier missile projects for the Russian army. He was considered one of the best military scientists of the day. He was also considered to be a complete fruitcake."

"Not much has changed there," Capek deadpanned.

"I thought he was dead."

"No," Bolan replied.

"What did he say?"

"He kept going on and on about a neutron bomb. I was hoping you could shed some light."

Bolan could now see her head bob as his eyes adjusted. "Oh, yes, the four-phase nuclear reaction process."

"What exactly is this?" Capek asked.

"Neutron technology utilizes fusion-fission in its explosive core to create the effects it does. Any nuclear weapon requires isotopes of particular elements in enriched quantities, such as plutonium and tritium. The enrichment of the isotopes is usually produced artificially in a process known as the cascade effect. To produce neutron energy is difficult but highly possible."

"Okay," Bolan interjected, "but how could he manage to do this without being detected?"

"Well—" she began, but Bolan raised his hand.

The sound of footsteps approached, and the Executioner knew the enemy was about to open the door. He only had a few seconds to put his plan into action, and he was going to need the cooperation of all to pull it off.

"Get ready," he told Capek as he stood to one side of the door and directed the pilot to stand directly in front of it.

He turned to Faithe and added, "Lay down and play you're out cold."

"What—?"

"Do it," he whispered harshly.

"What are you doing?" Capek asked.

"Getting us out of here."

And at the sound of a key turning in the lock, the Executioner prepared his ambush.

10

Capek took a step forward as the door opened.

The muzzle of the AKSU appeared, and Bolan pressed his back tightly against the wall as the first soldier stepped through and began to shove the Croat pilot backward with the point of his assault rifle. Capek stepped backward, raising his hands to take the guard off balance. A second guard started to enter and as he came into view, Bolan made his move.

The soldier leaped forward and encircled the man's neck with a muscular forearm. His other hand grabbed the brown-orange forward stock of the AKSU and shoved it downward as he pulled back tightly on the guard, separating the two and making any defensive response ineffective. The first guard whirled to the noise of the scuffle, but Capek jumped on him before the sentry could do anything about it.

Bolan twisted the weapon from the guard's grasp and tossed it away in Faithe's direction. "Now!" he shouted as he twisted inward and kicked out the back of his enemy's knee.

Faithe was off her stone table in a second, scooping up the AKSU before it had stopped skittering across the floor. She raised the weapon in the direction of the combatants, helpless to do anything—she didn't want to risk killing the wrong people.

Bolan's opponent collapsed under the force of the Executioner's assault, and he finished the guard off with a rabbit punch behind the ear. The man sunk under the onslaught and collapsed to the frozen wooden floor.

Capek wasn't faring as well. His opponent was a man of equal size and weight, and a trained soldier. The guard had lost a grip on his weapon, but it dangled from his shoulder by the strap. The sentry managed to land an uppercut to Capek's chin. The Croat pilot's head snapped backward, and a dazed look crossed his eyes although he managed to remain conscious.

The Executioner latched on to the guard's left wrist, wrapping his fingers around the metacarpal bones and applying a pressure point in a viselike grip. Bolan stepped outward, snatched the guard by the collar and performed a sweeping motion as he stuck out his right leg. The sentry tripped as he fell backward and landed hard on the floor. Bolan leaned inward, pressed his knee against the back of the man's left shoulder and popped the bone out of the socket. He landed a knife-hand strike against the soldier's windpipe and crushed his larynx. The man's screams died in a gurgle of blood that bubbled from his mouth.

Bolan paused to catch his breath as Capek reached down, still a bit unsteady on his feet, and relieved the spasmodic enemy trooper of his AKSU. The Executioner snatched the PM pistols from the sentries' holsters. He would have preferred something a bit more reliable than the Makarov, but he knew the weapons were made of high-quality alloys, and the special 9 mm Soviet cartridges it fired would be plentiful.

"Now what?" Faithe asked. She stood with hand on hip, holding the AKSU muzzle up and looking at Bolan with a furrowed brow.

"We split," he said.

"You're planning to fight your way out of here?"

He shook his head, slightly irritated—this wasn't the time for her sarcasm. "I'm planning on destroying that thing."

"What thing?"

Bolan sighed.

"Mishenka is planning to launch his missile against America," Capek explained. "Blanski plans to destroy it, and I can't say I blame him."

"Wouldn't it be better to get out of here and warn someone instead?" Faithe asked.

"Look, I don't have time to argue with you," Bolan replied. "You want to get out of here, then you're on your own. This is my fight, and I'd prefer we part company over having someone drag me down who's not on board a hundred percent."

"I'm with her," Capek announced, jerking his head in Faithe's direction. "I have found in my experience that it is better to live and fight another day than die without any chance."

"This isn't up for a committee vote," the soldier snapped. "I have a mission to accomplish and that's what I'm going to do. If you two want to split, go for it. But none of us stands a chance standing here talking about it."

A silence fell on the cell that was as cold as the air. The three looked at one another, and Bolan felt he was losing the battle. Nonetheless, he meant what he said. Men like Gavril Mishenka didn't care about life, especially not when the motive was revenge. In the Executioner's line of work, there was only one way to deal with that sort of cold hatred. You melted it with fire and brimstone.

"So you plan to do this no matter what?" Faithe asked.

"No matter what," he said quietly.

"We stand a better chance together, then, my friend," Capek said with a nod.

He yanked the charging handle on the AKSU as a statement of his readiness. Faithe traded looks again between the two men and then followed Capek's example. She tossed a curt nod at the Executioner. Bolan turned without a word and exited the cell, sweeping both pistols in front of him and tracking for any targets. He'd memorized their movements through the complex, and he knew the general direction and distance to the launch pad.

The first resistance presented itself in a rather nonthreatening way, four soldiers crowding the hallway in pairs. Their weapons were slung. The were obviously returning from somewhere above, fully clothed in their protective arctic-style camouflage and thick, fur-lined hats.

Bolan jumped to one side of the corridor as Faithe and

Capek took the other. The Executioner lined up both of the Makarovs and squeezed the triggers simultaneously. The first trooper went down milliseconds after the red holes appeared in his chest area. The second guard followed a moment later as Bolan snapped off two more rounds, the 9 mm slugs punching through this one's throat and skull.

Blood sprayed the other pair a moment before Capek and Faithe opened fire. The AKSUs danced in their fists as they hosed the remaining duo with autofire. Two volleys of Soviet rounds hammered into their flesh, causing them to dance under the impact before they crashed into one another in the narrow confines and dropped to the floor.

Bolan rushed forward, shoving the pistols into the pockets of his parka and retrieving an AK-74 from one of the fallen guards while Faithe and Capek covered him. The assault rifle was bulkier than his companions' AKSUs, but it chambered the same ammunition and it was a formidable weapon. Especially in the hands of Mack Bolan. The Executioner also relieved one of the others of a couple of flash-bang grenades and what looked like an older RGN grenade.

The trio continued through the catacombs, barely a few minutes into their journey before a siren sounded through the complex. There was no question now that the calling cards left at the cell had been discovered. Bolan cursed their misfortune. Within minutes he knew the entire complex was going to be on alert. He couldn't be sure how many troops Mishenka actually had at his disposal, but if the force he'd reckoned with so far was any indication, Bolan figured at least fifty.

The Executioner knew that he had no logical way of destroying Nadezhda with a few assault rifles. Even if they managed to get to the launch pad, shooting holes in the missile would only delay Mishenka's plans. Then they would die for nothing, as Capek had alluded earlier, and the U.S. would experience a blast and subsequent fallout unparalleled in the history of the atomic age.

The first trick would be to find their equipment and packs. Most likely, Mishenka's men would have stored the stuff in their armory. Bolan had no idea where it was, but it seemed like the most logical place to start looking. What troubled the soldier more than anything was that Mishenka had managed to keep his project a secret for this long. That was no mean trick—hiding the missile beneath the frozen wastes of Antarctica—especially in such a bitter and unforgiving environment.

The other issue came to how Mishenka had found a way to manufacture nuclear material without outsourcing his own country—or the resources of another—to produce the isotope concentration necessary in creating a neutron warhead. It would have taken a fine mind to imagine such a monstrosity of destruction, especially when Mishenka was obviously estranged from his government.

Bolan couldn't believe the guy was doing it on his own. He didn't have the technical know-how to manufacture a weapon capable of delivering a destructive force of that magnitude. He *had* to be getting his resources from somewhere—someone or something was supplying him food, medical equipment, computers and a score of other necessities. This icy compound hadn't built itself. That meant Mishenka was manipulating the situation or being manipulated.

And in either case, the Executioner knew his mission wouldn't end with the sabotage of Nadezhda.

GAVRIL MISHENKA JUMPED at the sound of the klaxon.

He was entering the launch laboratory when the alarm sounded, and he stormed past the computers and the lab technicians huddled around it until he reached his inner office. Ninakov and Trofimoff were standing near a video terminal, and snapped to attention upon his entry.

"What is going on?" he bellowed.

"It would appear that our prisoners have escaped, sir," Ninakov announced.

Mishenka snapped a puzzled look at Trofimoff. "Is this true?"

"It has been confirmed, Comrade General," the hardened assassin replied. To most his tone would have sounded disrespectful, but Mishenka had learned to tolerate the man. Although Trofimoff had been one of Colonel Vasily's cronies, the sniper seemed to switch loyalties as easily as a whore switched customers.

Mishenka didn't fully trust Erek Trofimoff; he didn't trust any man who wasn't motivated by either materialism or sense of duty. Trofimoff seemed spurred into action by nothing more than blood lust, and that made him both a fearless and untrustworthy ally. He was highly intelligent, not given to rash or impulsive decisions, and he planned each mission with the utmost care. Trofimoff would have smiled at Mishenka while simultaneously planning the easiest way to slit his throat.

Nonetheless, the assassin performed to standards and undertook any task assigned without hesitancy or question. He officially answered to no one but himself, but he was easily persuaded when one knew what buttons to push. Mishenka relied heavily on his knowledge of the human psyche to accomplish his goals, and this was a form of secret leverage he didn't hesitate to utilize when dealing with Trofimoff.

"How did this happen?"

"They ambushed their guards and stole weapons," Trofimoff replied. "There is no question that this Blanski is a trained soldier. I tried to warn you of this when I was picked up in Vostok. The others are followers, but this man is a leader. I have seen him in action, and he has proved to be a formidable opponent. I should have eliminated him when I had the chance."

Mishenka grunted his assent before saying, "What do you think he will do?"

"Try to destroy Nadezhda, of course. I told you not to leave him alive for long. Now he has proved more trouble than he's worth."

"I must know what they are planning to do, Erek. Do not question my methods."

"I am not questioning your methods, Comrade General," Trofimoff snapped. "I am questioning the necessity of them."

Mishenka chose to ignore Trofimoff's blatant disrespect, primarily because he knew the assassin was correct. Whether he liked it or not, the American had become a thorn in his side, and there was little chance Blanski was holding any information of value. Beside the fact, the woman was the expert in nuclear sciences. That made her very dangerous, because if she knew what he was up to, then she would know how most effectively to stop him.

"Inform Colonel Raustov to assemble his commandos. I want them taken alive if at all possible, Erek." Mishenka jabbed his finger at the man and said, "The woman must be taken so without question. If the other two resist and you are forced to dispose of them hastily, then do so. But Anika Faithe *must* survive. I wish to deal with her personally."

"Understood, Comrade General," Trofimoff said, and he exited the room quickly.

BOLAN TOOK a branching corridor rather than heading in the direction of the missile. His pack contained enough explosives to disable the warhead. The key would actually be to destroy the launch pad. The missile itself wouldn't matter if the Executioner could disable its ability to be deployed. That was the priority, and although he didn't want to admit it, Bolan knew that taking out Mishenka was his secondary concern.

Bolan proceeded down the subcorridor, taking the lead with Faithe in the center and Capek providing rear cover. The Croat pilot was proving a particularly effective associate. Both Capek and Faithe could hold their own, and that left the Executioner able to concentrate on the task at hand.

A pair of commandos rounded the corridor on the run, the sound of their boots slapping wood the trio's only warning. Bolan went low as the troops raised their AKSUs and hosed the area with autofire. Chips of ice and plastic flew off the walls, dropping the visibility to the immediate front and rear to almost nothing.

One of the 5.45 mm rounds smashed through Capek's side, ripping flesh and nicking a rib. The pilot screamed with the trauma, sucking a ragged breath through clenched teeth as he teetered on his heels. He managed to brace his shoulder against one wall and slide to the ground.

Bolan raised the AK-74 as Faithe fired off several quick shots to force the enemy duo to seek cover. She then turned to help Capek while the Executioner triggered his first salvo. Several of the slugs punched through the ankles of one gunner, dropping him to the ground.

The other commando managed to make it behind the wall where the corridor intersection in a Y-pattern. Bolan's second burst chipped away bits of wood and plastic, narrowly missing the trooper. The Executioner turned his face in Faithe's general direction.

"Faithe, give me some cover!" he yelled, trying to make himself heard above the indirect burst of autofire the commando sent their way.

The woman turned from Capek after shoving her scarf inside his parka, raised her AKSU and hosed the area with a fusillade of the special Soviet-made ammunition. Bolan took the opportunity to pull one of the flash-bang grenades from his coat, yanked the pin and tossed the bomb down the hallway. It rolled to within a few inches of the commando's position. Bolan tucked chin to chest, threw gloved hands over his ears and opened his mouth.

The flash-bang did its work, shattering the commando's eardrums and temporarily blinding him with the bright flash. Bolan got to his feet, surging forward with the AK-74 at his hip. The commando dropped his weapon and tried to get to his feet, but a few well-placed rounds from the Executioner's assault rifle put an end to that idea. Bolan dropped to one knee, stripping several magazines from the AKSU and tossing them in Faithe's direction.

She pocketed them and then helped Capek to his feet as Bolan covered them. The three met at the intersection, and the soldier studied the wounded pilot a moment with a practiced eye.

"You all right?"

"I will be fine," Capek replied in a pain-racked whisper, "assuming I don't bleed to death first."

"Hang tough," Bolan said.

"I don't think he can go on, Blanski," Faithe interjected.

"I am okay...really," the pilot insisted.

"What, Anika?" Bolan snapped. "You'd prefer he just lie down right here and die?"

"There is no—"

She never finished as Bolan turned to the sound of more troops entering through a door at the end of the corridor. He shoved them into the adjoining hallway even as the commandos raised their weapons and began to fire. The Executioner barely escaped the attack, one round tearing through his thick parka and nicking the flesh on his forearm.

"You're hit?" Faithe asked.

"Hardly," Bolan said, pushing them toward the opposite end of the corridor. "You and Capek go."

"What are you going to do?" she asked.

"Even the odds little. Move!"

Faithe obeyed without argument this time as Bolan withdrew the RGN from his coat. The Russian grenade was similar to the Diehl DM51s in that it could be used defensively or offensively. The fuse combined a time-impact mechanism, exploding either on impact or after four seconds. Within the first second or so of activation, two pyrotechnic units inside burned away and engaged an impact plunger. If the grenade was still in midair after four seconds, a separate pyrotechnic would set off the detonator and initiate explosion.

Bolan waited until his comrades were far enough down the corridor and he heard the leapfrog approach of the enemy before yanking the pin and rolling the grenade toward the intersection. He then turned and sprinted for Capek and Faithe, hearing the yell of panic from the troops just before the explosion.

The blast was nearly deafening in the confines, and it seemed to shake the very foundations of the area as the RGN exploded. The lethal radius of the grenade was only about eight yards, but in those close quarters that was plenty. The icy walls melted upon impact, and the secondary concussion cracked several of the wooden-and-plastic reinforcements. Bolan and his two allies pushed through an adjoining door as sections of the other corridor began to collapse. The lights blew out along the corridor they had just traversed, but there was enough in the adjoining room by which to see.

Bolan skidded to a halt, surprised by the sudden clack of many assault rifles. A tall, lean man dressed in a Russian officer's uniform and wearing the rank of a colonel stood in front of a ten-man squad of commandos with arms folded and a chilling smile.

"It would appear your escape has come to an end before it actually started," the man said in a hoarse voice.

The Executioner raised the last flash-bang, thumbed away the pin and greeted the man with an equally frosty expression. "Think again."

11

White Sands Missile Range, New Mexico

Hal Brognola buckled his seat belt as the plane prepared to touch down at White Sands Missile Range. He looked over and studied the passive face of his escort. The man lay with his head back, eyes closed, totally relaxed for all intents and purposes.

But the Stony Man chief knew Hermann "Gadgets" Schwarz better than that.

"You awake, Gadgets?" he asked.

"Yes," The man replied, although he didn't open his eyes and didn't move a muscle. "I've been awake."

"Can't sleep, eh? We'll be on the ground in a minute anyway."

Schwarz opened his eyes and studied the big Fed for a moment. "What's wrong, Hal?"

"What do you mean?" Brognola asked.

"Come on and cough it up," Scharwz replied. "I've known you long enough to figure out when something's bugging you."

Brognola paused, then finally admitted, "I'm concerned about Striker."

"He can take care of himself, Hal. You know that."

"Yes, I do, but I'm concerned he's going to get blindsided this time around, because of what may be going on here at White Sands. That's why I decided to come here and look into the matter personally."

"Whatever Mack's up against in Antarctica," Scharwz said, "probably has very little to do with what's going on here."

"Okay, maybe so," Brognola agreed.

He knew exactly what the former commando was doing. Scharwz loved to play devil's advocate, and he would push something from every angle until a reasonable or logical answer presented itself. It had become an old habit between these two, and Brognola couldn't say that he minded. That was just the way they did things, and it kept the Stony Man chief's thoughts off the more mundane matters. He tapped the file folders he'd perused during the flight.

"But how do you explain the lack of background material on Faithe or Pordello? Prior to around the same time frame, neither one of these people even existed. There are some smatterings of Pordello's time in high school, but the diploma he submitted when he entered the Army is from a facility that doesn't exist anymore."

Schwarz canted his head with an expression that told Brognola he wasn't surprised. "Military records have never been kept that well, particularly during the time Pordello entered the service. I imagine the only accurate information we will have on him is more recent military files and his involvement with this SLAMS project."

"That's another thing entirely. Striker said he was suspicious of an Air Force colonel named Ivan Wicker, who's apparently the brains behind SLAMS. Despite this Wicker's on-again, off-again battle with mental illness, which has been controlled rather well with medication, he seems to be the most accessible as far as information is concerned."

"Any other players?" Schwarz asked with a contemplative nod.

"Yeah," Brognola replied, flipping through the folders until he found the one he wanted. He passed it over to Schwarz and said, "There's this Lieutenant Kyle Makowski. Barb's description, as I recall was 'recruiting-poster officer.'"

Scharwz chuckled as he skimmed the file.

"So," Schwarz said finally, closing the file and handing it

back to him, "you're concerned that one of these could be a mole planted by whoever sabotaged this missile-defense project."

"It's the only theory that makes sense," Brognola said matter-of-factly. "There's no question that our saboteur or saboteurs had inside information. How exactly they did this is beyond me, but evidence would suggest they managed to pull it off undetected."

"How so?"

"The first two agents sent out here to investigate the SLAMS problem never arrived."

"Supposedly," Scharwz interjected.

"What do you mean?"

"Didn't it occur to anybody that maybe they did arrive?" Schwarz offered. "Look, Hal, if there is somebody on the inside who's doing dirty deeds dirt cheap, then it's possible those agents arrived, but somebody's turning White Sands into the Bates Motel. They check in but they don't check out. You see?"

"That hadn't occurred to me before," Brognola had to admit. "You think it's possible somebody killed those men?"

Schwarz shrugged. "It's always possible. Didn't you mention earlier that somebody tried to punch Mack's ticket when he got here?"

"Yes. Actually, I think the only reason they didn't try to take him down when he first arrived was because we kept his trip top secret."

"Who knew about the two agents that disappeared?"

"Pordello was the only one told, and whoever he told."

"That is suspicious," Schwarz admitted, "but it will narrow down our list."

The two men ceased further conversation as the military Learjet touched down.

The airfield attached to White Sands was primarily used for small-plane landings, but it was large enough to handle cargo planes, as well. No commercial liners were allowed to land, obviously, not even in the case of an emergency. Although that didn't matter since there was a small field in nearby Las Cruces. No plane or chopper was allowed to enter White Sands airspace without express permission from the base commander, but this was an exception. Pordello had been told that the President was sending a courier seeking information and nothing more, and that was good enough for permission to be granted.

Harold Brognola didn't kowtow to anybody. He was one of the most important members in the Man's covert-operations arsenal. While he had superiors in that position—such as the attorney general—Brognola didn't tend to worry too much about that. The President kept any potential problems out of Brognola's hair, leaving the Stony Man chief open to operate as he saw fit. That left Brognola with a considerable freedom of movement and action, and he wasn't about to back down from any highbrow brass like Pordello.

That quickly became apparent to the Army officer, judging by his expression as Brognola and Schwarz stepped from the aircraft.

"General Pordello, I presume?" Brognola stated.

"Yes, sir?"

"My name is Harold Brognola—" he gestured to Gadgets "—and this is my technical expert, Mr. Swanson."

"A pleasure, gentlemen," Pordello replied easily. "I would like you to meet my adjutant, Second Lieutenant Tom Mundy."

The men shook hands in turn, and then Mundy led them to a waiting military sedan. The adjutant climbed behind the wheel, with Pordello riding shotgun and Schwarz and Brognola in back. An MP sedan and a Hummer filled with fully armed troops accompanied the sedan from the airfield to the base proper.

"This is quite an operation you have here, General," Schwarz observed.

"Thank you, Mr. Swanson," he replied. "I am very proud of our accomplishments here. I hope our little escort doesn't make either one of you gentlemen nervous, but we've had a considerable amount of trouble lately, and I'm not taking any chances."

"I assume you realize," Brognola interjected, "that this 'trouble' you've had is exactly why we're here."

Pordello nodded but didn't look at Brognola. The Stony Man chief was about to open his mouth and demand the arrogant officer's attention, but Schwarz put a hand on his arm and cautioned Brognola with a barely perceptible shake of his head. The big Fed leader realized the mistake of barking at Pordello here. Demeaning the officer in front of his assistant wouldn't be the proper way to handle it.

Brognola clammed up until they arrived at the headquarters building. Mundy showed them to a spacious office and offered refreshments. Brognola declined but Schwarz happily accepted.

Pordello joined them a moment later. "I apologize for the delay," the general said as he seated himself behind his desk. "An important call from the Pentagon."

"General Pordello," Brognola began, "I'm going to come right to the point. The President is very concerned about what's been happening here at White Sands. Frankly, so are we."

"I understand perfectly, gentlemen," Pordello said, sitting back in his chair and crossing his legs. "But I assure you that there's nothing to worry about. As I've already told the Chair of the Joint Chiefs, everything is under control."

"It would appear that everything is *not* under control, General," Brognola snapped. "Not only has somebody managed to sabotage the SLAMS system, but they obviously have infiltrated an agent into this base. We're here to find out who that is."

Pordello didn't say anything. Rather, he opted to trade looks with Brognola and Schwarz. The Stony Man chief knew the Army officer was thinking furiously about this new proposal. Brognola hadn't presented it in such a way that would have suggested voluntary cooperation, and he'd done it this way purposefully. He wanted Pordello off balance; he wanted this man uncomfortable and worried. Worried men made mistakes, and if Pordello was involved with the saboteurs—if he was in fact the agent they were looking for—he would eventually make a mistake.

And Brognola would be there, ready to pounce.

"May I ask you a question, Mr. Brognola?" Pordello finally asked. "Just what exactly are the bounds of your jurisdiction here?"

"I'm the Justice Department's liaison to the White House, General," Brognola told him. "The President has assigned me to investigate this matter, since the original agents who disappeared were all members of federal law enforcement agencies. So I'd say your base falls into my jurisdiction, wouldn't you?"

"This Agent Blanski was from the NSA," Pordello countered. "That isn't considered law enforcement."

"Agent Blanski doesn't work for me, General," Brognola replied. "The other two agents did. And since they were civilian agents and not military investigators, their disappearance and everything related to it falls under the auspices of federal law-enforcement authority. Now, would you like to call the President and challenge his decision in this? I have his direct number."

"I have his direct number, too, sir," Pordello said, obviously miffed now and smoothing his jacket of medals by standing and yanking on it. "I am the commanding officer on this installation, Mr. Brognola, and I would suggest you keep that in mind. My authority is absolute at White Sands."

"Sit down, General Pordello," Brognola growled.

The officer looked at him for a moment, then at Schwarz before taking his seat. Despite the charade, the Stony Man chief knew Pordello was cornered on this one. Brognola had the real authority, and the White Sands Missile Range commander had nothing to say about that.

"In my official capacity," Brognola continue, "I could have declared a state of emergency and closed this installation to all outside personnel. Moreover, I could have initiated a full-scale investigation into the incidents here, appointed a joint study commission from the Pentagon and temporarily removed you and your command staff from their positions until such time as my investigation was concluded. I could have also seized anything and everything on this base related to the SLAMS project. I don't wish to do any of these things, and I don't think you want me to. So don't try to pull the wool over my eyes, General, because you and I both know where that will lead us."

Pordello sighed, removing his glasses and rubbing his eyes. He pinched the bridge of his nose, returned the spectacles to his face and replied, "What do you really want?"

"Cooperation," Brognola said, "and nothing more than that. I want to interview every member of your staff who knew anything of significance about SLAMS, and anyone who knew these agents were coming. I also have documents, signed by the President, that will allow full disclosure to Mr. Swanson in all areas regarding the SLAMS project."

"A witch-hunt, in other words?"

"No, a fact-finding mission. If you're not hiding anything, General, then you have nothing to worry about."

"I am *not* hiding anything, sir," the general replied. "I simply don't want a bunch of paranoid needle butts from a civilian agency nosing into military affairs. The SLAMS project and everything about it is a matter of national security. Moreover, it is a military matter and should not fall under the jurisdiction of civilian authority in any way, shape or form."

"With all due respect, General," Schwarz spoke up, "the President of the United States disagrees with you. If some terrorist organization or foreign military power has managed to steal the SLAMS technology, then that is a matter of national security, as well, and it needs to be dealt with."

"No one is trying to horn in on your operation, General Pordello," Brognola added. "Moreover, you are fully entitled to continue calling the shots on this installation. We just want some cooperation so we can get to the bottom of it."

"So you're basically telling me I have no choice in this," Pordello replied. "Even though I'm the commander of this post and responsible for everything that happens, I have to bend over and kiss your collective asses until this state of emergency is concluded."

"I guess it's all how you want to look at it," Gadgets quipped with a grin.

"Look, we could sit here and debate this for days," Brognola replied, "but we don't have that kind of time, and I don't imagine you do, either."

"You would be correct in that assumption," Pordello said.

"Then can I assume we'll have your cooperation?"

"You may. But I'm telling you this much. One bit of trouble and you're both out of here. I'll take my chances with the President afterward."

"There won't be any trouble," Brognola promised him. Yet, even as he said it he wondered if he would be able to keep that promise.

SCHWARZ STOOD in the bunker laboratory and launch command center and cooed like a contented dove.

If there was anything that could get the electronics genius's attention, it was buttons, computers and more buttons. The operation at White Sands was impressive, to say the least, and the technology was even more so. The most impressive part about it, however, was the antimissile project. There was no question that its creators were highly skilled in the areas of electronic surveillance and counterintelligence. The two men he now stood with were absolute wizards, if not a little on the strange side.

Schwarz could immediately understand why Bolan was suspicious of Colonel Ivan Wicker. The USAF officer was allegedly ruled a fruitcake, yet he was more or less the third most powerful man on the base. Schwarz would have thought—after the debacle surrounding the fire in Los Alamos—that the psychological screening for military scientists would have been a bit more thorough. Yet it seemed Congress and the rest of the country hadn't learned that nuts weren't put in charge of such sensitive projects. They either finally blew a gasket and turned their inventions against the country, or they sold information to America's enemies.

After all of the crazy things that had occurred—former presidents selling missile secrets to the Chinese and high-ranking Pentagon members who were double agents for foreign powers—it would have seemed that those in charge would have become a bit more careful. But alas, that wasn't the case. There were more nuthouse candidates and insane politicians in charge than ever before, and all it did was make more difficult the jobs of every member of Stony Man.

"So, Mr. Swanson," Wicker said, jarring Schwarz from his daydreaming, "what do you think of our little operation here?"

"Very impressive," Schwarz admitted. He didn't want to give the guy too big an ego.

"We're very proud of the SLAMS project," Wicker continued, looking around the complex and puffing out his chest. "There's no other system like it in the world."

"You mean how foolproof it is?" Gadgets asked. He couldn't help himself, poking a few jibes at Wicker. There was no real way to tell if the man was a complete whack or not, aside from the fact he seemed completely locked up in his own genius. Wicker seemed like the kind who got off on his own inventiveness, and that made for a very dangerous operator.

Wicker seemed to ignore Schwarz's comment. "You would be surprised at what SLAMS can do. It is the ultimate in missile defense. Nothing has even come close to it."

"Well, somebody has managed to find a way to counteract it. And that's dangerous."

"I realize this," Wicker said, tossing Schwarz a furious look. "It is only a matter of finding a way to counteract the danger."

"That's what I was sent to help you do," Schwarz said

Wicker scoffed at that. "Do you know anything at all about SLAMS, Mr. Swanson?"

"No, and that's probably a good thing. I might be able to offer your some more objective views on what's happening."

To this point, Lieutenant Kyle Makowski hadn't said a word. "Perhaps Mr. Swanson is correct, sir."

"What did you say?" Wicker asked. "Have you completely lost your mind, Kyle? This man isn't even in our league. I can tell simply by the way he speaks."

Schwarz wasn't moved by that. He knew Wicker was simply taking up the game of dodge-and-parry, but it was a little late now. Schwarz had tired of the game now. Besides, it was only fun when he could get a rise out of someone. Someone as gullible as Carl Lyons, for example. He had to admit he missed his *compadres,* and he wished he had them with him now on this mission. Ironman would have slapped that stupid look right off Wicker's face. Schwarz couldn't suppress the smile that came from that imagery.

"And what is so terribly funny, Mr. Swanson?"

"Nothing. Inside joke I thought of. So, why don't you boys tell me about SLAMS."

12

Pole of Inaccessibility, Antarctica

Mack Bolan released the grenade mere seconds after the pin fell loose. He tossed it in the Russian colonel's general direction while pulling Faithe and Capek backward by their collars and shoving them in the opposite direction.

The officer and his troops grew wide-eyed and scrambled to get away from the bomb as quickly as possible. Since it didn't look much different from an RGN or other standard-issue grenade, they had no idea that it wouldn't blow them to kingdom come.

The Executioner wasn't as worried about that as he was concerned that they were now forced to take the other hallway, which was in a condition that he rated shaky at best, at least from a structural standpoint. They got through the door, and it closed behind them just as the concussion grenade blew.

"It won't take them long to recover from this," Capek told Bolan. "We must get out of here."

"No," Bolan said. "We have to find our packs. There's enough explosives there to take out that missile."

"They will just rebuild Nadezhda," Faithe told him.

The Executioner frowned, shaking her words away but then stopping himself in the dismissal. At that moment it wasn't how she had made her statement, but the content itself. As they scrambled through the debris in the hallway, he began to think back to their previous conversations. While every moment wasn't vividly clear, he didn't recall ever discussing the missile project with Faithe.

When they reached the other end and got through a doorway, Bolan waited until Capek was ahead of them before turning and grabbing Faithe by the throat. He shoved her against the wall and put the rapidly cooling muzzle of the AK-74 against her cheek. She put up her gloved hands and made a sound that bordered on a squeal.

Capek turned and his jaw dropped in shock. He lifted his weapon and pointed it at the Executioner. "What are you doing? Let her go this—"

"Back off. I'm saving both our skins," the Executioner replied.

He turned his attention back to Faithe. "You know, I had to wonder how they kept hounding us at every turn. It just seemed like Mishenka had been onto us since the beginning of this whole thing. And now I know why. We had a rat among us. A big one. You sold out yourself and your country to the Russians, didn't you?"

"I don't know what you're talking about!" she said, trying to pry his fingers loose from her throat. The more she struggled, the tighter he squeezed.

"You don't actually expect me to believe that," Bolan replied.

Capek jacked the slide on the AKSU and flipped the switch to full auto. "Let her go!"

"Capek, I'm not going to tell you again to lower your weapon."

"And I am not going to tell you again to release Dr. Faithe."

"If she even is a doctor," Bolan said, "think about it a second. You and I were both with Mishenka when he called that missile Nadezhda. But she wasn't with us then, and I never mentioned the name before. So how did she know what it was called?"

It seemed for a moment as if there were nothing but the three of them beneath the frozen plains above. A harsh silence had fallen on them—no sounds of pursuit, no cracking of automatic rifles or exploding of grenades, just silence and the sound of three people breathing heavily with exertion and adrenaline.

"That is true," Capek said, lowering the muzzle of his weapon. "How did you know this name, Dr. Faithe?"

"He's lying," Faithe insisted, Bolan having released enough pressure to allow her to talk normally. She looked him in the eye and insisted, "You *did* tell me. Back in Vostok."

The Executioner shook his head. "No way, lady. There were only three people who knew that word, and you weren't one of them. I didn't even know it actually referred to the missile until just a few hours ago, which makes you the liar. Now you've got about three seconds to explain, or I'm going to cut down on our liabilities."

"You may kill me," Faithe finally snapped, "but you will never escape alive. I am your ally, whether you think of me as such or not."

"I'm listening."

"I did not sell out my country. I am Russian I have been since birth. I was born in Moscow."

"What?"

"We do not have time for this," Faithe said at the sound of approaching troops. "I will explain, but you must trust me for now."

"Do you know how to destroy this missile?"

"Yes, but we will have to come back to do it."

Bolan released her but shook his head. "That's not an option. There's a storm only a few hours out. My people said that once it hits, I could be trapped here a very long time. If that's the case, so be it. But I'm not leaving until that missile is destroyed."

"Even if you destroy the missile," Capek said, "it is obvious we cannot kill all of these men, my friend. They will just seek us out and destroy us. We cannot run forever."

"I'm not interested in killing them all," the Executioner snapped. "I'm just interested in destroying that missile." He snatched the AKSU from Faithe. "You're done holding weapons for now until I know more."

"You expect me to die down here?"

"I expect you to stay out of the way," he told her.

He turned to Capek. "We need to find the armory. That's where I'm guessing they're holding the explosives I need. Even if I can disable the launch pad, that will stall them enough for us to get out of here and send back an air strike."

"This sounds like a good plan," Capek agreed. "What do you have in mind?"

"I'm betting Mishenka will want to take us alive," Bolan said. He jerked his thumb at Faithe and added, "At least her. Maybe we can use that to our advantage."

"Perhaps, but for this moment I think we had better be on the move."

"Agreed."

Bolan shoved Faithe forward and said, "You stay between us."

The three continued in the direction they had been heading. The door connected to another corridor, and it wasn't long before they found the armory. True to Bolan's assumption, they found his backpack and it still contained the HE C-4 he'd brought with him on the mission. It wasn't much—only fifteen pounds—but it was enough to accomplish the task ahead. They also grabbed a few extra magazines for the rifles, and Capek shouldered the pack Faithe had carried that contained some survival equipment.

In a few minutes, they were on the move and headed toward launch ramp. They encountered the commandos trying to negotiate the obstacle course of fallen braces and large chunks of ice upon their return. There weren't quite as many as Bolan initially noted in the group; the flash-bang had obviously had a more detrimental effect than originally hoped for.

The officer cried something in Russian and pointed at the group, but the Executioner and Capek were already prepared for the encounter. The troops were jammed inside the confined space of the crumbling hallway, and the duo decided to take advantage of this fact. Bolan and Capek opened up with their assault rifles, pouring on the firepower and chopping the enemy to shreds.

Several rounds struck the Russian colonel's head, nearly decapitating him as he fell under the vicious ambush. Bolan cut down three more troops, Capek keeping pace with every one of his shots. The commandos who weren't immediately cut down took cover behind the fallen barricades, trying to take out their attackers. But the soldier and his Croat companion had the cover of the door on their side, and the shooting was ineffective. Within moments, the corridor was littered with bodies.

As the echo of the stuttering weapons died down, it was replaced by the ugly boom-boom sound of stressed walls that had reached their limits. The ceiling began to collapse around them, and Bolan suddenly realized their near fatal mistake. The cacophony of automatic rifle fire had created shock waves harsh enough to cause an avalanche.

Bolan and Capek whirled, the Executioner dragging Faithe by the coat as they began to sprint back in the direction of the armory. The thunderous effect of collapsing walls and ceilings reverberated down the hallway, followed by an icy mist. Darkness shrouded the hallway as every light implanted along the walls went out. The Executioner stopped, knelt unslung his backpack and dug around until he found the flashlight.

"Blanski, are you still with me?" Capek asked.

"Yeah," Bolan growled as he engaged the switch. The flashlight cast a bright beam ahead of them.

"Let's move out."

They continued along in the darkness, Bolan taking up the rear left wall, shining the light ahead of Capek. They reached the armory and pushed open the heavy wooden door. There was light inside the armory, and the soldier breathed a sigh of relief. They might need to conserve that precious light for same later point. He clicked the off button and replaced the flashlight.

"Sit down there," Capek told Faithe.

"We must get out of here, Blanski. There is no way we can get back to the launch pad now. If we do not find a way out soon, we are finished."

Bolan nodded his understanding and then turned and

looked at Faithe. "Okay, before we go farther you have some explaining to do. Start talking."

"What do you want to know?" she asked. The tone in her voice was filled with resignation, but Bolan wasn't going to trust that alone. He tried to keep in mind that she had hidden the truth from the beginning. He wasn't about to blindly start trusting her now.

"Why don't we start with who you really are?"

"My real name is Anika Faithe," she said. "My father was an American businessman, and my mother Russian. She was a concubine for a very powerful man named Borysko Luvanovich."

"The crime lord?" Bolan asked, his eyes narrowing.

"He is not a crime lord," she said icily. "He is a respected member of the Russian business community and my adoptive father. You see, the American businessman who fathered me refused to acknowledge his responsibilities. My mother would have been forced to give me up for adoption or risk raising me in secret, had it not been for Borysko. This man eventually realized the error of his ways. I took care of him quite neatly, just as I was assigned to do with General Mishenka."

Bolan nodded. "So you were sent to assassinate him. By whom?"

"By Borysko, of course. You see, Blanski, you don't know everything as you believe you do."

"I'm not the delusional one, lady," the soldier warned her. "How does my country and your position with the NSA come into all of this?"

"False credentials were provided for me by connections within your government. When I reached eighteen, my father felt it might benefit both him and members of the committee if there was someone inside the military working in R&D. I was the perfect choice. They forged transcripts, paid off U.S. officials and eliminated those who were uncooperative, and then they managed to get me into one of your universities.

"When I got out of school, I joined the meteorological-weapons division to give myself a way into this society. When the cold War finally ended, there was no more need for me to be there. I volunteered to serve in the Gulf. My job was to gather intelligence about U.S. Army military tactics and feed this information to my father. With the disbanding of the KGB, and the separation of our great country, it was only natural I manage to get into the NSA. It was my connections here that brought me to Antarctica, and my ultimate assignment— the elimination of General Gavril Mishenka."

"Except you hadn't counted on one thing," Bolan told her.

"What?"

"Me."

"COLONEL RAUSTOV IS dead, Comrade General," Erek Trofimoff told Mishenka. "He and his troops were slaughtered by this American and his friends."

"No..." Mishenka whispered. He then jumped up and slammed a meaty fist on his desk. "No! This cannot be!"

"I'm sorry," Trofimoff replied. "There is nothing that can be done to change this. However, the roof has collapsed in the main southeast corridor, and they are trapped in the armory section. They can go nowhere."

"But they can, Erek," the general said. "Don't you see this? Anika Faithe knows this complex thoroughly. In that case, she also knows of the ladder well that will take them outside to freedom."

"To attempt to venture to the outside now would not be freedom, Comrade General. It would be suicide."

"Perhaps for many," Mishenka replied, "but not for this Blanski."

"What do you mean?"

"He is resourceful, Erek. You said it yourself. And I know for a fact that Anika will not stop until she has completed what she came to do."

"Which is?"

"To kill me, of course."

"She is not with the Americans?"

Mishenka snorted and Trofimoff wanted to reach out at that

point and choke him to death. There was too much mystery and too many secrets surrounding Gavril Mishenka. He wasn't the open and hardened realist that he wanted everyone to think he was. No, this man was sly and dangerous; he was like a slippery eel, and Trofimoff didn't like that one bit. It was difficult to read such men. He never knew what they were going to do. But he also knew that Mishenka considered him dangerous, as well, and their arm's-length alliance was probably the best thing for both men.

"Do you know who sent her?"

"Of course," Mishenka snapped. "It was her father, that damn Luvanovich!"

"Borysko Luvanovich?"

"You know him." It wasn't a question.

"Of course I know him," Trofimoff replied. "I used to work for him. Until he decided he wasn't going to pay me for a contract because he didn't believe I was the one who killed the target. I stayed with him for many years. I had been a faithful worker. I do not like this man. I do not trust him. It would be my pleasure to eliminate the woman for you. It would serve a double purpose for me."

"Absolutely not, Erek," Mishenka warned, shaking his head emphatically. "You are not to harm her. It is to Luvanovich that I owe the assistance for building this complex and supplying us with all of our equipment. These were troops he paid to train, although I hardly find them to be impressive. His commandos are only watered-down versions of real soldiers." He barked out a laugh and added, "Why, my own troops are better than his commandos!"

"What do wish me to do, then?"

"I wish you to do absolutely nothing. Let them escape to the surface. There is nowhere they can go, and no habitable place they can reach in time to avoid the storm with the exception of air transport. Our planes are well guarded. If they make any attempt to steal one, my men will deal with them."

"Can you be certain of this?" Trofimoff asked. "This Blanski has proved to be quite a challenge. I cautioned you before about underestimating him, and now many of your commandos are dead. He is a formidable opponent."

"Then it is up to you to destroy him, Erek. You have been well compensated for your services. Now, as a professional, I expect you will earn some of that money."

Trofimoff narrowed his eyes. He had to remind himself to stay calm, while at the same time trying to find some way of telling this egotistical simpleton that he didn't work for him. Erek Trofimoff worked for *nobody* but himself, and he would be damned if some narrow-minded military has-been would tell him what to do and when to do it. Particularly when it wasn't Mishenka who had even paid his fee.

Moreover, this idiot had squandered all of the resources given to him by Luvanovich. While there was no love lost between him and the Russian mobster, there was definitely no honor in working under a slothful and wasteful man like Mishenka. It was time that he put this man in his place.

"I will do what I think needs to be done, Comrade General," Trofimoff stated quietly. He knew the tone had captured the man's attention when Mishenka snapped a surprised look at him. "Therefore, I will keep my own counsel on my actions. I was hired by Colonel Vasily to perform a function. However, you saw fit to eliminate him and so that makes my contract null and void."

"How dare you—"

"No!" Trofimoff reached into his coat and gripped the butt of his pistol. Mishenka was a crafty one, and the assassin wasn't about to take risks. "How dare *you!* Do you think that I'm some idiot who will bow to your every whim?"

Trofimoff stepped forward, keeping his hand on the Glock 21. In a clipped tone, he continued, "You do not frighten me, Comrade General, and your ridiculous plan to launch Nadezhda against the Americans does not impress me. Any man can kill millions of people with a mass-destruction weapon, but it is the ability to kill a single man professionally and personally that is impressive. I will not destroy this Blanski because you order me to. I will do it because it will be my pleasure. Do we understand each other?"

Mishenka said nothing at first, and Trofimoff knew the man was thinking furiously about taking advantage of the situation. Nonetheless, the fact of the matter was that this man thought of himself as a glorified military statesman, while Trofimoff knew he was capable of killing anyone quickly and dispassionately. Especially from long range through a rifle scope.

"Were it not for the fact I am a man of honor," Mishenka replied coldly, "you would be dead right now."

"I'm sure," Trofimoff replied. He took his hand from his coat. "I will wait for Blanski on the surface, since you are convinced he will come. And when I finished with him, I will take my leave of you and your revenge against the Americans. I have other work that awaits me."

Mishenka nodded slowly, and Trofimoff left the room. But as he did, he made sure that he didn't fully turn his back to the Russian officer. If he had, he was certain the general would have shot him in the back.

"THERE IS a much greater threat than Nadezhda," Faithe told the Executioner. "Even if you destroy this missile, you will not stop Mishenka."

"What are you talking about?" Bolan asked. He had more or less turned his attention from her while he and Capek searched the armory for anything they could use to blow out the rubble that was blocking their exit.

"The isotopes used to make Nadezhda work are not developed here," Faithe explained. "Did you ever think about that, Blanski?"

Bolan stopped searching the armory to look her in the eye. "You really are a scientist."

"Of course," she said. "I was trained by some of the finest minds in Russia. And in your country, as well."

"Where are the isotopes for this warhead being manufactured?" the Executioner demanded.

"You remember Pyotr?"

"At Vostok, yeah. The scientist from the Ukraine."

"It is he who developed the isotopes necessary to create the neutron cascade effect. It is he who first drafted the blueprints for Nadezhda so many years ago. He was once a faithful servant of the country and my father. And he still is, although he is determined that the comrade general has gone mad. That is when they sent me to destroy him. I had not been afforded the opportunity to reach General Mishenka until now."

"I was your excuse," Bolan observed.

"You were my insurance," she replied, "and you fell perfectly for it."

"Well, it doesn't look as if any of us will retain the upper hand," Capek interjected. "There is nothing here that we can use to clear the hall. And you, my friend, do not have enough explosives in that bag to do the job, I think."

"Foolish men," Faithe said. The Russian spy rose and walked to one of the racks that was empty of any weapons. She pulled forward on a handle, and the six-foot high rack swung outward on hidden hinges to expose a ladder. Daylight streamed down through a hole that reflected off the plastic rungs. The two men stared at her as she turned and put one hand on her hip. "I do not care about whether Nadezhda is launched anymore, Blanski. But I must complete my mission to eliminate Mishenka. So we will make a truce?"

"One thing at a time, lady," Bolan said. "First, we get out of here. Then we'll talk about truces."

13

White Sands Missile Range, New Mexico

"The project began in 2001," Ivan Wicker told Hermann Schwarz, "when the President mandated full research to begin on a suitable antimissile device."

Schwarz nodded at that. He remembered the scandal surrounding the disclosure of missile secrets to the Chinese, and how the Man, newly elected at that time, began a serious defense project to squash the threat of a massive enemy missile attack. Despite the fact the United States hadn't been invaded by a foreign power since Pearl Harbor, Americans were still uncomfortable with the idea that the Chinese were privy to missile secrets.

When the new President took office, he immediately began to address these concerns regarding the security of the nation, allowing for the manufacture of weapons and increased research in the area of defense. The new budget called for tax relief in both the private and public sectors, and this freed enough cash for increased revenues in defense spending and technological advancement.

"SLAMS is an acronym for Satellite Linked Anti-Missile System," Wicker continued. "I first got the idea several years ago, but it wasn't until I met Lieutenant Makowski that I realized my dream could be a reality."

"In what sense?" Schwarz asked.

"Well," Makowski chimed in, "I'd been serving with information-technology engineers in the Army. We were trying to come up with new and better ways of sending communications that couldn't be intercepted. This was when we stumbled onto the MXT signals and realized what they were capable of doing. The progression from there was simply a natural one."

"What exactly are MXT signals?"

"It stands for Multi-Executable Timing," Wicker announced proudly. "These signals stem from Army studies in particle-emission technology."

"You're talking like particle-beam weapons?" Gadgets asked with excitement.

"In a matter of speaking." Wicker began to pace as he added, "The SLAMS satellite emits a series of vertical laser beams, which provide the framework for a grid. Ostensibly, these beams are invisible...virtually undetectable by enemy sensor equipment."

Wicker went to a control panel and pulled up a three-dimensional image of the satellite. The imagery technology he was showing the Able Team commando had Schwarz amazed. Stony Man and Kurtzman's cybernetics team utilized some of the most advanced equipment in the world, but this went beyond anything even they were able to do. The entire concept had him fascinated.

"Phase one of the SLAMS is actual detection of the threat," Wicker continued, pushing another button. "We immediately enter phase two, activating the SLAMS satellite and deploying the lasers. When they reach Earth, a ground-based reflector retransmits the lasers horizontally and provides a targeting array for any inbound missile."

"The grid is large enough to lock on to as many as six missiles at a time," Makowski added. "We were only testing it against one when the accident occurred."

Schwarz shook his head. "We don't think that was any accident."

"Perhaps not, but let us maintain our focus for the moment," Wicker rebutted in a professorial tone. "Once a missile is targeted, we then initiate phase three, or deflection. A large radio-frequency dish reads the vector information programmed into the missile computer. And this is where Kyle's brainchild is realized." Wicker looked at the young officer and nodded, a signal that Makowski could take it from there.

Makowski seemed happy to oblige, grinning as he pushed another button and the display changed again. Sparks of yellowish light seemed to pulse from the dish of the three-dimensional satellite graphic. The light shot across the grid of laser light and terminated in squares randomly, turning to a fiery red and then soft green color within the squares before dissipating.

"What you're seeing here, Mr. Swanson, are Multi-Executable Timing signals. They're more or less bursts of particle emissions. They reroute the computer's point of reference, changing the latitudinal, longitudinal and ground zero numbers. Regardless of the destination of the missile, the curves and geographical surface of our planet is unchanged. Most ICBM's are smart, if you will, and the onboard computers know where they are at all times. So any change in reference points will, of course, cause the missile to alter course."

"So you're saying these signals don't change the programming," Schwarz concluded, "they just change the way a missile looks at the position."

"Precisely!" Wicker interjected triumphantly. "It might seem a bit complicated, but I can simplify it for you."

The Air Force colonel walked to a nearby desk and picked up a yo-yo. "Let's pretend that I am a launch site and this is the missile. If I fire the missile—" he shot the yo-yo straight out "—it goes where I direct it. However, if I were to change position—" he turned sideways "—this would change the position at which I fired the missile. It would not change the actual direction I fired it, but rather alter the initial position from which it was fired. The same is true for SLAMS." He set the yo-yo back on the desk and folded his arms.

"Absolutely amazing," Schwarz said with a sigh. "It's so simple in concept. I wonder why nobody thought of it before now."

"Oh, it's been theorized a thousand times," Makowski replied. "It wasn't until we invented MXTs that things really took off. Colonel Wicker added the idea of Differing Quotient Light signals to form a grid. Only through the testing did we come to realize that DQLs could contain MXTs and provide the stability for missile deflection."

"Kind of a 'you got your chocolate in my peanut butter' thing?" Schwarz quipped with a smile.

Both men laughed and Wicker said, "That's exactly what is was."

Schwarz was thoroughly impressed. These two men were extremely knowledgeable, and he was certain that Wicker bordered on brilliant. Many of their enemies would have paid a heavy price to sway either of these men over to the other side. America was damn lucky to have them, and the Able Team commando felt privileged in some sense.

He liked both of them, and he was finding himself hard-pressed to believe either was capable of selling his country down the river. Nonetheless, he had to keep his personal feelings in check. Good humor didn't necessarily rule out a spy or saboteur, and it was that kind of thinking that had allowed for so much espionage to go unchecked during the cold war. Americans were very trusting of their fellow man in a peculiar sense—perhaps they were victims of their own culture.

At any rate, Schwarz knew that this was serious. Somebody on the other end of the spectrum was as bright as these men. Someone in Antarctica had managed to find a way around the SLAMS system, and that was bad news. If the enemy was resourceful enough to bypass the brilliance of military scientists like Makowski and Wicker, then that made them a formidable threat. They had to find out who had fed the fish on this end. If these two *were* straight, then they had to find who was selling America's secrets and put a stop to it.

And at that moment, Schwarz wondered how Hal Brognola was holding up.

"I'M NOT HERE to suggest you don't run a tight ship, Major Kranz," Brognola stated. "I'm just suggesting that these are very odd events under the circumstances."

Major Mark Blaine Kranz, provost marshal of White Sands, studied the big Fed with a pained expression. The guy was definitely not happy to have some Justice Department suit nosing around in his backyard, and he'd made no bones about that. Nonetheless, he knew Brognola was there on the authority of the President of the United States, and that seemed to shift his attitude some. The guy was obviously more impressed by Brognola's credentials than Pordello had been.

"Well, sir," Kranz replied, "just as long as we understand that if there's a problem with any of my people, I want to know about it. I have both the protection of the civilian population here, as well as military security, to think about. Those take precedence above any investigation, and I'm sure the President would agree."

"I'm sure he would," Brognola said in an empathetic tone. "And as I've already said, Major, I'm not here to step on toes. I'm just here to find out what happened to two U.S. agents."

"Fine."

Brognola took a deep breath before continuing. "Did General Pordello tell you that these men were coming to investigate the missile accident?"

"No."

"Either of them?"

"No."

"Don't you think that's strange, Major?"

Kranz didn't answer at first, and Brognola could tell the man was thinking carefully about his reply. Undoubtedly he felt some loyalty to Pordello, albeit the Stony Man chief couldn't imagine why. Pordello was as slick as a snake and as wily as a wolf, and that made him untrustworthy. The only reason Brognola could fathom Kranz's lack of response would be he was hiding something. Or, if the general was playing for the other team, it was possible Kranz was part of the conspiracy.

"It may be strange to most people, but not me," Kranz said. "Jonathan is a pretty closemouthed individual. He knows how to keep quiet, and I would imagine that's a good trait for a man in his position."

Brognola had already thought of that, however, and he had an answer ready. "Fair enough. But don't you think it would have been wise to communicate this to your office for the sake of security? After all, you said yourself that this is your primary responsibility. I would think this is something *you* should know, of all people."

"What's your point, Mr. Brognola?"

"My point is that there doesn't appear to be any communication going on here."

"I thought you said you here to find out what happened to your men."

"I am."

"Sounds to me like you're scrutinizing the way we do things at White Sands."

"I'm scrutinizing the way Pordello does things, yes," Brognola snapped.

The head Fed was going way out on the limb here, and he knew it. This could go one of two ways. He knew that if word of what he'd said got back to Pordello there would be trouble. The President had authorized Brognola to come out to White Sands and evaluate the situation. He hadn't authorized a full-scale investigation into officers of impeccable record without gathering all of the facts.

But Brognola couldn't help himself. He was sure Pordello had something to hide—maybe it had something to do with the SLAMS project and maybe not. Nonetheless, he couldn't pull punches now. He had to get Kranz on his side right now or all would be lost. He had to make the guy believe there was something amiss, and either Kranz was for him or against him on that. He hoped it was the former.

"Why are you pushing this issue with Jonathan Pordello?" Kranz asked in a suspicious tone.

"Why do you find it necessary to defend him?"

"I've known Jonathan a lot of years. He recommended me for this position," Kranz said. "He's as much a friend as he is my commanding officer, and I pride myself on being loyal to both."

"Even if they betray that trust by selling out to the enemies of this country?"

Kranz's face took on a dangerous hue at that point. "What do mean? Are you accusing Pordello of espionage?"

"I'm accusing him of nothing. I'm just curious to know why he withheld this information from you."

"I'm sure I don't know, but I'm guessing he had his reasons."

"Did he inform you about Agent Blanski's arrival?"

That caused Kranz to drop the defiant expression and sit back in his chair. His gray eyes watched Brognola carefully, probably probing the big Fed for any sort of impropriety, but Brognola simply waited for an answer. He couldn't let Kranz off the hook now. He just about had the officer where he wanted him, and to let up now would have caused him loss of any hope at all.

"No," Kranz said quietly.

"Listen, Major Kranz, it would seem to me that you're on the up-and-up," Brognola said. "I need help with this and I think you can be trusted. I'll admit that I'm very suspicious of Pordello's actions. He didn't tell you about Blanski's arrival, and he didn't tell you about the pending arrival of the previous agents. He freely admitted to me less than an hour ago that he told his XO and adjutants. Hell, even his assistant knew. So why is it everybody else knew but you didn't?"

"What are you getting at?"

"I'm not looking to hang Pordello out on a wire," Brognola said. "I'm just looking for a reason why you didn't know about these agents. Moreover, several men dressed as MPs tried to take out Blanski within hours of his arrival. We've identified these men as foreigners. Somebody had to supply them with the uniforms and weapons. Aside from you, the only one with that kind of authority would be Pordello. So unless *you* sent those men after Blanski, that leaves few others in the way of suspects."

Kranz appeared to be thinking very hard about what Brognola was saying. He was winning the guy over quickly, and now it was time to put the icing on the cake. "I know you had nothing to do with that attack. Blanski says he followed Mundy out to that ambush site. Pordello's XO was out of town at the time. That doesn't leave much to doubt."

"Okay, Brognola," Kranz finally replied in a conciliatory voice. "Let's suppose for a moment that you're correct. I'll even go so far as to say that maybe Lieutenant Mundy and Jonathan Pordello are in cahoots with a foreign power. What proof do you have?"

"None yet," Brognola admitted immediately. "That's why I need your help."

"Okay, I'll look into this." He jabbed a finger at Brognola and added, "But you don't do a damn thing until I've had a chance to look this over. Don't go poking your nose where it doesn't belong. If there's something to be found, I'll find it. Are we clear?"

"We're clear."

"Now, if you'll excuse me I have work to do."

Brognola nodded and left the office. Once outside the MP headquarters, Brognola climbed behind the wheel of the borrowed government sedan and dialed a number into his cellular phone. There was clicking a few bursts of static before Kurtzman's voice broke through on the other end.

"What's up, Hal?"

"A lot, I think," Brognola replied as he pulled out of the parking lot and headed toward the guest billets. "There's little doubt in my mind that Pordello's up to something."

"Well, Barb did that digging like you asked."

"And?"

"She came up flat empty. Before military service, Jonathan Pordello didn't exist. No schooling, no social security, not even a driver's license."

Brognola nodded, even though he knew Kurtzman couldn't see him. "A mole."

"Yeah, probably inserted by the Russians or Chinese."

"My guess would be the Russians, based on what Jack told us."

"We think so too."

"Okay, Bear, here's what I want you to do. I—" Brognola never finished his sentence as an explosion erupted in the road ahead of him.

A large chunk of pavement exploded upward in the red-orange flash of light, and Brognola dropped the phone as he jerked the steering wheel to avoid the blast. The sedan bounced onto the curb and rode the sidewalk, fishtailing as the big Fed tried to keep it under control. He finally slammed into a telephone pole, his head striking the B-post and opening a gash over his left eye. The windshield spiderwebbed and the impact jarred Brognola's teeth as the vehicle lurched to a halt.

His vision was blurred as he struggled to extricate himself from the dashboard, which had intruded into the passenger compartment. Brognola staggered from the vehicle in time to see four men approach. It was a hell of a time for a fight, but the big Fed had seen action before and he wasn't about to just curl up and show his belly.

Brognola reached beneath his coat and retrieved the Colt Combat Commander .45-caliber pistol he carried in the field. He raised an unsteady hand, gripping the weapon tightly as he squeezed off the first shot. The 180-grain .45-caliber round went wide of the intended target. He readjusted his aim and fired again.

The four men dressed in garb similar to the Executioner's skintight blacksuit fanned out. They were toting submachine guns, and they lined themselves up to take Brognola. The Stony Man chief left his position and rushed for cover behind his sedan. He managed to duck in time to avoid the first volley of rounds as the reports from the SMGs echoed through the air. The 9 mm bullets zinged past or ricocheted for the trunk of the sedan.

Brognola lay behind the rear tire, panting and cursing himself for not seeing the attack coming. Well, it was no time to beat himself up. He could do that later—*if* he managed to walk away from this alive. He risked exposing his head a moment to pop off a few rounds from the Colt before ducking behind the trunk again. He was clearly outgunned, and it wouldn't do any good to blow off all his ammunition. He needed a plan, but one wasn't coming to him right at the moment.

The squeal of sirens through the air seemed to cause the staccato of autofire to cease. Brognola looked to his right and saw several MP sedans approaching, as well as a Hummer. It was either additions to the attackers or the cavalry, and as the first vehicle screeched to a halt and the MPs emerged, Brognola knew he'd just found relief.

The military policemen immediately drew their weapons and opened fire, trading shots with the nameless gunmen. Brognola got into the fray, coming to his feet and emptying his pistol in their general direction. The other MPs dressed in full battle gear jumped from the Hummer before it had come to a complete stop. They leveled their M-16s and made short work of the four men, one of whom had already dropped under the initial defense.

As the sounds of gunfire died, another vehicle pulled up and ground to a halt. It was a government sedan with a single dome light on the driver's side, the kind that magnetically attached to the roof. Brognola lowered his pistol as he saw Major Mark Kranz emerge from the sedan.

The guy looked over at the dead quartet, watching as his men carefully converged on the bodies, their weapons held at the ready. He turned to look at Brognola with a look of unabashed shock.

"Now do you believe what I'm telling you?" the Stony Man chief asked.

"I'm all ears, Brognola," Kranz replied.

14

Pole of Inaccessibility, Antarctica

Mack Bolan was the first to emerge from the underground complex, looking skyward and frowning as Faithe and Capek followed. Dark was approaching rapidly. The storm was coming, and it had no intention of cutting him a break.

The Executioner turned toward the east and saw three shapes in the fading twilight. He estimated that they were at a distance of maybe fifty yards. One was rectangular and large, with a very tall tower similar to the one he'd seen back in Vostok. The other two were definitely choppers, but Bolan couldn't tell what kind from that distance. Not that it mattered. The use of a chopper would give him a fighting chance to finish the job of destroying the missile pad and getting out intact ahead of the storm.

"What do think, my friend?" Capek asked Bolan, squinting to study the source of Bolan's interest.

"I think we need to pilfer one of those birds."

Bolan turned and pinned Anika Faithe with an ice-blue stare that was as cold as their present surroundings. "How much time do we have before that storm hits?"

"Perhaps an hour or two." She shrugged and added, "Definitely not longer than that."

"It's enough."

"To do what?"

"Destroy that missile pad."

"You are crazy, Mike," Capek rebutted. "We just came out of that hellhole. Now you wish to go back in?"

Bolan looked at Capek coolly. "Like I told you before, Luva, you can drop out at any time here. I can't leave now. Not with the thought that Mishenka will make good on his threat to launch Nadezhda against my country."

"This I can understand," Capek said after a pause.

Bolan knew he probably could. The man had fought for and defended his own country against its enemies. The pilot was much like the Executioner in that regard. He knew what was at stake, and he understood Bolan's need to eliminate the threat. Thus far, he'd proved himself a faithful ally. And although the soldier preferred to work alone, he'd need Capek to agree to fly him out of there.

"Then you can also understand I need your help. I can't fly that aircraft, and I'm not sure the good doctor here knows how to, either." Bolan shot her another flat look and added, "Unless the Russians trained you to fly, as well."

Faithe didn't say a word, but just sniffed disdainfully. It was just as well. Bolan didn't trust her any further than he could throw her. She'd used him to get to Mishenka, certain that the general would be so focused on the Executioner that he wouldn't consider her a threat. In some respects, Bolan had to wonder if Faithe hadn't made her verbal blunder on purpose. It was possible she had some other nefarious scheme in mind. It was even probable she was actually working for Mishenka.

If the woman wanted to kill this madman, then Bolan didn't care a bit. It would save him the effort. Just as long as she pulled her weight and didn't get in his way, it didn't matter who pulled the trigger. It was one less thing Bolan had to worry about and that was just fine with him.

"What is your plan?" Capek asked.

"That depends. What's inside that building, Faithe?"

"That is Avdotya Station."

"Is there another secret entrance there that will take us back inside the bunker?"

"Yes."

"Okay, we take out any enemy guards and grab one of those choppers. Once we've secured our position here, you'll stay above while I get back down there and find a way to blow that missile pad."

"I will go with you," Faithe announced.

"No, you won't," he told her.

"We had a deal."

"We had nothing," Bolan said. "I'm going to be on a tight schedule, and I don't have time to be worried about whether you're going to put a bullet in my back."

"If I'd wanted to kill you, I could have done so already," she said. "In many respects, we're on the same side, Blanski. The difference is that I have not forgotten my *true* mission. You are apparently more worried about me than you are Mishenka or Nadezhda."

"Cut the psychoanalysis," the Executioner snapped. "You want to come along, fine. But you'll have to take your chances because there's no way I'm going to put a gun in your hand."

"Then I shall stay with Capek."

Hairs stood on end on Bolan's neck. It seemed to him she'd given in just a bit too easily. He wasn't worried about the Croat pilot; Capek would shoot her if he thought she was trying to pull some monkey business. But Faithe had nearly convinced him once before that she was on the straight and narrow, and he seemed less experienced with the feminine wiles. If he succumbed to her stunts, it was almost a given that Bolan's mission would be finished.

He would just have to take that risk.

"Suit yourself," the Executioner said with a shrug.

He turned to Capek. "Shall we?"

The man nodded and the trio set out for the choppers, Faithe keeping back a considerable distance. There was no real cover, so they didn't bother trying to conceal their approach. They would have to get inside the fire zones of any sentries quickly and neutralize opponents on the run. Bolan knew they only needed control of one chopper. A frontal attack was probably the last thing the enemy was expecting—any attack was probably unexpected.

They were within thirty yards of the nearest chopper, and Bolan could now see that one of them was Capek's Mil Mi-6, while the second was a Mil Mi-24 Hind. The first resistance appeared in the form of a group of soldiers clad in the arctic-camouflage suits and cold-weather parkas. There was a team of three guards assigned to each chopper, plus a pilot. That meant the guards probably doubled as gunners and crew. The chopper teams were obviously determined to defend themselves, and they immediately fanned out to meet the threat.

They were a moment too late as the Executioner and Capek opened up with their assault rifles. The first burst from Bolan took a gunner high in the chest, spinning the man and dumping him to the ice-packed ground. The soldier immediately followed up with another controlled burst. The slugs tore open the man's belly, some punching through and ripping out the lower spine. This man collapsed, his blood staining the snow and ice.

Capek proved equally effective, dispatching the second chopper team with unmatched ease. His first set of 5.45 mm rounds took two crew members of the Mi-24 Hind before they even realized they were under attack. The pilot, wearing officer's insignia, managed to find cover behind the Mi-24 before Capek could bring him down. The Croat dived to ground as the enemy pilot ripped off a few shots from a 9 mm Makarov.

Capek groaned at the pain in his side. Bolan thought the man had fallen under those shots but he quickly realized the Croat pilot had simply dropped to avoid being ventilated with autofire. The Executioner shot the rest of the troops who had been watching the Mi-6, then circled on the left flank and began to provide some covering fire.

The fourth man from the Mil Mi-24, who had also managed to find cover, came to his feet and nearly lost his balance trying to repel the soldier's surprise attack. Bolan dropped the AK-74 level to his hip and opened up, spraying the man with a sustained burst. The gunman's trigger finger curled reflexively on the AKSU he was holding, and several rounds went skyward before the man fell to his knees. His eyes opened wide as one of Bolan's rounds punched through his forehead and blew out the back of his skull. The man flopped onto his belly like a dead fish.

The pilot turned when he saw he was now alone, outgunned and flanked on two sides. He dropped the Makarov and raised his hands in surrender. Bolan quickly stepped forward and frisked the guy for weapons as Faithe helped Capek to his feet. Once he found the guy clean, Bolan moved him over to the pair with a nudge from the muzzle of the AK-74.

"You speak Russian," Bolan told Faithe. "I want you to interpret for me."

"What do you want to know?" she asked.

"Ask him how we get back inside undetected."

Faithe translated the message, and based on the Executioner's functional level of Russian he knew she was more or less using his words exactly. The guy made a short, heated reply, and Faithe's interpretation caused Bolan to scowl. The Executioner reached into his coat and retrieved the Makarov. He made a show of checking the breech by drawing back slightly on the slide, then put the weapon to the man's temple.

"Ask him again," Bolan told Faithe.

She did.

This time the guy began to talk rapidly. It didn't appear the pilots were as faithful to Mishenka as the other misguided soldiers who had died for the ruthless scientist. Within a minute, Bolan had all of the information he needed to make a successful penetration, and a clear set of directions for getting to the missile pad.

Bolan noticed a change in Capek's pallor. The guy looked woozy on his feet, and his face was lacking color. "What's wrong with you?"

"I think I opened up my wound. I could feel a rip and some bleeding on Faithe's patch job. I think it needs to be redressed."

"All right," the Executioner replied. "You and Faithe stay with our new friend here. Have the chopper ready because I'll probably be headed back in a big hurry."

Capek nodded. "I will be all right. Be careful."

GENERAL GAVRIL MISHENKA was prepared for war. The time had come and he could no longer wait. At the moment, however, his scientists were counseling him to wait. What aggravated him more than anything was that his trusted aide was agreeing with them. He sat in his office discussing it with Moriz Ninakov, and the young man just didn't seem able to understand the gravity of the situation.

"You must be patient, sir," Ninakov protested. "These men are trusted associates. They know what they are doing, and Dr. Karamov agrees with them."

"Whether or not I trust their opinions isn't the point, Moriz," Mishenka contended, looking through the windows at the group of physicists and weapons developers.

These were veteran scientists of the former Soviet Union, and some of the brightest minds on the face of the planet. Two of the men had served with Pyotr Karamov and transferred their loyalties along with the distinguished scientist. The others were either members who had worked closely with Mishenka during his career in the Russian army, or those he'd managed to recruit with promises of money and prestige.

"And you know," Mishenka continued, "how much I trust Pyotr's judgment. But the fact of the matter remains that we are running out of time. If do not send Nadezhda on her maiden and only voyage now, this American, Blanski, and that witch, Anika Luvanovich, will surely try again."

"But Comrade General," Ninakov replied, "Erek has already assured you he will take care of—"

"My dear Moriz," Mishenka said, raising his hand to override his aide's protests, "you put too much faith in others. Erek is a hired gun and nothing more. This man is an expert, do you understand? Look how many of our best troops he took out single-handedly. His skills as a combatant would appear virtually inimitable."

"He had assistance," Ninakov replied.

"He has what he thinks is assistance," Mishenka reminded the youthful protégé. "It is only through my foresight that I will be able to prevent this man from ruining our plans. So you do not have to worry. Simply follow my orders and you will see the glory of the CCCP come to pass once again.

"Soon," he whispered, "we will know victory."

MACK BOLAN PREPARED his descent into Capek's proclaimed hell.

The soldier was attired in full battle dress, wearing the backpack filled with the high-explosive plastique and a few flares. The ammo belts contained all the spare 5.45 mm rounds and a few more RGN time-delay/impact grenades, all of which they had acquired from the armory.

Bolan pushed aside his thoughts and concerns for Capek. The Executioner had decided to keep the other pilot alive—just in case—and if things went sour there was still a good chance they could get out alive. After all, the Russian pilot had proved his will to survive outweighed his loyalties to Mishenka's cause. The guy would obviously fly them out of there if he knew a storm could end up trapping them there for a very long time.

Several staff inside Avdotya Station immediately reached for their side arms when the Executioner popped through the door. The soldier was ready to deal with the situation. He took the first guy hard, the bullets of his AKSU chopping through the man's sternum at a cyclic rate of 800 rounds per minute. The gunman was slammed against a wall by the impact.

A second and third man split up and tried to flank the Executioner, but Bolan was ready for that. He'd already hefted a grenade—thanks to the advice regarding troops strength provided by Faithe—and he let it fly. The HE grenade exploded on impact, blowing one soldier's foot off while the other was peppered with fragments and scorched with the explosive blast of the RDX-wax filling.

Bolan moved through the main operations area and continued down a corridor until he reached the bunk room. Beyond it was a toilet facility, including a sauna. Once through the cleanup area, he found himself faced with a computer lab. The place was unattended, which didn't surprise him in the least. According to Faithe, this time of year was when the Australians were off and the Russians had the station. Nobody cared what went on here at Avdotya, so it didn't really matter. The Executioner imagined the Aussies had no idea what was going on beneath them, and by the time they returned Mishenka had his people back into place and everything looked normal.

It was an ingenious setup in many respects, and Bolan couldn't help being impressed. It almost seemed like a paradox, coming face to face with Mishenka after all of these years. Rumors had flown that Luvanovich was behind much of the KGB's and GRU's secret weapons projects in those days, but there wasn't enough information at the time to follow up with it. In the soldier's wars against the KGB, Mishenka and Luvanovich were two that had eluded him, escaping his rage over the death of his beloved April.

When he was finished with Mishenka, he'd make it a point to penetrate the USSR and take care of Luvanovich, as well. While rumors floated that Greb Strakhov was alive, Bolan knew better. That matter was closed entirely, and there was no point in thinking about it now. He had to concentrate on the mission ahead.

Part of that mission greeted him shortly after Bolan found the hidden entrance behind a mock wall in the computer lab. He was descending a set of spiral stairs when he saw a group of commandos ascending them through the plastic grating. The Executioner froze a moment, not quite sure what was happening. The commandos were moving at a pace that looked preparatory—almost as if they were expecting him.

Bolan wasn't about to give them a chance. He looked over the curved railing and saw the drop was five yards, give or take. He slung his AKSU and vaulted over the side without hesitation. Several of the climbing Spetsnaz turned as the figure streaked past them and dropped to the wooden floor plates below.

Bolan took the shock to about the knees before executing a shoulder roll to absorb most of the impact. He tucked his chin to his chest, landing similarly to the way he learned to land in jump school at Fort Benning. The soldier came to his feet and risked a look back. The soldiers were crammed onto the spiral staircase and weren't aware of the threat until Bolan was already aiming the AKSU in their direction. The Executioner fired, curling his finger slowly around the trigger and holding the weapon steady. Some collapsed under the vicious onslaught, while others were literally flipped over the railings and crashed to the ground below. Less than ten seconds elapsed before the bolt locked back on an empty chamber.

Bolan flipped the smoking muzzle to his left, dropping the spent magazine and slamming a fresh one home as he studied the carnage. A half-dozen bodies were strewed across the fire zone now, and the Executioner threw them a quick nod of satisfaction. The sound of boots slapping flooring commanded his attention, and he whirled in time to see a fresh cluster of commandos rushing toward him.

Bolan realized at that moment what was really going on. These troops had been ready for him. Their escape had been no accident—it had been planned from the beginning. The soldier had suspected that and had developed a contingency plan. He'd prepared himself to meet a copious amount of resistance. Mishenka would do everything to prevent the Executioner from destroying his Nadezhda.

Even as he prepared to meet his new attackers, the Executioner was surprised at a sudden announcement in Russian over the complex speakers. Bolan couldn't understand all of it, but he was certain he knew what it meant. They were planning to launch Nadezhda.

Bolan dropped to the floor as the enemy opened fire.

15

White Sands Missile Range, New Mexico

"I think Pordello is definitely our man," Hermann Schwarz told Brognola.

"I disagree," Brognola replied.

"What?"

The two men sat in their quarters, drinking coffee and discussing it over a table stacked high with maps, personnel dossiers, military file jackets and a slew of computer files just sent by Kurtzman via secured electronic transmission. Brognola had his laptop and was studying the information he'd downloaded from Stony Man's database.

"The Bear turned this thing with Pordello over to Hunt Wethers," Brognola explained. "Hunt did some digging and came up with information regarding this guy."

"You mean we have some inkling of his background?"

"Not entirely. There's some real inconsistencies in his story here, so I asked for a second meeting and requested clarification. He accepted, and that's what makes me much less suspicious of him now."

"Well, even his own boys, like Kranz, think there's some truth to what you said."

"I'm not sure I trust Kranz," Brognola admitted. "As a

matter of fact, I don't trust anyone here. Present company excluded, of course."

"Thanks." Gadgets snorted good-naturedly.

"There's something definitely awry here at White Sands. Everybody's just a bit too closemouthed and secretive."

"What do you expect from a bunch of landlocked technical geeks?"

"I believe there's someone near and dear to Stony Man that would qualify as one of those 'technical geeks,'" Brognola replied.

"Yeah," Schwarz agreed, "but I'm not landlocked."

"Touché."

There was a brief rap at the door. Brognola looked at Schwarz in time to see him draw a Glock Model 23 from shoulder leather. He locked gazes with the Stony Man chief for just a moment before nodding and dropping the pistol beneath the table. It would be out of sight but ready for trouble—Brognola knew he couldn't be much safer than with one of the Able Team commandos playing guardian angel.

The big Fed opened the door and stepped back to allow Pordello to enter. Brognola was a bit surprised to see the Army officer, but he was relieved to see he was alone. That meant there was little chance Pordello had brought trouble with him, and even less that he'd been followed.

"Good afternoon, General," Brognola greeted him. 'What can I do for you?"

"You requested a meeting," Pordello replied as he stepped in and removed his cap. He was attired in his Class A uniform, and the only sign of informality was the fact his black tie was loosened and the top button undone.

"A bit overdressed for the occasion," Schwarz observed with a disarming smile.

Pordello actually returned the smile and nodded. "My wife and I are attending a dinner tonight in honor of the mayor of Las Cruces."

"No end to political functions," Brognola said.

"Agreed."

"Have a seat."

Brognola closed the door and Schwarz took the time to make a show of returning the pistol to his holster. The general seemed neither surprised nor bothered by the fact that the Able Team commando was armed. Obviously, nobody in his right mind would have been surprised, considering some of the events that had transpired over the past few days. Nonetheless, Pordello obviously couldn't help commenting about it.

He nodded at Schwarz. "I take it that electronics isn't all you're into, Mr. Swanson."

"You could say that," Schwarz replied.

Pordello sat down and briefly scanned the contents of the table. "You've been busy, I see."

Brognola returned to his seat and gathered the files into a neater stack, while Schwarz rose and got the man a cup of coffee. Once they were all seated again, Brognola cleared his throat and fixed the career Army officer with an astute gaze.

"Listen, General, I think we've gotten off on the wrong foot," the Stony Man chief began apologetically.

"You're damn straight we have."

"I'd like this to be water under the bridge. We need your cooperation here."

"Ever since you got to my post you've been nothing but trouble, Brognola. I've attempted to be courteous, but you don't seem to respond to that. You don't want to hear the truth. Maybe it frightens you."

Brognola's voice had a hard edge to it as he stared at Pordello with a level expression. "I think there's very little left in the world that frightens me, General. You'd be surprised what I've seen over the years. I've sent men out to do things you couldn't even imagine doing yourself. And I lie awake many nights wondering if I've done the right thing. So don't think you can lecture me about truth. I know more about truth than you ever will."

"Speaking of truth," Schwarz interjected, obviously making an attempt to keep the peace, "we finally got some information on your sketchy past. To this point, you've been suspected by several high-ranking members in the Pentagon of military espionage, General. The President would like the truth, and so would the rest of us."

Pordello scowled. "I'm being accused of espionage?"

"Nobody's being accused of anything yet," Brognola replied quickly. "As I told you this morning, I'm here on a fact-finding mission only. Everyone at this point is suspect. Nobody, and I mean nobody, is above the law here. We just think you owe us an explanation about your past. Now would you like to provide that explanation, or should I call CID agents down here to do it?"

"Call who you like, Brognola," Pordello replied haughtily. "Do you think I'm afraid of the CID? I've not done anything to be afraid of, so you can take that back to your White House cronies."

"If you don't want to tell us what you have to tell us," Schwarz suggested, "then perhaps you'll feel more comfortable answering to a Senate panel. You see, there's something I think you need to get clear. Hal here knows a lot of very important people. Now, I know you're pretty high on the totem pole yourself. But he's just *teensy* bit higher. So cut the shit and let's get this out on the table once and for all. Okay?"

Pordello cleared his throat and shook his head. There was definitely something nagging at the guy's conscience, and Brognola just knew he had something to say. No, there was something he *wanted* to say, but it seemed as if he was holding back. It was as if something unseen was prompting the guy to keep his silence.

"Listen, I don't know what's going on," Brognola said, "but I don't believe you're involved. If you have an explanation for why there's no information on you prior to your enlistment in the military, now would be the time to spill it. Otherwise, I cannot protect you down the line."

"Come on," Schwarz added after a long silence. "You've got to talk to us."

"I'm not sure where to begin," Pordello finally said in a quiet voice. "And even if I did, I'm not sure you would believe me."

"Try us," Brognola prompted him.

He took a deep breath before saying, "The reason there is no information in my file is because I couldn't ostensibly exist. I'm the son of a woman who was an illegal alien in this country. My mother and father attempted to the cross the border when she was pregnant with me. She made it, but my father was shot and killed by a border patrol agent.

"Several months went by, with my mother living solely off the gratitude of others, or staying in churches and shelters. She worked a short time for a priest, but when she started to show, others began to talk about her. The priest was forced to send her away. But he helped her to settle into the home of friends in Raton, New Mexico. She worked for them, the Pordellos, and eventually they explained her to their friends as an orphaned relative they'd taken in. They treated her more like their daughter than like the hired servant she'd come to them as."

The story had both men absolutely fascinated, and Brognola could hardly believe what he was hearing. So this was Pordello's big secret, and the reason it would seem he'd been hiding something.

"After I was born," the general continued, "my grandparents made arrangements to keep us in the country. They paid a lot of money to see that my mother and I had an excellent life. I will always love them and be indebted to them for what they did. They never judged us for our heritage or culture. They simply accepted us and took care of us.

"When I finished high school, I joined the military immediately. My grandparents and mother wanted me to continue with the family business of running a restaurant, but I had my own plans. Before I realized it, I was applying to West Point and my grandfather's influence got me accepted. It is too bad that neither he nor the rest of my family lived to see me graduate."

"How did they die?" Schwarz asked.

"My grandfather of a heart attack, my mother of cancer and my grandmother, who outlived both of them, of old age and a broken heart. My grandmother arranged to leave her entire holdings to charity, so that I wouldn't be placed in any kind of uncomfortable position that would leave someone asking questions. You see, in those days they could explain away my mother. I, on the other hand, was quite another matter.

"So that is my story, and that is why there's nothing about my life. For the first many years of my life, I didn't really exist. No social security number, no birth records."

"How did you manage to get into the military without a social security number?"

"Forged birth certificate and other documents," he said. "My grandfather had met a person or two during World War II who worked for various state and federal agencies. It wasn't difficult."

"That's why it seemed you had just suddenly appeared," Brognola surmised.

Pordello nodded in agreement. "And why it probably appeared I was a spy, perhaps inserted by a foreign government. I would imagine many of these acts performed by my late grandfather will come back to haunt me. I'm sure now I will be out of military service. But at least I will be out with my name cleared, and my conscience much the same."

"Hardly," Brognola said, sitting back and sticking a fresh, unlit cigar between his teeth. "You've served your country with distinction to this point, General. You have a perfect military record, and you are one of the President's most trusted officers. You have a family of your own now. Grandchildren, even, according to your file."

"Yes, I have two."

"It wouldn't serve any purpose to ruin your career, sir," Schwarz said, echoing Brognola's sentiments. "We're here to find the real enemies of the country."

"Then you won't have to look very far," a voice said behind them.

The trio turned to see Kyle Makowski standing in one of the bedroom doorways, and there was no mistaking the sleek outline of a Beretta 92-SBF pistol in his fist. Also known as the M9, the weapon was the standard side arm for officers and other select groups in the military. The lieutenant now held it on the threesome in a surprisingly steady grip. He'd come in so quietly that they hadn't even heard him—probably through a window. That was the work of a marked professional, not some amateur youth making a wanna-be sucker play.

Still, Makowski looked a bit out of place standing there with the weapon. More out of place than anyone would have thought. It was the boyish features, charming good looks and harmless expression that made it strange. But now Brognola sensed something feral in the young man's eyes. Something he hadn't detected during the meeting with him and Wicker that morning.

It explained quite a bit. The one person they wouldn't have expected was now there to show them the error of their thinking. Schwarz was probably kicking himself more than anybody—he'd told Brognola earlier that Makowski and Wicker were probably the last two people he suspected. But it made perfect sense to the Stony Man chief now, and he couldn't believe his eyes in some ways. In other ways, he wasn't the least bit surprised. The whole experience here at White Sands was becoming one paradoxical déjà vu after another.

"Lieutenant!" Pordello exclaimed. "What in God's name do think you're doing?"

"Keeping you from making a mistake, Comrade General," Makowski replied in a calm voice.

"Comrade Gen—?" the officer began, but Schwarz shushed him.

"You look surprised, Mr. Swanson," Makowski said.

"Not really." The tone in his voice held an edge that chilled even Brognola. "We knew somebody was close enough to the SLAMS project to feed intelligence to the enemy. Whoever was feeding that intelligence also had to be pretty familiar with how to disable it."

"You're quite clever," Makowski interjected.

"You must think we're fools," Brognola said, picking up right where Schwarz had left off.

They had to keep the guy talking, had to keep him occupied for a little bit longer while Schwarz formulated some plan.

"Do you honestly think," Brognola continued, "that we weren't eventually going to find out who was behind the sabotage of the SLAMS system?"

"Blanski didn't figure it out," Makowski replied with a chuckle. "He walked right into the trap we had set for him. And you just couldn't leave it alone. You had to come back here and start poking around in places where your nose didn't belong. I tried to warn you through Blanski. The general tried to warn you. But still you would not listen."

Brognola looked at Pordello and squinted his eyes. "You were behind this?"

"No," Pordello stammered, exchanging looks with Brognola and Makowski. "I don't know what he's talking about."

"Oh, your precious General Pordello a spy?" Makowski said "Perish the thought. I heard him tell you this morning. You see, I'm not only an expert in electronic warfare, I'm also an expert in electronic surveillance that is undetectable by most standard bug sweeps, and even some advanced ones."

"So how much are these people paying you?" Brognola asked. "I hope it was enough to make it worth selling out your own country."

"Spare me your sick nostalgia and patriotic speeches, Mr. Brognola," Makowski said, sneered. "I watched my parents slave away for the greater glory of the armed forces for many years. They retired poor, broken hearted and with the thankless praise of this republic of damnation. I was happy to sell out to the Russians. How did you know they were behind it?"

"We didn't for sure," Schwarz said menacingly. "Until now."

"Well, for all the good it will do you. There is no one else staying in the guest billets at this present time, and no else will be close enough to hear the shots."

"That truly is sad," Schwarz said, shaking his head. "You know why?"

"Why?"

"Because that means nobody will hear you die."

Schwarz pushed the table up and away, yelling for the others to get behind it as he unleathered the Glock 23 and brought it into play.

Makowski remained calm, stepping back behind the frame of the bedroom door as Pordello and Brognola took cover. The focus remained on Schwarz, which was probably what the Able Team commando was counting on. This gave Brognola time to draw his own pistol and even the odds. The Colt Combat Commander roared in Brognola's fist, and a bullet shattered Makowski's elbow before the kid got off more than two shots. The youth's weapon was knocked from his grasp and skittered across the floor.

Schwarz had rolled away from the table and was coming to his knees as the round from Brognola's weapon found its mark. The veteran commando set up his shot and pumped out a double tap from the Glock 23. Both .40-caliber S&W cartridges missed, taking out splinters of wood from the door frame as Makowski ducked out of sight.

"Stay here," Schwarz ordered the other two men.

He launched himself toward the door, entering the bunk room just in time to see Makowski leap through an open window. Schwarz took the room in two strides and threw himself through the window, as well, palms smacking the sandy ground as he rolled and came to his feet.

Makowski was trying to stumble through the dark, glancing behind him to see where Schwarz was. The kid was much younger and more nimble than the Able Team commando, but he'd fattened up on easy times over the years at White Sands, and what's more he was wounded. The guy wasn't going far. Schwarz caught up with him less than fifty yards later and tackled him. His pistol jammed muzzle first into the dirt, and he left it there as he hauled the kid to his feet by the collar.

Makowski swung wildly with his left fist, and Schwarz easily ducked the attempt. He landed a rabbit punch to Makowski's body, then followed with a left jab and then a right uppercut. The blow from the beefy-armed combatant knocked Makowski's smaller frame into the air. The traitorous officer landed hard on the ground. He looked over and saw Schwarz's abandoned weapon lying nearby. The young man snatched it from the dirt and whipped it in the Able Team commando's direction. Schwarz backed away, raising one hand and starting to protest. Makowski obviously didn't want to hear it.

He squeezed the trigger.

The weapon exploded in his hands as sharp pieces of metal flew in every direction. Superheated fragments and gunpowder peppered Makowski's face. One of those fragments was traveling fast enough to penetrate bone and the brain protected beneath it. Makowski's head snapped backward from the impact as the powder burned itself into his face.

Schwarz stood there for a long moment, breathing heavily and shaking his head. He knew that enough dirt, sand and rocked had clogged the barrel to make the weapon unsafe. Obviously, Makowski hadn't.

Brognola and Pordello joined Schwarz outside a moment later as the sounds of sirens approached.

"Another sad loss of life," Pordello whispered. "And another damn tragedy."

"Yes," Brognola agreed solemnly. "Another young hopeful whose life had been snuffed out by the promise of something better."

"The problem is that there's nothing better than good, old-fashioned, American freedom," Schwarz concluded. "The kind of freedom we fight for every single day of our lives. That's the real tragedy."

And they all knew he was right. It was a tragedy when anybody with potential like Makowski could be duped by false hopes and suckered into scams that offered a greater tomorrow. Makowski had been as much a victim as a player in the game. He'd allowed himself to become blinded by something intangible.

16

Pole of Inaccessibility, Antarctica

The enemy autofire came so close to Mack Bolan's sprawled form that he could hear the bullets pass his ears.

It was a hell of a situation in which to be—although he'd been in much worse. The odds and the enemy's advantage were rapidly dwindling under the soldier's marksmanship. For every five rounds they wasted with short, uncontrolled bursts interspersed with grabbing cover, Bolan managed to drop another with one well-placed shot. He'd estimated ten and they were now down to four.

He rose to one knee as he steadily depressed the trigger and swept the muzzle in a corkscrew fashion. He hammered the corridor with bullets, keeping the heads of his enemy down, continuing his spiral pattern while he yanked another RGN from his pocket. He manipulated the pin beneath his boot, leaned his weight forward and yanked on the grenade. He let the bomb fly with a side-handed toss and then rolled away from the area as the bolt locked back on the smoking AKSU.

The remaining troops burst from cover, hearing the Executioner was out of ammunition and eager to make their kill. They all noticed the grenade just a second before it landed next to them. There was no time to avoid it as the impact fuse detonated and the HE filling went up. The blast was most effective in such a confined area and all four men fell under the slag-hot fragments that shredded their flesh.

They toppled under the onslaught, and two of them who remained alive received their final sentence a moment later when Bolan blew them away with rounds from the fresh magazine he'd loaded.

Bolan pressed onward, storming through the hallway and stepping over bodies. He was like a ghostly wraith of death incarnate—an angel and specter of destruction. Nothing would stop him from his goal now. He wouldn't *let* anything or anyone stop him. As he continued along the icy hallways, he heard another announcement come over the loudspeaker. It sounded like a number: ten minutes, maybe.

There was a sudden, basslike thrumming through the cavern, and then it stopped as abruptly as it had started. Mack Bolan was running out of time.

EREK TROFIMOFF ENTERED Mishenka's office and snapped, "Blanski has broken through your pitiful band of resistance, Comrade General. He's going in the direction of the launch pad. I would advise that you head for the surface."

"I'm not going to run, Erek."

"It is not running," Ninakov reminded his master in a high-pitched voice. There was no mistaking the fear in his tone, and Mishenka felt a pang of disapproval. "It is a tactical retreat. There is no point in waiting here to die, sir. We must go now. The storm will be here within an hour, according to our forecasters, and once it has arrived we will be trapped for six months."

Mishenka didn't want to accept the fact that it was time to leave, but he knew there weren't many options. It was only a matter of time before the last of his troops would fall beneath the guns of Blanski. He *had* proved himself to be troublesome—just as Trofimoff had predicted—and Mishenka wasn't going to be his victim. Nadezhda was in launch mode now, and there was nothing Blanski could do to stop that.

"You are correct," Mishenka finally conceded. "It is not the right time to throw ourselves away. We must go to Vostok and await the results of our launch."

"How will you disable the defense system set up at White Sands if you're not here?"

"I will not have to disable it from here. It can be taken care of either remotely or through our operations at the research station in Vostok. Dr. Karamov can disable SLAMS, and if he is unable to do so, then we have our people at the other end."

Trofimoff scowled with a derisive laugh. "Do you honestly think that your mole at White Sands will sacrifice himself for the greater glory of your alleged Russian empire?"

"He has proved himself completely reliable. Anyway, it does not matter. He knows that I can do it from my end, so it would not benefit him to try overriding the MXT signal commands. He does not have the counterfrequency codes necessary to repel the missile, and he could not possibly get far enough away from the base for it to make any difference. Anyone within approximately three thousand square miles of White Sands will feel Nadezhda's revenge."

He turned to Ninakov. "Find Major Orlov and tell him to prepare what's left of Raustov's commandos. We will need an escort to the surface. Tell him to clear the corridor of debris caused by Blanski and his people. We will use the armory exit."

Ninakov nodded and rushed out of the office.

Trofimoff raised an eyebrow. "It would appear you have developed a healthy respect for this Blanski. Taking the back way out?"

Mishenka could feel the anger rise from his belly, roiling in his chest and causing his face to flush. He'd never liked Trofimoff, and now the assassin was mocking him. That was quite all right—he'd find a way to dispose of Vasily's stooge once and for all. Trofimoff had outlived his usefulness. If Blanski didn't kill him, the storm probably would.

"We wouldn't even have to worry about him if you had done as you said you would," Mishenka said in a mocking tone.

"I will kill Blanski when the moment is right."

Mishenka couldn't contain his laughter. He detected just a trace of trepidation in Trofimoff's voice and he realized that the assassin was as intimidated by Blanski as he was. He had the same healthy respect as Mishenka; otherwise, he would not have been able to identify it so readily in Mishenka's behavior.

"I realize your cowardice prevented you from attempting to stop Blanski," Mishenka taunted him. "However, I know that it doesn't matter much now. You may accompany Orlov and the others. I will choose to overlook your acid tongue this time. However, when we have reached Vostok, you are on your own."

"There will be another opportunity to kill Blanski," Trofimoff reasoned. "A perfect opportunity. That is the difference between a professional and an amateur. A professional knows how to wait for his kill. What do you plan to do about this Faithe woman? She is waiting on the surface."

Mishenka smiled, his heart thudding in his ears with renewed anticipation. "I have already taken care of that little issue."

BY THE TIME the Executioner had made his way through the deserted corridors to the launch pad, the portal had already opened. Snow and chunks of ice were still falling from where the heavy-duty hydraulics had pushed away large plates buried beneath the surface.

Bolan stood on the catwalk and studied the launch area below. He had only minutes to set the charges and get out of there. If the missile firing was initiated before he could plant the charges, he would be incinerated and this whole attempt would come to naught. He had to get down there and fast.

The soldier studied the catwalk a moment and then looked to the launch pad again. There was some kind of entrance down there, but he didn't have time to go searching for it. He'd have to do this here and now. Bolan reached into an external pocket and withdrew a tightly coiled bundle of rope. He undid the clip holding the bundle in place and tossed it over the side. The seventy-five-foot rope fell short of reaching the floor.

Bolan tied a quick bowline knot around the railing of the catwalk, then ducked between the gap between the catwalk and the railing itself. He immediately lowered himself over the side, holding on to the railing with one hand while he leaned back and tested the rope strength with his full body weight. Convinced it would hold, he launched himself off the side.

The Executioner descended the rope hand by hand, muscles tensing with the strain as he strove to control his speed and prevent rope burns. He reached the bottom of the rope in less than a minute, then dropped the rest of the way to the frozen ground. There was no wood or plastic here, but rather a heavy pad made from a material with which Bolan was unfamiliar. He ignored his curiosity and kept his thoughts on the matter at hand.

Bolan slung the pack off his shoulder and knelt. He began to retrieve the C-4 and blasting caps from the bag, looking around often to make sure nobody attempted to spring a nasty surprise. If they chose this moment to ambush the Executioner, they would get the nasty surprise. The soldier quickly made preparations, removing the last of plastique and then walking to the missile. He tapped the shell of the thing, pressing his ear to it. A frown crossed his features and he pulled his head away from the missile. He looked at the thing disgustedly, shaking his head. Even if he were able to destroy the launch pad, it wouldn't be enough to stop the missile from getting off the ground. He wouldn't have to set blasting caps. When that thing fired, it would create enough heat and pressure to blow the plastique, but because of the way C-4 blew it wouldn't have any effect. There was at least 38 mm of homogenous armor protecting that launch cone. He didn't have enough plastique to do any real damage beyond maybe leaving a scorch mark.

That was it, then. He'd have to find a better use for his explosives. He'd have to go to the source of the launch area and stop it there. And the more time he stood here thinking about it, the less his chances of finding the launch controls before it was too late. Undoubtedly, Mishenka would have the place secured. He'd cross that bridge when he came to it. He returned the C-4 to the pack as he formulated his plan.

Once that was complete, Bolan went to the opening he'd noticed; it was actually more of a scuttle hole, barely three feet at its maximum height and width. The Executioner squeezed his way through the hole, pack in front of him and the barrel of the AKSU ready for action. At least if someone decided to appear at the other end and shoot at him, the pack would provide him enough cover to give him a fighting chance.

He reached the other side and climbed out of the crawl way. He was in a circular room, maybe eight feet in diameter. The room was empty except for a ladder that led up the side of the wall to a ledge perhaps twenty feet above. Bolan slung the pack and immediately began to ascend it. He reached the ledge and found himself facing a thick plastic door.

He looked through the view slot in the door and saw the laboratory he'd been searching for. Several men in lab coats busied themselves around computers, and as Bolan was set to make his entrance, he detected a rumbling sound emanate from below. He noticed one of the men in the laboratory speaking to an associate and pointing excitedly at some kind of radar screen. The missile was active and set to launch.

Bolan looked to his right and saw two guards standing near a plate-glass window that led to another office beyond the lab. The Executioner saw Mishenka and the dark-haired man who had first shown his face when they were incarcerated. He didn't know who the tall, muscular man in the leather coat was, but he didn't really care. It was more important that he find a way to abort the launch. Then he'd deal with Mishenka and his colleagues.

The Executioner burst through the door and rushed toward the two men talking with animated gestures over the radar screen. He swept the muzzle of the AKSU in the direction of the guards, cutting them down on the run with a series of controlled bursts. Bolan reached the scientists in a matter of seconds and pointed the smoking assault rifle at them.

"Either of you speak English?" he asked.

The two men looked at each other a moment before turning their attention back to Bolan and raising their arms. One of them stammered, "I d-do."

"Stop Nadezhda," the Executioner ordered him. "Abort the launch."

"We cannot stop it!" he exclaimed. "I-It is t-too late. Please do not sh-shoot us!"

"I'm not going to shoot you," Bolan said firmly but calmly. "Stop the launch."

"I cannot stop the launch!" he yelled again. "It is unstoppable!"

Bolan looked at the guy a moment before finally shaking his head. There was no point for either one of the men to lie. The look on their faces was genuine fear, and they knew he might shoot them dead if they didn't comply. These were scientists and scholars, not lunatics. They had nothing to gain by disobeying him. The Executioner spun in the direction of the office—prepared to meet a new threat—but Mishenka and the dark-haired man were gone.

They obviously had more important matters to attend to, and now that the missile was going to launch and there was no stopping it, Bolan thought he knew what those matters were: escape and evasion. Well, the Executioner had played that game a time or two himself, and he knew how to play it well.

Bolan whirled. "Get away from those consoles."

The scientists moved aside, and Bolan depressed the trigger of the AKSU. He began pouring lead into the consoles, trying to destroy the equipment that would guide the weapon. In a few seconds, he shattered screens and laid waste to thousands of dollars' worth of electronic equipment.

"Get out of here!" he ordered the men.

They bolted from the room, their associates joining them when they saw the destruction that lay ahead. The sound of the rumbling had now increased, and the Executioner knew it was time to go. He could no longer do any good here. He had to pursue Mishenka and the mysterious stranger. It was time to even the score.

The Executioner wasn't sure where the missile was headed

but he knew there was little he could do about it. Based on the tests he'd seen at White Sands, he knew there was a pretty good chance the SLAMS device could stop the missile. But there were no guarantees. Moreover, Mishenka knew that he would have to disable the SLAMS technology before he could use the weapon, which was probably what he was concentrating on doing now. He wouldn't be able to stop the missile from here, because Bolan planned to blow the lab to kingdom come.

He had to have a satellite area somewhere else, a place where he could disable the SLAMS deflection technology. The original signals had been traced through Admundsen-Scott Station from the Pole. That meant that those signals could be sent from just about anywhere. Bolan was betting on Vostok as the alternate point of origin.

The Executioner quickly pulled the C-4 from the bag. He planted the charges through the room, inserting a blasting cap in each one. He then left through the office and cleared the outside door before activating the primer switch on the electronic detonator. With a push of the button, the Krai erupted into smoke and flame. Ice, snow and debris blew through the office, clouding the immediate area. As the echo of the blast died, Bolan could hear Nadezhda preparing to come to life.

The Executioner headed out in search of Mishenka. It was time to bring that maniac to his knees and wipe away his twisted dream with one swift stroke.

AT FIRST, it started as just a slow rumble, then the ground began to tremble. It seemed as if the entire ice shelf would collapse beneath them. It was no hideous monster—no earthquake or other natural disaster. But whatever it was, it was emerging from the snowy and ice-packed plateau of the Pole of Inaccessibility like a demon unleashed.

It took Anika Faithe a moment to realize that her apparition was anything but—they were actually hydraulic doors rising from the ground, emerging slowly and steadily like the coffin of some great ice creature. She stared through the cockpit of the Mil Mi-24 Hind, frozen in place like a statue as the entire chopper rumbled with the event.

"What is happening?" the Russian pilot asked her.

"Nothing for you to worry about," Capek replied in flawless Russian.

Faithe turned to look at him with complete surprise. She had finished dressing his wound and they now sat in the Hind waiting for Blanski to get back. Except that now she wondered if that was what they were actually waiting for. The reality of the situation came to her quite abruptly when she saw that Capek now had his AKSU trained on her, and she had been posting guard on their Russian guest.

"What do you think—?"

"Shut up," Capek cut in, "and hand over your side arm. Slowly, my dear. I don't want to shoot a woman of taste and beauty, but I will if provoked. Or if I sense any trickery."

Faithe was too stunned at that moment to try trickery. It was actually surprising to find Capek acting this way. Perhaps he was working under Blanski's orders, but it wouldn't have made sense. He had originally been the one to give her one of the two Makarov pistols Blanski had lifted off the deceased. Now he was telling her to give it back. She realized she had been duped. Capek had caught her unaware by luring her into thinking he trusted her. Then, when her guard was down and she felt she had no reason to consider him a threat, he turned the tables on her.

"You're most clever, Luva," Faithe said, sitting back and folding her arms defiantly. "How did you manage to fool all of us for so long? Are you working for Mishenka, as well?"

"I'm working for your father, Comrade Luvanovich. You see, I know that you told Blanski only part of the real story. And I also know why."

"And just what do you perceive is the rest of the story?"

"If you are referring to the truth," he replied, raising an eyebrow, "I know that you are not here under sanction from your father. I have known Borysko Luvanovich for many years. I have worked as a security agent for him in one capacity or another."

"I have never heard him speak of you."

"Of course not!" Capek said, sneering. "Do you honestly believe that your father told you everything? He did not tell you all, just as you did not tell him all. It's only natural that we who serve from the shadows live in a world of lies. We live so deep in our cover that many times we forget what the truth is. Every now and again, we must come out of it."

"You speak excellent Russian. Just the hint of eastern port accent. Your instructors must have trained you well."

"They trained me well enough."

"So what exactly is your mission here?"

"I am here to do three things," Capek replied triumphantly. "First, I am supposed to make certain that Nadezhda leaves her nest just as planned. Second, I am to escort General Mishenka back to Vostok. Last, I was ordered to do something that will bring me very little pleasure."

"Which is?"

"To kill you, of course. All of you."

17

Mack Bolan passed through the corridor that had been blocked by ice and debris—the one that led to the armory—and saw that it had been cleared. The soldier also noticed the cluster of sentries, obviously posted there to cover Mishenka's escape. Bolan ducked behind the wall where it intersected with the other corridor in time to avoid being torn to shreds by autofire.

The Executioner yanked the last two grenades from his coat and pulled the pins. This time, he let the numbers count down to one while he immediately tossed the other. The sentries saw the first one in time to back up, but they weren't prepared for a second one to come immediately behind it. The twin blasts shook the foundations of the corridor and brought the entire ceiling down.

Bolan knew they were cut off from him. He'd neutralized the threat and given Mishenka only one way out of the frozen depths. It would lead him right to the surface and into the waiting arms of Capek. The Executioner stopped to listen, cocking his head to one side and fixing on a distant sound. The boom-boom kept increasing in frequency, coming closer and closer.

The place was set to go up—Mishenka had booby-trapped the complex.

Bolan whirled and sprinted down the corridor to the door where he'd first encountered the cluster of commandos. He knew the corridor went through the bunking area and circled back to the entrance where he'd descended from the research station. He ran like a bat out of hell, his muscular legs pumping at a furious pace. Bolan gulped the frigid air, sucking life-giving oxygen and pushing himself for all he was worth.

The explosions continued to approach, increasing in tone at an exponential rate and threatening to overtake the soldier. The Executioner reached the spiral staircase, using the railing to pull himself forward as his cramping legs took the steps two at a time.

Another rumbling overtook the explosions, just barely detectable beneath blast after blast. The missile was off the pad and headed skyward. The Executioner's worst fears had come to realization. That weapon of terror was on a direct course for God knew where, and there wasn't a thing he could do about it. Even as he reached the research station building, Bolan could hear the explosive concussions continue.

The entire experience was ominous for him. Despite his best efforts, the ICBM would more than likely complete its destructive mission. Mack Bolan offered a brief, silent prayer to the Universe for those who would experience her devastating power.

GENERAL GAVRIL MISHENKA watched with tremendous satisfaction from the Mil Mi-24 Hind as Nadezhda lifted up and away in a soul-trembling experience of power unleashed. Blue-white flame poured from her tail cone, and red-orange balls of superheated gas from the launch left the smell of rocket propellant in the air that was detectable even inside the chopper. Mishenka beamed with pride, turning to look at the faces of his loyal comrades. They were seated on the various benches lining both sides of the belly. Capek and Trofimoff sat together, the Croat pilot keeping his weapon trained on Faithe, who was wedged between them.

The blades of the chopper began to spin faster as the Russian pilot Blanski had taken prisoner was now behind the controls, warming the machine for liftoff. It would take them approximately three hours to get to Vostok. The missile would have done its work by then. Nadezhda would have set America on the brink of chaos. There would be no stopping them now.

"We have cause to celebrate and rejoice in our victory," Mishenka boomed. He could barely contain his elation.

"You have done a great thing today, sir," Ninakov commended him.

"You haven't done anything," Trofimoff cautioned. "We do not know if it has worked yet."

"It will work," Mishenka said in an exasperated voice. "You must learn to have much more faith in destiny, Erek."

"I have faith only in that which I can directly control."

"And thus, you have no vision. No ability to see beyond the mere surface impression. No idea what great things you can achieve when you set your mind to it. Killing men has made you shallow and one-dimensional. You cannot see beyond personal survival. That is a dangerous path."

"I create solutions to problems in my chosen profession," Trofimoff muttered.

"Yes, but I create countries and nations. Kings and world leaders will bow before the new order of the CCCP. The Soviet Union will be once again great, and no one will dare oppose her now. Once more, people will tremble at the thought of Russia and her great might. The *new* Russia for a *new* world. We shall be victorious!"

"I wouldn't think quite yet," Faithe interjected, nodding out the window of the Mi-24.

All eyes turned as Blanski burst from the power station and began sprinting in the direction of the Hind.

"Liftoff!" Mishenka barked at the pilot.

Blanski started to raise his weapon as Mishenka felt the chopper vibrate under the increased power to the engines. A lump formed in his stomach as the Hind left the frozen plain. Darkness seemed to cover the entire area in moments, the sun now completely gone from the horizon. Light glinted off of the approaching bands of dark clouds. It seemed that the world had gone dark in the twinkling of an eye.

Mishenka could see Blanski aim carefully for the tail rotor, but the night was suddenly lit with the fiery explosion of the station. Debris rained down on him, knocking the troublemaker to his knees and finally depositing him onto his belly. The last of the explosive charges sent flames skyward, the concussion rocking the Hind and threatening to tear it apart. Blanski wasn't moving, becoming a speck rapidly as the chopper continued to rise.

"No!" Faithe screamed.

She jumped from her seat, pushing the muzzle of Capek's AKSU toward the ceiling as she leaped for Mishenka's throat. Capek fumbled with the assault rifle, careful to keep his finger off the trigger as he tried to recover from Faithe's sudden and explosive maneuver.

Mishenka reared away, stunned by the lithe form that came toward him. He could see vengeance and hatred in Anika Faithe's eyes as she reached for his throat. She was stopped short by Trofimoff, who reacted quickly and grabbed her by the edge of her parka.

"You bitch!" he snapped.

The assassin yanked on her, pulling her backward and encircling her throat with an arm. He wanted to break her neck there—Mishenka could see it—but instead he apparently thought better of it and held himself in check. Trofimoff stood, dragging the ferocious woman away from them and toward the door. She kicked backward at his shins, trying to rake his face with her nails and get a bite hold on his hand. He pulled tighter, holding her at bay while he opened the door.

"You love Blanski so much?" Trofimoff said. "Join him, then!"

He disengaged the locking mechanism, threw back the handle and pulled the door open. Before Mishenka or anyone else could react to his violent outburst, he shoved her roughly out the door.

"What are you doing?" Mishenka screamed, coming out of his seat even though he knew it was too late.

Faithe's body sailed downward, spiraling the some thirty yards before smacking the icy plain. Mishenka didn't see the body hit the ground, the darkness returning as the flames from the station rescinded. Nonetheless, he knew it was too late. They couldn't suffer a delay.

Trofimoff closed the door, his chest heaving with the exertion. Mishenka stood there, the two men staring at each other as the chopper moved away from the scene. The Russian officer couldn't believe what he had just witnessed. Trofimoff had no conscience, no soul of any kind. The general was half tempted to open the door again and toss the assassin pig out with similar malice, but a quick look in the direction of his troops quelled his rage. It wouldn't do to show the same lack of control that this worm had shown. Trofimoff had obviously been looking for an advantage; he couldn't be trusted.

"You did that on purpose," Mishenka spit. "You defied my order just to spite me. We had an agreement. You were supposed to leave the woman to me."

Trofimoff shrugged. "What difference would it have made, Comrade General, whether she was to die now or later? There is no hope for them now. They will freeze to death and their bodies will soon be buried beneath the unforgiving ice. They will never be found."

Mishenka threw an appealing expression in Capek's direction, but the Croat pilot just sat there with a smirk. He'd not wanted to deal with Faithe any more than Trofimoff had. Mishenka knew he was losing control of the situation. Everything he'd worked for had just gone up in smoke and flame. He could only take comfort in the fact that within an hour Nadezhda would have impacted somewhere on the White Sands Missile Range.

He returned to his seat, staring daggers at Trofimoff as the assassin returned to his place next to Capek. When the first opportunity presented itself, he would order both of the men shot to death by firing squad. And he would make sure to hang their bodies where his troops could see them.

WHITE-HOT DAGGERS of pain stabbed the nerve centers along the Executioner's back.

The shrapnel and debris from the explosion had lanced his

body with fragments from neck to legs, and it took every ounce of energy just to remain awake. The concussion effects of the blast had nearly knocked him into a comatose state. Had he actually become unconscious, he knew he probably would have frozen to death.

Something deep down burned in his gut and drove the Executioner to get to his feet. He shook his head to clear mental cobwebs. He was bleeding from several large wounds, yet the blood was freezing almost instantaneously. In a sense, that was good. It would plug the holes until he could find medical attention.

The barely perceptible shape of a body called for his immediate attention. Bolan secured his weapon and gritted his teeth from the jarring pain as he rushed to the still form. Even in the darkness, Bolan could see it was Anika Faithe. His eyes swept over her body, looking for bullet holes. Nothing there, but her leg was pretty messy. A bone was protruding through the right lower calf. Broken fibula and probably damage to the tibia, as well.

He leaned close to check her breathing.

The Executioner jumped as Faithe screamed suddenly. He pulled back in time to see her eyes snap open. She moaned, trying to move and reach for her leg, but Bolan put a hand on her shoulder to restrain her.

"Take it easy, Anika," he said. "You broke your leg."

"How?—" She swallowed hard, her voice hoarse and her breath coming in gasps before she finally managed to ask, "How bad is it?"

"It's not good."

She laid her head back and moaned again. She was going into shock—probably blood loss combined with hypothermia. It didn't make a damn bit of sense to the Executioner. Someone had thrown her from the Hind, obviously, but they hadn't tossed Capek. That made Bolan angry, and it made him suspicious. He wondered for a brief moment if that was by design.

"I don't th-think," Faithe began, shivering under his hand before continuing, "that I'm going to m-make it."

"Just hang tight. We'll get out this," Bolan said grimly, even though the very idea was ludicrous.

"I mu-must know something."

"What?"

"I must know that y-you believed me when I said I—I hadn't...b-betrayed you."

"I believe you."

The Executioner's heart went out to Faithe. He'd been pretty harsh on her, and his own war was probably going to have another casualty. It was becoming apparent that she wasn't the real enemy after all. He'd misjudged this woman—she really had been trying to stop Mishenka's evil plans. That didn't excuse the fact that her foster father wanted Nadezhda for himself, but Bolan knew that wasn't her fault. Mishenka would have launched the missile whether Anika Faithe existed or not.

"You must st-stop him, Blanski," she stammered, breathing more shallowly now. "Don't let him do this."

The warrior's heart was heavy, but he choked back his emotions and just nodded. In his darkest hours, there had always been a glimmer of hope. This time, there was no hope.

Yet something deep down spoke to Bolan. There was something inside of him that guided his movements and his thoughts. He'd always related it as a sixth sense—the same sense that warned him when trouble was close at hand. It was an intuition he'd never been able to explain, but it had saved his life countless times. And it looked as if it was going to save him again.

Bolan looked to his right and noticed the Mil Mi-6 Hook still setting there in the howling, windy darkness. The first signs of the storm were approaching from the northeast, and if they didn't get out of there soon it was going to mean trouble. Nonetheless, the Executioner didn't have the first idea how to fly the chopper. Piloting was always left to Grimaldi—he wished his friend and faithful ally were with him now. The Stony Man ace could have flown that Hook right through the storm and probably never batted an eye.

"Any idea on how to fly that Mi-6?"

A strange expression came over Faithe's pert features. "Th-there is a chopper nearby?"

"Yeah, the one Capek flew us in."

"G-get me to it," she said, a new excitement reaching her voice. "Get me to it. I can fly it."

"With your leg like it is?" the Executioner challenged her.

"I can tell you how to f-fly it."

Well, that was all he needed to hear. This was neither the time nor the place to argue with the woman. If she said she knew how to fly it, then he had to trust she wasn't just delusional. At least if they froze to death it would be inside an aircraft. Bolan had her bend her right leg at the hip, then propped the wounded limb between Faithe's two hands.

"Hold on," he said.

Bolan grunted with the pain that shot through his back and legs as he lifted Faithe off the icy ground and moved quickly to the chopper. He set her down gingerly so he could disengage the door handle. He then loaded her into the Hook and followed behind, closing the door.

"P-put me in the copilot's seat."

Once that was accomplished, he went through the back of the Mi-6 Hook until he'd located a medical pack. He rushed back to the cockpit even as he heard the first whine of the rotors. The instrument panel lights were now glowing, and Bolan could feel the deck plates beneath his boots vibrate as the twin-turbine engines started to warm.

The Executioner wedged himself into the cockpit the best he could and began to use bulky field dressings to pack the wound. Faithe screamed several times, but it couldn't be helped. He had to get the bone covered to reduce the risk of infection and stop the bleeding. Once the leg started to thaw some, there was a chance it could start bleeding again.

"You must not worry...about m-me," she said hoarsely. "We m-must go b-b-before the storm."

"It won't do me any good if you pass out from blood loss while we're in midair."

"I will be fine. L-let's get out of here."

Bolan looked at her a moment as he tied a knot over the dressing. He then squeezed his big frame into the pilot's chair. She began to give him instructions, slowing her breathing and doing her best to take him through each process step by step. In a few minutes, the chopper blades were turning and picking up speed. Bolan cranked the heater, welcome for the relative warmth. This hadn't been the first time he'd ever worked the controls of an aircraft, but it wasn't something he did regularly.

"Note to self," he muttered. "Have Jack teach me to fly one of these crates."

The chopper began to rumble and Faithe was shouting to be heard over the noise. Bolan looked around and quickly spied a headset. He donned it, then did the same for Faithe.

"Is that better?" he asked.

"Yes," she said, still barely audible. The thought of hope had obviously given her renewed strength, though, because she'd stopped stuttering and hesitating. Perhaps she was also being rejuvenated by the heat that was now cranking full blast into the cabin.

"Okay, there are two switches," she said. "They're range finders that keep you oriented. They are green and orange."

"Got it."

"You must think in three-dimensional terms when flying a chopper."

"Understood."

"The handle in your right hand is the collective control. It changes both sides of the swash plate's angle of attack and gives the chopper lift. As you pull up on it, the chopper will leave the ground. The handle directly in front of you is used for the cyclic control. If you move it you will have tilt and direction."

"What about the foot controls?" Bolan asked.

"They control the tail rotor, which gives you rotational direction and thrust. You must keep yourself balanced with the foot pedals. Put them to the floor, pull back slightly on the collective control and push forward on the cyclic control."

Bolan followed her instructions to the letter, pulling steadily on the collective control handle. The rotor speed began to increase and he felt a slow shudder go through the cabin. A moment later, he watched as the ground began to fall from them. The chopper was airborne! The thing started to feel like it was going to turn, putting them in a spin.

"Now, use the right and left foot pedals to balance yourself and keep the chopper pointed straight ahead."

The Executioner did as ordered and the spin slowly decreased until he had what he felt was better control. It was absolutely amazing that she could talk him through something as complicated as flying a chopper. It seemed that Grimaldi always handled these birds with such great ease, but Bolan's nerves were ragged right at the moment.

"You are doing fine," Faithe advised him softly. "Just keep control. I will tell you as we need to change direction, watching the range finder. Then I will tell you how to change that direction."

Bolan nodded slowly, concentrating on keeping the chopper level and not putting them into a spin from which they couldn't recover. It was complicated to do but easy to understand. As he continued to pull back on the collective control, he watched the digital altimeter continue to count upward. The chopper started to tilt forward a bit too much, and he eased back on the control some to keep them in a forward direction, rather than down.

Bolan looked over at Faithe, and she was watching him. She smiled and nodded, her face pale and weary in the luminescence of the instrument lights.

"You are a natural, Blanski."

"Lots of help," he quipped, then returned to concentrating on his flying.

18

White Sands Missile Range, New Mexico

"General, I think we have a problem," Colonel Ivan Wicker announced.

Pordello had just entered the bunker with Brognola and Schwarz in tow. "What is it?"

Wicker pointed to a flashing blip on the three-dimensional monitoring systems. "Our satellites have picked up some activity in Antarctica. Approximately twelve minutes ago, we detected a signal variance originating from the geophysical research station in Vostok. This signal was a feedback loop, coming from a set of subsystem signals somewhere within the ice shelf. Shortly after that, our radar detected this."

"Isn't that where your people suspected the signals originated that redirected our test missile?" Pordello asked Brognola.

Brognola nodded. "We sent Blanski in there to find out what was going on. Despite what I'd told you before, he does work for us. I can't disclose everything to you, General, but suffice it to say that there's a little more to me and Mr. Swanson here than meets the eye."

"Why am I not surprised?"

"Someone tried to kill our pilot, but he managed to pull out of it. He's at a hospital in Halley Bay. But we haven't heard a word from Blanski. Last time he was seen, it was accompanying a military scientist to Vostok."

"What do you think it is, Ivan?" Pordello asked.

"We believe it's a missile, sir," Wicker replied quietly. "Type is still unknown."

"Any idea of its target?" Brognola said.

"It's still too early to tell. It doesn't appear to be taking any direct course, whatever the target. To be sure, it has an odd vector and until it begins to level out we can't be sure of direction."

"What's going on, Mr. Brognola?" Pordello demanded. "Who's behind all of this?"

"We're not sure," the Stony Man chief replied, "but we think it might be a Russian deserter named General Gavril Mishenka."

"What?" Wicker interjected. "What makes you think that?"

"The intelligence we have is sketchy. Our one link was Makowski, and we have no way of confirming the information now. However, he mentioned 'the general' when he was popping off at our quarters. He wasn't talking about you, General Pordello, so I can only assume he meant Mishenka."

"Who is this Mishenka?"

"Well, he was supposedly a deserter from the Russian army. A highly decorated officer who was officially ruled later to have died by his own hand."

"Suicide?" Pordello asked.

"Maybe," Schwarz interjected, "but our people are skeptical about that. His body was never recovered. There is apparently a cemetery where he's allegedly buried, but we've got no concrete proof to support that."

"Especially since nobody trustworthy has ever claimed to be an eyewitness to the identification," Brognola added. "All we have are the official reports from the Russians. We hardly find that to be conclusive evidence. I think our theory is correct."

"So let me get this straight," Pordello said. "You think that some former Russian army officer might be the brains behind sabotage of the SLAMS project?"

"It's very possible."

Pordello said nothing for a moment, and Brognola could

tell this had taken him completely off guard. The theory probably did seem weak, considering the circumstances, but there was no question the Russians had their finger in the pie here somehow—whether officially or unofficially remained to be seen. Makowski had confirmed this before his death. Nonetheless, it probably seemed shocking for a man like Pordello. He'd moved up through the ranks during the cold war. This kind of threat had probably not occurred to him for many years, and now the idea of conflict with the Soviet Union had brought about a refreshed view.

"Is it possible he's working under Russian sanction?"

Brognola shook his head. "Unlikely. I don't think the Russians would go to this kind of trouble. We believe if this is Mishenka, he's working on his own."

"Okay." The general turned to a nearby phone. He picked up the receiver, punched in a four-digit number and spoke briefly with his executive officer, who had returned to the base under a state of emergency.

After the incident with Makowski, Pordello had sent Kranz and his men to arrest Lieutenant Tom Mundy under suspicion of espionage. Mundy was sitting in the detention facility at the provost marshal's office now, awaiting Brognola and Pordello to come and question him. They were very suspicious that he had been the one to arrange the disappearance of the two federal investigators, as well as the attacks on Bolan and Brognola.

When Pordello had completed ordering his XO to close the base and go to full security alert, he made another call from the bunker. "This is General Jonathan Pordello of White Sands Missile Range. Get me the Chair of the Joint Chiefs. Tell him we have a Def-Con 3 situation."

As Pordello waited, Brognola turned his attention to Wicker. "It would appear we owe you an apology, Colonel."

"Why is that?"

"Well, this is rather embarrassing, but we suspected you of being our traitor."

"It wouldn't be the first time, Mr. Brognola."

"Colonel, what's the situation at this point?" Schwarz asked. "If that missile *is* headed toward America, how long will we have?"

Wicker looked at the screen a moment, then walked to a nearby computer terminal and began to type something very quickly into the terminal there. Schwarz moved a bit closer to see what he was typing, and he was amazed to see the guy working that fast. It looked as if he was putting in code, since he was using English letters, numbers and symbols but they were insensible. A few moments later, new information came on the screen.

"Given present speed and elevation," Wicker finally said after looking at the information only briefly, "I would say that any impact on the East Coast will occur in twenty-nine minutes. Midwest would be thirty-two. Mountain regions, including ourselves, would be twenty-six, and Pacific I'd guess at about thirty-seven. Of course, those times could vary given when the missile changed direction."

"Colonel?" a controller called. Brognola and Schwarz followed Wicker over to a nearby terminal. The controller continued, "We have confirmation on our bogie. It's a cruise-type weapon, Soviet architecture, but beyond any normal classification I've ever seen. I would have to say larger than any class III or IV missile."

Wicker nodded. "It's probably an ICBM, Nick. Maybe a nuclear warhead."

"Our sensors aren't powerful enough to detect that this early, sir," the controller said, "but I would have to say that's probable. We'll know more as it enters mid-Atlantic airspace."

The USAF officer turned to Brognola. "What do you think?"

"I think," he replied, "we're going to have to assume it's a mass-destruction weapon until advised otherwise. I need to get in touch with my people and let them know the situation."

"Do you think you can stop it, Colonel?" Schwarz inquired.

"I'm not sure. If it gets close enough, SLAMS might be able to repel it. We've only conducted one live-fire exercise on the SLAMS device." He waved his hand in the general direction where the dud missile had crashed through one of the billets and added, "You see the results of that."

"True," Brognola said, "but that was under different circumstances. Makowski had sabotaged the first test."

"He'd allowed for sabotage of the first test," Wicker countered. "But that doesn't dismiss the fact that those signals interfering with the SLAMS satellite came from a local point in Antarctica. They were undetectable because of the amount of internal activity, and I've not yet found a way to filter those signals yet."

"Colonel Wicker, we have ultimate faith in your abilities. You'll come up with something."

"I wish I had more faith in myself. When it came to this part of things, Makowski was the real genius."

"Colonel, is it possible to jam those signals?" Schwarz asked.

Wicker appeared to think about it a moment. "I suppose it is. But again, that's grossly dependent upon whether or not we can identify them."

Schwarz rolled up the sleeves of his button-down shirt. "I know a few tricks. I need a secured Net-link and an independent terminal."

"You've got it."

Schwarz turned to Brognola. "Hal, you'd better get Aaron and his team on the line right away. I have a feeling the next twenty-nine minutes are going to be the longest of our life."

"Agreed."

Antarctica

"I CANNOT BELIEVE that I did not see through Capek's cover," Faithe murmured. "I must be getting lax spending so many months in solitude at Admundsen-Scott Station."

"Don't beat yourself up," Bolan replied. "I didn't catch it, either. It should have been obvious, but I was so focused on what I was doing that I missed it entirely."

"What do you mean?"

"Didn't you notice something different about that Hind they tossed you from?"

"The external tanks?"

Bolan nodded, looking at her in the dim cockpit. "How far do you think it is from Vostok to the Pole?"

"Perhaps seven hundred kilometers, maybe eight hundred."

"Yeah. If memory serves, the maximum range for a Mil Mi-6 Hook with a four-ton payload is a thousand klicks, at best. He didn't have anywhere near that weight, but he certainly couldn't have done our drop round trip. There are no fueling points between here and there, so he had to have fueled somewhere closer than Vostok."

"So he came to the research station."

"Exactly."

"But that makes no sense... Wait. You're off course. Adjust for about twenty-degrees southwest. There. Much better, Blanski. It's almost as if you have flown before."

"I can't say it's the first time I've ever been behind flight controls. But it certainly is the first time for a Russian cargo ship."

"Ah!"

"Your leg?"

"Yes," she replied tightly, her voice barely audible in the Executioner's headset. "It is becoming more painful."

"The cold was probably numbing the pain."

"I wish it were cold again."

"I can take you back—"

"I believe an appropriate response would be to shove it, Blanski."

At least she had maintained her dry sense of humor. She was a tough act to follow, and despite her allegiances the Executioner had to admit he liked her. There was something sensible and earthy about Faithe, something that didn't quite belong in the company of men like Mishenka and Luvanovich. The relationship between her and the former Russian KBG/GRU agent was a troublesome factor. He couldn't bring himself to tell her that he planned to attend to some unfinished business with Luvanovich when all of this was over.

"Capek said something strange to me," Faithe said, intruding on the Executioner's introspection. "He said that my father sent him to kill us. He said all of us, as if he were referring to General Mishenka, as well. This does not make sense that he would then ally himself with the enemy."

"Maybe he had financial incentive."

"I am not so certain of this," she replied in a challenging tone. "Capek was very cool, very professional. There is something else behind all of this. I do not believe my father would have sent him to kill me."

She stopped a moment and groaned as another wave of pain ran through her. Bolan was becoming very concerned for his ally-turned-enemy-turned-ally. The pain wouldn't kill her but the blood loss might. Despite the fact he'd dressed the wound the best way possible and tied bulky dressings, he could see the blood was beginning to soak through the bandages.

"You're bleeding again," he told her.

"It is okay," she said. "I will be fine."

"I'm pushing this thing for all it's worth," he said.

"It will take us several hours to get to Vostok, even at our present speed."

"We don't have that kind of time."

"There will be nothing you can do to stop that missile, Blanski," she reminded him. "Even if you could arrive there right now. Nadezhda is capable of reaching any point in the world within a time span of fifty minutes or less. It travels at unbelievable speed."

"I know that," he said quietly. "There's nothing I can do about the missile. Or the poor people who will experience the effects. My country will take a very long time to recover from this. All I can do now is prevent it from happening again."

"Do you think that your defense system will be able to stop Nadezhda?"

"I don't know," Bolan replied honestly. "All I know is what I've seen, and from that I can tell you it works. As long as they can keep Mishenka from tampering with it again, we've got a shot."

"I hope so."

The Executioner looked at her with surprise and she stared back at him. He couldn't believe what she had just said. It didn't make any sense. She was here to kill Mishenka because Pyotr believed that the good comrade general had flipped his lid. Yet there was little doubt Luvanovich had planned to use the missile for his own selfish purposes anyway. To that end, Bolan found it hard to believe that the Communist controller had experienced some change of heart through the years.

"Why do you look at me so?" she asked him. "I do not wish for millions of people to die any more than you do, Blanski. I am not inhuman."

He had to admit the thought hadn't occurred to him until that moment.

"I do not wish to kill anyone not deserving of death."

Bolan noticed she'd begun to slur her words. Her speech was also becoming less audible and slowed down tremendously. At moments, it was as if she were even searching for the right words to use. That indicated impaired brain function, probably from blood loss. If she survived the trip, it would be a miracle.

There were a few minutes of silence before the Executioner spoke again. He needed to keep Faithe awake, keep her concentrating. "What can you tell me about this weapon? You were explaining something about neutron cascade effects. You said Pyotr was the one who actually developed the isotopes for the missile?"

"Yes," she said, taking a deep breath. He could tell she was trying to stay awake as well. "When General Mishenka was first appointed to the R&D team, Pyotr was a young and ambitious scientist at the time. Many believed he was a genius. Both of these men let their ambition get the better of them. When General Mishenka approached Pyotr about the possibility of a neutron bomb, he discovered that the scientist had already been working on the design plans for years. At first, Mishenka thought he would kill Pyotr and take credit for the plans. But he changed his mind when Pyotr told him that if he were to die, the schematics would fall into the hands of the other major powers. General Mishenka decided to recruit Pyotr instead."

"And in so doing," Bolan concluded, "he also created a liability."

"Yes."

"Mishenka then starts to call his own shots, and Luvanovich decides to scrap the project. Except Mishenka has Nadezhda completed and ready for launch. He discloses his plans to launch the missile against America, so Luvanovich sends you to solve that problem."

"Now you understand why it is so important I stop him."

"Yeah, I understand. But you're right about one thing. That doesn't clear this mystery with Capek."

"What are you going to do, Blanski?"

"I don't know yet," he said, "but I know I'm going to stop this insanity. I hope Mishenka and all his cronies enjoy the cold."

"Why?"

"Because they're never going to leave it."

White Sands Missile Range, New Mexico

"WE HAVE DIRECTION and speed," Aaron Kurtzman told Hermann Schwarz.

The pair was talking to each other via the phone. Wicker was working nearby with several of his men, attempting to find a way to isolate the jamming signals being transmitted by an unseen enemy.

"According to our calculations, that missile is headed straight for White Sands."

"Right down on top of our heads?" Schwarz asked excitedly, looking at Wicker when the Air Force colonel took notice of what he'd said.

"Yeah."

"That's not good, Bear."

"You think?"

"Can you stop it?"

"We have no way to stop the missile or jam the transmissions that would disable SLAMS. Hunt has been busting his ass since Hal sent that information to us. We might have a chance."

"Talk to me."

"We can filter the transmissions jamming the SLAMS satellite through this end. We can then identify those signals and retransmit them to your location. As long as you can see them on that end, you should be able to find a way to jam them from the source."

"That's it?"

"That's it, buddy," Kurtzman replied. "We can do little more with no time. We're not even sure we can keep those signals visible that long, because a lot of it is going to have to do with changing weather patterns. There's a storm brewing over most of the Antarctic continent. I would say that if we don't hear from Mack soon, we're not going to ever hear from him."

"We can't worry about him now," Schwarz snapped. "Just do what you can on your end. We'll have to figure something out from there."

"Sounds good. And Gadgets?"

"Yeah?"

"Good luck, man," Kurtzman said quietly.

The Able Team commando could hear the emotion in the man's voice, and he knew there was a pretty good chance they weren't going to make it out of there. But there was no way in hell Gadgets Schwarz was going to jump ship now. He had to stay and do something to help Wicker. He had to find a way to help defend his country from the jackals who had bent themselves on wiping out every last shred of mom, apple pie and the American way.

He set down the phone and turned to Wicker. "Our people said they could make the signals visible, Colonel. It will have to be up to us from there. Do you think you can jam those signals if you can see them?"

"We could probably modify the SLAMS satellite's computer to produce a variable jamming frequency. It would reduce the effectiveness of the deployment grid considerably."

"Meaning?" Brognola asked.

"Meaning that we will only have a small windows of opportunity to repel the missile. The functionality of the SLAMS device will be greatly impaired by this."

He rushed over to another terminal, sat down and began to type. Brognola went to stand over him, watching his every move as Schwarz watched both men with interest.

"What exactly are you planning to do?" the Stony Man chief asked hesitantly.

Wicker talked as his hands flew over the keyboard. "The ground dishes serve as reflectors for the DQL signals. They form the box, if you will, that we use to change the location reference inside the missile's guidance system. We now have to modify those dishes to provide jamming instead, because the signals affecting the missile are being fed through the SLAMS satellite itself."

"So how will you repel the missile?" Schwarz asked.

"We'll have to do it with a local dish here on the base," he said, his voice filled with uncertainty. "That only leaves us a single grid, which can cover only a small portion. If the missile changes direction at the last minute, there will be no way to compensate in time."

"Meaning?" Pordello asked, joining Brognola.

"Meaning, we can all kiss our collective asses goodbye."

Brognola looked at Schwarz and there was a ghostly color to his cheeks. "Bear's certain?"

Schwarz nodded slowly. He could understand Brognola's reticence—Wicker was committing himself based upon their information. But there was no question about Kurtzman's skills or those of his team. Schwarz would have trusted the Bear's guesses before he would have the facts of most people, and he could think of no one he would have preferred working for them on the other end more than Aaron.

"Twenty minutes to contact," the controller announced grimly.

And everyone in the room waited for the moment to come. A moment that would either end in victory, or a very sudden and permanent defeat. And as that time drew nearer with every sweep of the analog clock second hand, Schwarz began to wonder if they could really pull it off.

And he couldn't help but take a moment to hope and pray that Mack Bolan—his longtime friend and ally—was alive.

19

Vostok, Antarctica

Dr. Pyotr Karamov watched with a mixture of disbelief and anticipation as the missile continued unimpeded toward White Sands Missile Range in New Mexico.

He couldn't believe that Mishenka had actually been insane enough to unleash the weapon against America; neither could he help himself in anticipating the effects. The United States was about to suffer a horrific blow. As the creator and designer of Nadezhda, Karamov had to admit he'd never thought it would come to this. He knew Mishenka was a crazed man, but he also realized some would have considered him the same for developing such a devastating weapon.

A neutron bomb was capable of unmitigated destruction. It didn't react immediately upon impact, not in his mind, anyway. The first thing that would actually happen was fission of the atomic particles that waited to unleash their awesome power. The isotopes would excite in the nuclear material he'd extracted with the laser technology in an adjoining building there at Vostok. The pair of atoms would split in two, and the fission effect would open channels within the warhead.

The trigger inside would produce an explosion and subsequent blast that would turn most of White Sands and Las Cruces into hot ash within a matter of seconds. Little could survive the thermodynamic temperature of critical mass in a neutron bomb. Then there would be a secondary effect a few moments after the fission effect. The shock wave would be caused by the two fission atoms colliding with each other and causing the fusion effect. Over minutes that would lead to hours, a concussion wave would begin to spread in every direction. The blast was theoretically powerful enough to sheer off large sections of landmass at their weakest points, but it would take actual impact and probably days before any quantifiable measure could be made of the end effect.

Karamov couldn't imagine what it would be like to observe the explosion from a great distance. While he wanted to be present to see the power of Nadezhda realized, he was also smart enough to know that he was presently in one of the safest places on the face of the whole, rotten planet. Karamov had once used his skills to help his government. He'd once locked himself away for days trying to find more efficient methods of solving the energy crisis in his country.

But his true talents lay with research and development for the Russian military. With the banning of nuclear arms in the former Warsaw Pact countries, there was little need for men like Karamov and Mishenka. But Borysko Luvanovich had felt differently. In a form of protective exile, Luvanovich had sent the two men to Antarctica to develop the superweapon designed to bring down the enemies of Soviet doctrine and the New Republic.

However, it wasn't Mishenka who was supposed to launch the weapon, it was to have been the decision of those spearheading Luvanovich's upcoming coup. This was too soon. Nadezhda was now to be wasted on Mishenka's own plans, perhaps his own personal bid for power. Not that it mattered. If it worked, Karamov could build a dozen more, a hundred more if necessary! He would continue to design them; perhaps let others build them while he retired in leisure, with the pretty American woman waiting on him hand and foot. Perhaps Anika Faithe would notice him, come to appreciate him for his talent and charm rather than judging him on looks alone like most of the American women did.

In either case, there were less than twenty minutes left to American life in the Southwest. Karamov continued to watch the missile close the distance to its target, occasionally monitoring the signal used to jam the SLAMS satellite. He could see the satellite powering up, watching the readings as the computer began to go through the detection phases and prepare to deploy the grid.

Karamov smiled as he stabbed the switch that activated the jamming frequencies.

And the missile got closer...

White Sands Missile Range, New Mexico

"THERE THEY ARE, Colonel!" Pordello shouted, watching as the frequency signals began to appear on the computer screen.

Schwarz continued to monitor the computer transmissions coming through from secured satellite communications at Stony Man. They weren't taking any chances this time around. The Farm had experienced too many attacks in the past, and they couldn't allow hackers or even their enemies to know from where the assistance was coming. Even if their plan didn't work, Stony Man would go on.

Either that, Schwartz thought, or the rest of the guys will be collecting their pension checks.

"They're definitely coming from Vostok," Brognola observed.

"Yeah," Schwarz agreed.

"Stand by, I'm going to bring the jamming program on-line," Wicker announced. He completed tapping the keyboard and then jumped from his chair and rushed to a nearby computer console. He stabbed some buttons in certain sequence, flipped a few switches and then began to flip a set of very distinctive red switches to the off position. As he did so, the three-dimensional grid began to disappear, fading a little more as Wicker flipped the switches.

But as he did so, Schwarz began to notice the signals disappearing, as well.

"It's working...it's working!" he shouted, laughing.

Pordello and Brognola began to shake hands, and Wicker grinned as everyone in the room let out a cheer. They knew it would all be a downhill ride from there. The SLAMS device had already proved itself before, and now it had done it again. With a little help from bright and astute scientists in Ivan Wicker's league.

The Air Force colonel finished shutting down the last of the other deflectors and then turned to the controller. "Nick, make sure that you let me know as soon as the missile comes into grid range."

"Yes, sir!" the man said jovially and threw a mock salute.

"We're not out of the woods yet, are we, Ivan?" Pordello asked solemnly.

"No, I'm afraid not, General. Unless we can stop this thing once it enters range, we have to assume the worse."

"I suppose I'd better call my wife," Pordello said.

He looked at Brognola. "Aren't there any calls you have to make?"

The Stony Man chief shook his head. "No, if this thing actually hits and I don't come home tonight, my wife won't have to ask questions. She'll know exactly what happened and where I was when it did."

"And what he was doing," Schwarz added.

The two men looked at each other as Pordello simply nodded and left for another room where he could have some privacy. Not that it would matter. None of them would be there in less than fifteen minutes if that thing hit, and Pordello would die only a few seconds before his wife. Then again, they had no idea what was about to happen. It was possible this whole thing was a hoax, although Schwarz wasn't betting on it.

"I just want you to know, Gadgets—"

"Stop, Hal," Schwarz said, standing and shaking the big Fed's hand for possibly the last time. "There's no guarantees in life and we both know it. No guarantee we're going to live from one minute to the next, and no guarantee we're going to die today. So let's save it until we know for sure."

"Then it will be too late."

"It's never too late, boss."

Schwarz smiled and Brognola obviously couldn't help but break into a grin himself. The two men knew that whatever needed to be said already had at one time or another. If they died, it would at least be in each other's company, and there wouldn't be any need to muck up the moment with a lot of awkward and unhappy conversation. Death would come quickly, and whatever was beyond that was anybody's guess. Schwarz was just happy to have someone close by to call a friend, and it seemed Brognola felt the same.

Schwarz turned to Wicker. "You said you only had a small window to repel that missile."

"Right."

"How small?"

"Five miles, give or take."

"But then there will be some extra time to deflect it."

"No, Mr. Swanson. That's five miles for the entire ball of wax. From deployment to deflection."

"At the speed that thing is currently traveling, you're only talking about a few seconds!"

"Yes, 46.79, to be exact," Wicker replied calmly.

"Can it be done in that time?"

"I don't know," Wicker said through gritted teeth. "But I'm sure as hell going to give it my best shot. I have no more wish to die today than the rest of you."

Vostok, Antarctica

EVERYTHING APPEARED to be operating smoothly. Within an hour or two, Mishenka would arrive and they could then leave for the mother country. The storm wouldn't reach them in time to impede their takeoff, provided that Mishenka and his people didn't dally. The storm had already crossed over the perimeter of the Pole of Inaccessibility, so that meant either Mishenka was trapped or they had made it out.

The plan was for Mishenka to contact Karamav by radio at a certain point in the storm movement. If he didn't hear from the general in that time period, he would simply have to gather his belongings and take off on his own. Karamov watched the cluster of monitoring panels with excitement. The missile was still on course. The SLAMS satellite appeared to be operating at full power, but it would be ineffectual.

Karamov smiled as he thought about how those idiots at White Sands were probably running around, banging into one another and scrambling to figure out why the satellite wasn't deflecting the missile. That was if they even knew where the damn thing was. Obviously they had spotted Nadezhda, or they wouldn't have had any reason to activate the SLAMS device. However, it wouldn't do them a shred of good.

Karamov didn't notice the spikes on the instrumentation at first. Less than ten minutes remained, and the missile was on course. The other grids had begun to disappear, an effect that Karamov thought somewhat peculiar. He'd not seen this before, but he could only assume that it was some effect caused by their jamming. The reflector grids on the other end probably weren't seeing the transmissions anymore and were shutting down automatically.

A warning alarm began to sound on the panel, so quietly at first that it didn't even get Karamov's attention. He abruptly detected the subtle hooting and went to the instrument cluster that measured the signal effectiveness. The needle was spiking repeatedly, showing an inconsistent transmission. Karamov turned some the squelch and configuration dials slowly, attempting to make minute adjustments at first, but nothing he tried was working.

Puzzled, the Russian scientist went to another screen and

noticed the missile was still on course. The other grids were gone now—all except for one over the White Sands base. It flashed on and off like a net, the red lines crisscrossing in a cube pattern. The coverage couldn't have been more than perhaps twenty-five square miles, but it was there.

Why wasn't it disappearing?

Karamov checked another scanning device and saw that his signal frequencies were reading triple zeros across every transmitter. His eyes widened as he realized what was happening. The reflector dishes throughout the country were being used to jam the signals. He had to remodulate those signals on a higher and more variable frequency. He rushed to the configuration console and began to type furiously. He attempted to induce a new frequency level but it had no effect. The frequency wouldn't transmit.

"What in the hell is going on?" Karamov muttered to himself.

He went to the power terminal and made sure the tower outside was transmitting. All instrumentation showed it was operating at peak performance, full power engaged. It wasn't the transmission site. Karamov returned to his instrumentation and checked the SLAMS satellite signal rerouter. It was operating at full capacity. It was operating so well that it was, in effect, sending his signals right back to the satellite now.

They were jamming him! They were reflecting his own signals back to the satellite and causing them to be dispersed into space. Karamov began to type into his keyboard, switching between the terminal and frequency configuration panel, but it did him no good. Finally, his eyes swept over the display panel as Nadezhda entered the grid.

White Sands Missile Range, New Mexico

"HERE IT COMES," the controller called to Wicker.

"Detection complete!" Wicker replied.

"I minus thirty-four seconds," the controller returned.

The missile entered the grid display now, flashing a bright yellow as it crossed into the grid. The speed at which it appeared to be traveling through the grid seemed strange to what Brognola and Schwartz had seen in the recall of the previous demonstration. That was because they didn't have grids displayed of all of U.S. airspace now, but rather only a very small portion of it.

"Preparing deployment!" Wicker called to his staff.

The red grid lines began to pulsate as the MXT signals began sliding down the DQL laser light. They all stood silent, breath bated, as they expected to see the return of the jamming signals. However, they never appeared. The missile continued to draw closer to the *X,* and everyone in the room began to sweat. They all knew they were sweating because it manifested itself in the air as an odor—it was the unmistakable smell of fear and adrenaline.

As the blip grew in size and color intensity, Pordello entered the room. "What's the status of the ICBM?"

"I minus nineteen seconds!" the controller announced from across the room.

"I guess that answers my question," Pordello grumbled.

"Deployment complete," Wicker said, "and initiating deflection."

"I minus fifteen, fourteen, thirteen..."

The controller continued counting down and the missile drew nearer. Schwarz turned at one point and looked at Brognola and Pordello. He nodded, somewhere around eight seconds. They returned his gesture at six seconds. Wicker looked at the men, sadness ever present on his features at four seconds. And at two seconds...

"Deflection!" the controller announced. "We have deflection! Target is turning and outbound!"

A cheer went through the complex, and Brognola thought in that moment he was going to have a coronary. The missile began to turn upward, headed toward the sky and an unknown fate. There was probably enough fuel left inside the weapon to get it out of the gravitational pull of Earth, and that was the important thing. If it actually entered an orbit, a highly unlikely event, they could send a mission team up later to retrieve the weapon.

But in any case, the threat was over and they could rest easy now. And Hal Brognola wondered what had become of the Executioner.

20

Antarctica

Mack Bolan's heart sank over the next couple of hours as he realized that millions were probably dead.

He felt it even more so when he looked over and saw Anika Faithe slumped in the seat. She'd stopped talking to him about fifteen minutes before that. He thought she'd just drifted off to sleep, but a quick check for a pulse confirmed the worse. Anika Faithe had passed into another plane of existence. She had probably suffered from internal injuries, as well as the open fracture, and slowly bled to death.

It was a hell of a way to go.

The Executioner could feel the rage start to well within him. He knew he had to be close to Vostok because the fuel tanks were almost empty. As if some nameless deity were reading his mind, the lights of Vostok and the landing pad appeared in the distance through the cockpit of the Mi-6. The other chopper was already on the ground, and the Executioner knew that there was probably a tremendous amount of excitement among Mishenka and his men.

They were probably drinking, toasting one another with champagne and bragging about their victory against the imperialist Americans. Yes, the capitalist pigs who thought noth-

ing of others but only of themselves and their financial gain. Bolan had heard the same cultural hate and filth spewed for years from those like Mishenka, and he was getting sick of it. Men like Mishenka, Capek and Luvanovich just seemed to never cease existing. For every one of them that he cut down, a new one sprang into place like a mutation of the same, multiheaded monster.

The Executioner watched as the landing pad near the research station drew nearer. He had no idea how to land the chopper, but he willed himself to remain calm. He moved the left pedal and started to circle as he decreased speed and rotated the collective control. The chopper slowed tremendously, the cockpit shuddering as if the aircraft were going to stall. The soldier hesitated but then remembered that in order to continue lift he would need additional power.

Bolan pulled up slowly on the cyclic control, and the shuddering decreased rapidly. He continued to spin until he was an estimated two hundred yards from the site. He couldn't see a thing in the dark, but he wasn't about to turn the lights on. At this distance, he was hoping the winds would hide the noise of the chopper from those inside the buildings. It wasn't as if anybody was going to be standing guard outside in that environment. He stopped his spin and began to decrease the throttle by pushing down both pedals slowly in conjunction with the cyclic control. The chopper descended, lifting some, and descended, lifting and dropping as Bolan tried to keep things in line. He hit the ground a little harder than intended. The force was enough to jar Bolan out of his seat and cause the left landing-gear strut to snap. There was a sound of tearing metal as the strut pushed through the floorboards in the cargo area.

The chopper canted to one side, but Bolan quickly recovered from his surprise impact and killed the engine. The blades began to spin down and the Executioner was out of his seat in a moment. He got to the cargo area of the Hook and began to search through the locker type storage beneath the seats. His search for weapons came up fruitless and he cursed himself. Well, he'd just have to take what he could find once he got inside the station.

Bolan secured his gear, checked the action of his AKSU and verified the load. He counted about a dozen rounds left in the magazine on the weapon, another 30-round clip in his belt, and the two 9 mm Makarovs with some rounds in each were still in the pocket of his parka. It only took one bullet to kill Mishenka. Until he reached the lunatic general who had been responsible for killing millions, he would have to make every shot count. Easy enough to do with only a skeleton crew remaining.

The Executioner left the chopper, tossing a mental farewell to Faithe on his way out.

He proceeded toward the Vostok main research station at a full sprint. He could see activity in the near distance, the single flashing strobe of the Lockheed P-3C Orion jet that had brought him and Faithe there two days earlier. The pilots were on loan and had agreed to wait as long as possible. It looked as if they had waited long enough and they would probably be leaving within a half hour. It would be enough time for Bolan to finish his business here. If he didn't catch them, it wouldn't be long before Stony Man sent someone to retrieve him.

Then again, it would actually be six months. The Executioner had no intention of staying in Antarctica that long.

Icy winds bit at his face, and he was numb within seconds. His trip across the frozen plain seemed to take forever when in fact he reached the building in less than a minute. The Executioner went through the door and took the first pair of guards completely by surprise. The two men were seated at a table, enjoying some hot coffee—they had bags near them and it looked as if they were planning to leave.

Bolan changed that idea for them in a moment, raising his AKSU and triggering two single shots at each before they could even bring their side arms into play. One of them wore the rank of a colonel, and blood spattered across the insignia as he was slammed against the wall by a double tap through the chest. The other officer with him fell next, his midsection destroyed by the 5.45 mm Soviet slugs fired at close range.

The warrior continued farther into the complex. He pressed onward, determined to find Mishenka and finish what he'd started. Bolan found the first two rooms empty, but the laboratory was another story. A single person was in there: Pyotr, the scientist from the Ukraine who had turned against all humanity and developed the Nadezhda missile. He now lay on the floor in a pool of blood, a single bullet hole in his forehead. The blackening marks around the entrance wound told the Executioner that Pyotr had been shot point-blank, and he was sure he knew who the triggerman was.

Bolan whirled and stormed from the laboratory, heading to the next building and sweeping it, as well. There were several more guards awaiting him here, the bulk of Mishenka's team. The men were completely surprised, and the soldier unleashed his fury. The first two guards tried to line up shots, but Bolan found cover behind a thick sofa.

Their AK-47 assault rifles stuttered loudly inside the confines of the small building. Bullets ripped through the fabric of the sofa, continuing outward on the back side, but they never struck their intended target. Bolan had rolled away from the cover, changing the selector to burst mode and making a beeline for a flank position. He triggered the AKSU on the run. The first short burst hit one of the guards and knocked him onto his back. The second soldier started to adjust his weapon, bringing the muzzle into new acquisition, but the Executioner was ready. Bolan dropped to one knee, raised the assault rifle and squeezed the trigger. The burst tore through the man's chest and neck, tearing away cartilage and bone. The man's knees wobbled a moment before he collapsed to the floor.

The remaining six soldiers had recovered from the shock of Bolan's assault and attempted to bring the Executioner down once and for all. He never gave them the chance, rolling out of the line of fire and taking cover behind a doorway. He dropped out the magazine and popped the last one into place even as the opposition opened up full auto.

Bolan waited for a lull in the gunfire and then popped around the corner. He triggered his weapon on the run, gunning down two who hadn't found cover yet before getting across the room. He realized that the door he'd come through was the only way out, and he was a long way from that. Bolan reached another doorway and got through just in time to avoid a fresh cluster of autofire. The Executioner was in the bunking area, and he saw the beds lined up there. The enemy was quickly advancing, keeping up a wall of fire and pinning him down. He knew he was outgunned and outnumbered, and if he didn't think of something quickly he was going to spend his final moments in Antarctica.

Bolan looked at the thin mattresses and a thought hit him. He reached into one of the deep, inner pockets of the parka and removed a flare. It had been there from when he'd used them out on the ice shelf. The warrior closed and locked the door, diving away from it in time to avoid the bullets that shattered the heavy wood.

The Executioner activated the flare and tossed it onto the bed. He watched as the thin, worn mattress immediately caught fire, and within seconds the entire bed was going. Bolan went and got a second mattress and tossed it crossways onto the first, leaving enough space between them to allow for air. The cramped quarters quickly began to fill with smoke. The smoke was thick and black and spread across the room like an angel of death.

Bolan quickly rolled beneath one of the bunks that was still covered, set the AKSU to full-auto burn and waited. The smoke got thicker but the autofire had stopped. He could no longer see rounds smacking through the door. The troopers were probably waiting just outside on either side, waiting for him to make his move.

Another minute or two passed before the Russian troops finally came through the door. The acrid smoke poured through the opening, the sudden rush of oxygen flaring up and crossing the murky expanse at ceiling level. The superheated gas ignited and the soldiers experienced immediate flashover as the outside air fed the fire. Flame rushed downward, threatening to engulf several of them. One immediately left the room while two others became human torches from chest up before they knew what was happening. They danced and screamed in the flames as the Executioner left his cover and crawled past them. He saw them stumble around aimlessly, screaming as flesh was seared off their faces.

Bolan left the black smoke like a raging specter, his iceblue eyes glinting in the firelight as the remaining quartet of guards dried to cope with the change in odds. The warrior cut them down before they could react, sweeping the muzzle of his rifle back and forth. They fell under the autofire and the Executioner threw the weapon aside when the bolt finally locked back on an empty breech.

He left the building and headed for the last building. This was probably the commons area, where they kept the food and storage. He opened the door and stepped inside. It was dark and quiet, surprisingly, and Bolan could hear only the faint hum of a generator. The heat seemed to be on, but there was no activity visible. Bolan waited a moment, crouching and letting his eyes adjust to the gloom.

The Executioner began to move through the darkness, his way lit only by what appeared to be a few emergency lights recessed into the ceiling. They were very bright, at that, but Bolan knew that was probably by design. The warrior sensed that someone was watching him, possibly waiting to pounce, and he would be ready when the moment came.

As he entered another room, he caught a glimpse of light off to the left. Through another doorway, he could see that Mishenka and Capek were preparing to leave. They were both carrying bags from the room and heading in his direction. Bolan ducked behind a nearby stack of boxes, crouching and waiting for them to pass. As they did, he reached out and snaked a forearm around Mishenka's neck. The Executioner was about to give them a send-off they wouldn't forget.

"Leaving so soon, Comrade General?" Bolan said tightly, holding the Makarov to Mishenka's head.

The general dropped his bags and stood erect. "What—?"

"Impossible," Capek stammered. "It is impossible you are alive...impossible you are here!"

"I have a few tricks of my own, Luva. Or have you forgotten all the fun we had together?"

Bolan pressed the muzzle of the weapon tightly to Mishenka's temple. "Tell me something, Mishenka. Was it worth killing all those people? Was it worth wasting the lives of millions to satisfy your own lust for power? The United States will never fall under the likes of you or the others who support you. And I won't rest now until your entire regime is dead!"

Mishenka began to shake, but Bolan soon realized he was laughing. His noises increased until he was laughing so hard he was choking beneath the warrior's hold.

"You imbecile!" he wheezed. "Do you think that killing me will change anything now?"

"No, but it's a hell of a good start," the Executioner said coldly.

Bolan released his hold on Mishenka. He brought the muzzle around to the back of Mishenka's head and squeezed the trigger. The report from the Makarov was deafening in the building. The 9 mm bullet smashed through Mishenka's skull and blew off the top of his head. Bones crunched under the impact, shattering in jagged shards and tearing away skin on the forehead. Blood and brain matter doused Capek as the general's stout body toppled forward.

The Executioner now trained his weapon on Capek, aiming center mass. The gun-for-hire tried to reach for his own weapon, but he never cleared it from shoulder leather. Bolan fired twice, squeezing the trigger and holding the tinier Makarov in a rigid grip. The weapon bucked in his fist, and one round shattered the killer's jawbone while the other went through the bridge of his noise. The force of the close-range impact lifted him off his feet and sent him crashing into the wall. He collapsed, leaving a dark smear as blood spurted from a severed carotid artery.

Bolan turned from the grisly scene, not giving either body a second look as he left the building. He burst into the cold night and began to head for the makeshift airstrip. It was time to bring this mission to an end. He could feel the pain returning to his back and legs, and he thought he might pass out before reaching the airstrip. It would be good to finally get out of Antarctica and back to...to where?

Anywhere but here would be good enough. He would probably head right for Halley Bay, since he could be there in a very short time. The doctors there could tend to his wounds, and he could check in on Grimaldi and see how the ace pilot was coming along. It would be good to see a friendly face.

Bolan felt the pain before he heard the shot. He felt the bullet go through the meaty portion of his shoulder and exit. He felt the impact of the round as it drove him to the ground, and he felt his head hit the ice. Darkness threatened to envelop him, but the Executioner willed himself to stay awake. It was unbelievable that someone was still left. Bolan wondered whom he'd missed and then he realized as the shooter first came into sight that it wasn't one of Mishenka's troops. It was the dark-haired man—the one with the cold blue eyes.

Bolan started to climb to his feet, ignoring the biting pain in his shoulder. Actually, it was beginning to diminish already with the cold. The man kicked him in the chest, knocking the breath from his lungs as he collapsed onto his back. The ice felt good against his shredded flesh. It numbed the pain and made Bolan's misery fade. He'd lost so much, watched so many die today, that he would have just preferred to lie there and freeze to death.

"I wanted you to know who it was who actually defeated you," Erek Trofimoff said. "I wanted you to see me, up close and personal. Mishenka, Capek, Luvanovich...all fools. All ignorant fools who thought that nothing could touch them. All weak and pathetic, being feckless and thinking that no other could capture a vision. Well, now I have shown them my vision. My vision is to kill you. To prove to you that I am the dark side of your conscience. You and I are alike—we kill for honor and distinction. I understand you more than you think."

"You understand nothing," the Executioner sneered. "You're nothing more than a crony who caved under the promise of greed. Now your master is dead and you have nothing. So you can kill me now, but it will mean nothing."

"Do you think I care if Mishenka is dead? He showed his incompetence when his beloved Nadezhda failed. He killed a brilliant scientist in a fit of rage. He was always wasting something. A fat, self-indulgent waster is what he was."

"What do you mean 'Nadezhda failed'?" Bolan asked.

"Oh…wait a minute. You did not know this, eh American? You did not know that his beloved missile was repelled by your country? Well, you have nothing to fear. Mishenka's miserable plan and the billions he spent to finance it have failed. You have nothing to fear."

Hope surged through Mack Bolan. New strength coursed through his veins, and he knew that if he was going to act it would have to be now.

"You do," he said quietly.

The warrior spun onto his side and caught Trofimoff in a leg-trip maneuver. The man fell backward, dropping his Steyr-Mannlicher rifle in the process. Bolan was on the man in an instant, hammering him twice in the solar plexus and knocking the wind from his lungs. The would-be assassin tried to rake out Bolan's eyes with his fingernails, but the Executioner was too fast. He caught the killer's right arm in a joint lock and snapped the elbow. Trofimoff screamed, trying to buck the Executioner.

Bolan weakened quickly, the surge of adrenaline wearing off, and Trofimoff seized the advantage. He twisted with enough force to knock the warrior off balance. Bolan fell off and rolled away from the attack as Trofimoff reached for a knife and yanked it from a belt sheath. The guy attempted to slice the Executioner open, but he missed. Bolan rolled away from the attack and got to his feet, rolling over his adversary's rifle as he did.

The Executioner sent the rifle airborne with a lift of his foot and snatched it in midfall. He pointed the muzzle at Trofimoff's chest and squeezed the trigger. The high-velocity round tore through the man's sternum and ripped out a section of his spine. Trofimoff sucked in a single breath as both lungs collapsed and all motor sensation was cut off from his brain. His eyes glazed over then rolled into the back of his head. He twitched just a moment before lying still.

"We're nothing alike," the Executioner stated.

And with that, he turned and staggered toward the plane.

Epilogue

Stony Man Farm, Virginia

If I never see another snowflake again, it will be too soon," Jack Grimaldi announced as he sat in a bedroom at Stony Man Farm.

"Hear! Hear!" the group of visitors chimed in simultaneously.

Brognola, Price, Kurtzman and the Able Team commandos were ranged around the Stony Man pilot's bed.

Grimaldi was damn happy to see them, and it felt good to be among the company of friends. Except he hadn't seen the Executioner since Bolan's return to Halley Bay. The entire incident had been close—too damn close. Nonetheless, his friend had performed admirably under the gravest circumstances. Each one of them had risked his life while the people of America slept in their beds, comfortable, unaware of the danger.

"Anybody seen the sarge?"

"He's in his own bed..." Price began to say, and she stopped herself when Lyons threw her a sly look. "What? He's recuperating."

"Recuperating, eh?" Lyons said, cocking an eyebrow. He looked at Rosario Blancanales and added, "Is that what they're calling it these days, Pol?"

Politician grinned. "Got me. I heard that—"

"All right, you two, don't start," Brognola growled.

"I'm feeling better," a familiar voice echoed through the room.

All eyes turned to see the tall, muscular form of the Executioner as he entered the room. He was moving stiffly, but he was moving and he looked rather odd dressed in ragged blue jeans and a flannel shirt.

"Hey, Sarge," Grimaldi said. "You're gonna make it, right? You're not planning on checking out of here soon."

"No way, Jack," Bolan replied. "I'm not planning on checking out for a while yet."

"You did a hell of thing, Striker," Brognola said. "You deserve to stand down and have some quality R&R."

"I can't rest, Hal," Bolan said. "Not while Luvanovich is still alive."

"We can always take care of him."

"No, I have to do it. This one's personal."

"All right," Brognola said. "I can't say you haven't earned the right to call your own shots."

"That's for sure," Schwarz agreed.

"Bolan turned his attention to Grimaldi. "There's something I need help with, Jack. How soon do you think you'll be up and running?"

Grimaldi was suspicious now. "I don't know. Doctor said a week or two yet. Why?"

"You probably wouldn't believe it if I told you," Mack Bolan replied with a chuckle.

James Axler
EQUINOX OutJanders
ZERO

As magistrate-turned-rebel Kane, fellow warrior Grant and archivist Brigid Baptiste face uncertainty in their own ranks, an ancient foe resurfaces in the company of Viking warriors—harnessing ancient prophecies of Ragnarok, the final conflict of fire and ice, to bring his own mad vision of a new apocalypse. To save what's left of the future, Kane's new battlefield is the kingdom of Antarctica, where legend and lore have taken on mythic and deadly proportions.

In the Outlands, the shocking truth is humanity's last hope.

Or order your copy now by sending your name, address, zip or postal code, along with a check or money order (please do not send cash) for $6.50 for each book ordered ($7.99 in Canada), plus 75¢ postage and handling ($1.00 in Canada), payable to Gold Eagle Books, to:

In the U.S.	In Canada
Gold Eagle Books	Gold Eagle Books
3010 Walden Avenue	P.O. Box 636
P.O. Box 9077	Fort Erie, Ontario
Buffalo, NY 14269-9077	L2A 5X3

Please specify book title with your order.
Canadian residents add applicable federal and provincial taxes.

GOLD
EAGLE®

GOUT24

ᴛʜᴇ Destroyer™

WASTE NOT, WANT NOT

Mayana—a South American country known only for a mass cult suicide—is poised to become the salvation of a trash-choked globe. A revolutionary device, the Vaporizer, can turn garbage into thin air and trash into cash for the beleaguered nation. But with the President scheduled to attend a global environmental summit in Mayana, Dr. Harold Smith smells trouble—and dispatches Remo and Chiun to the scene to pose as scientists.

Available in January 2003 at your favorite retail outlet.